"A wild, twisting crime thriller filled with secrets, betrayals, and complex characters that will keep you up until you reach the last darkly satisfying page. A five-star beginning to Debra Webb's explosive series!"
—Allison Brennan, *New York Times* bestselling author

"Debra Webb once again delivers with *Trust No One*, a twisty and gritty page-turning procedural with a cast of complex characters and a compelling cop heroine in Detective Kerri Devlin. I look forward to seeing more of Detectives Devlin and Falco."
—Loreth Anne White, *Washington Post* bestselling author of *In the Deep*

"*Trust No One* is a gritty and exciting ride. Webb skillfully weaves together a mystery filled with twists and turns. I was riveted as each layer of the past peeled away, revealing dark secrets. An intriguing cast of complicated characters, led by the compelling Detective Kerri Devlin, had me holding my breath until the last page."
—Brianna Labuskes, *Washington Post* bestselling author of *Girls of Glass*

"Debra Webb's name says it all."
—Karen Rose, *New York Times* bestselling author

THE
LAST
LIE
TOLD

THE
LAST
LIE
TOLD

DEBRA
WEBB

THOMAS & MERCER

Text copyright © 2022 by Debra Webb
All rights reserved.

Published by Thomas & Mercer, Seattle

www.apub.com

Amazon, the Amazon logo, and Thomas & Mercer are trademarks of Amazon.com, Inc., or its affiliates.

ISBN-13: 9781542035439
ISBN-10: 1542035430

Cover design by Amanda Kain

Printed in the United States of America

Mother-daughter relationships are so special.
An amazing connection of friendship, love, and respect.
I am so proud of the brave, strong, beautiful women
my daughters have become! The two of them provide all
the inspiration I will ever need to create characters like
Finley.

A lie told often enough becomes the truth.
—Vladimir Lenin

1

One Month Ago

2:00 p.m.

Riverbend Maximum Security Prison
Cockrill Bend Boulevard
Nashville

"It's time the world knew the truth."

Charlie was no fool. He knew the lawyer seated across the table thought he was a liar or crazy or probably both. The fancy bastard had a look about him that said he thought he was way better than Charlie. Well, that might be. For sure the thousand-dollar suit beat the hell out of Charlie's baggy prison uniform. But there were things Charlie knew that this big shot educated man did not, and that gave him leverage. There was nothing better than a little leverage.

"What truth is that, Mr. Holmes?" Theodore Siniard asked. He glanced at his watch while he waited for an answer. He was busy, with little time for games.

It didn't take a shrink to recognize Siniard was out of his comfort zone. Big man like him putting in an appearance at a place like this.

Siniard had that clever jingle that ran in all his commercials and blazed across all his billboards. *Need a hand? I'm your man!* He was the most famous lawyer in the Southeast—in Tennessee for sure. Charlie had been a little surprised when he showed up in person instead of sending one of his minions. Then again, the name Legard carried some serious weight in Music City. Legard Records was still the top label in the industry even five years after the founder's murder. Old Theo here would love nothing better than to reopen that can of worms and turn it upside down. Where there was money and fame, there was public interest and publicity to be gained.

Charlie smiled. He knew the Legard family's biggest secrets. He held the key to a mystery even they didn't fully understand. Secrets that would put Music City in a media frenzy. Might even make a hell of a movie. He decided to give the impatient man something to chew on. "The truth about who killed him, what else?"

Siniard's gaze narrowed. "You were charged and ultimately confessed to his murder. You've served five years of a life sentence. Don't waste my time, Mr. Holmes. If this is some attempt to rekindle a measure of publicity, you're wasting your time, and more importantly, you're wasting mine."

This time Charlie let the chuckle escape his throat. "And yet, here you are. Breathing the same air as me."

Siniard pushed back his chair and stood. "Don't call my office again."

Charlie waited until the arrogant man walked the few steps to the door, where he would call for the guard. Only Siniard could have managed a face-to-face with Charles Holmes on short notice and in one of the nicer interview rooms. Charlie was a bit of a celebrity in Riverbend. He wasn't exactly Charles Manson, but he wasn't a plain old generic convict either. He and the deceased Manson shared a little something besides first names. For one thing, a streak of evil that went bone deep. For another, a dedicated fan following. Charlie received dozens of letters every month from the people who loved him. He figured there were more, but the guards didn't want him getting a big head. All that was irrelevant, really. It was Legard's murder that had put Charlie on the map and opened the door to his claim to fame. Life was ironic like that sometimes.

"It was someone else who did it. Someone close to him," Charlie announced to the haughty man's back. "All I did was clean up her mess and try to protect her."

The words rattled the silence and stopped Siniard dead in his tracks.

Siniard turned around, surprise written all over his Botoxed face. "If that were true, why not speak up before now? Why wait all this time? *Why confess?*"

The attorney figured this revelation was a lie—an attempt to get Charlie a little publicity. A smile split Charlie's face again. This was going to be fun. "I would have done anything for her." It was true. He really would have. Nothing had ever made him feel so strongly for another person. There wasn't a drug in existence that could top the feeling she gave him.

Everything he'd done, he'd done for *her*.

But that drug had suddenly worn off, and the pain it left behind was unbearable. It was time to teach her a lesson. To show her what he could do if she tried to ignore him any longer. There were things this fancy lawyer didn't know—didn't need to know. He only needed the match that would light the fire.

Oh, and Charlie had the match.

This fire was going to burn deep, because it wasn't just *her*—they all had something to hide. They were all guilty to some degree.

Siniard stared at him, analyzing, searching for some visible tell that would contradict the statement. He didn't believe Charlie, but he couldn't walk away without being absolutely certain. Charlie knew the possibility was just too damned enticing for him.

"Again, I have to ask: Why not mention this during the investigation? You allowed the trial to play out for weeks before confessing. You enjoy games, Mr. Holmes. I do not." Siniard made a face that suggested no small amount of loathing. "If you're hoping for an appeal, I'm afraid you're far too late."

"I've done my research," Charlie said. "If new evidence can prove my innocence, I'm entitled to a new trial."

"You have evidence of your claim?" Siniard's manicured eyebrows reared up his forehead. "It was, after all, primarily your confession that convicted you."

"I sure do." Charlie might not have gone to college—hell, he never even finished high school—but he was smarter than people realized. Way, way smarter than anyone would guess. "Like I said, I was protecting someone. Emotion caused me to make a mistake."

Siniard gave a slow nod as if assessing his options. "All right. *If* you do in fact have credible evidence—"

"I do, and that entitles me to a new trial." Charlie was not taking any shit from this highfalutin guy.

"I'll need a name and the details," Siniard demanded, his tone thick with condescension.

Charlie grinned. Wouldn't he like to know. "You get me a new trial, and I'll tell you everything you need to know."

"Let me be clear, Holmes," Siniard warned, his posture stiff with indignation. "If we start down this path, I will not—"

"You will if you want the biggest case in this state's history," Charlie challenged. "You should stop beating around the bush and make this happen."

Siniard held his gaze without saying a word for long enough to make Charlie sweat. "I will need the name and the evidence before I proceed."

"No problem." Charlie sat back in his chair. The shackles he wore rattled with the movement. "Buckle up, Mr. Siniard. This is going to be a wild ride."

"Why now?" Siniard asked again. "Why wait five years?"

"Some things are worth waiting for." And this was worth everything.

Siniard's lips thinned with more of that glaring disgust. "Public perception is important, Mr. Holmes, but jury perception is key. I'm afraid we're going to need a better reason to sway the jury to our side."

Charlie had the perfect reason. One that was universally recognized and accepted. "I opened my heart to Jesus, Mr. Siniard. He won't let me live with this lie any longer. I have to tell the truth."

And that was the biggest lie of all.

2

Wednesday, July 6

1:30 p.m.

Metro Police, East Precinct
East Trinity Lane
Nashville

"Let's go over this again."

Finley O'Sullivan considered saying no, but that would only land her another extended period of the silent treatment while the detective pretended to confer with his colleagues. Spending more time in this eight-by-ten sterile-white interview room was not exactly how she wanted to occupy the rest of her day.

"How many times do you need to hear the same story, Detective?"

The question earned her a long look of frustration. Detective Ronald Graves was likely only a couple of years from retirement. He had the gray hair, the sagging jowls, and the slightly rounded belly to prove he'd done his time in a demanding field. But his indifference toward his physical condition hadn't dulled his keen mental acuity. The man was sharp.

He knew she was lying, and she knew he had every intention of proving it.

Better men had tried.

"Perhaps it's time you reconsidered council, Ms. O'Sullivan," he offered. "Despite what you see in the media, it is my job to look out for the best interests of *all* citizens, including those involved in cases where someone ends up dead."

Finley dug a little deeper for more patience. He couldn't possibly hope to drag this out much longer. "As I told you before, I *am* an attorney."

"But you're not practicing right now," he said, his gaze narrowed in accusation. "You're on probation, isn't that right?"

Ah, the intimidation tactic. She knew it well. Had used it all the time as an assistant district attorney for Davidson County. She executed a mental eye roll. *Former* assistant district attorney. After her famous crash and burn, she'd been given two options: be fired, or take probation and have her position reviewed in one year. *Six of one, half a dozen of the other*, her grandmother would have said. Either way, she'd lost her job, with the minor exception that she'd quit before she was fired. The media had, of course, had a field day with the story. "Hotshot ADA Bungles Case. Courtroom Meltdown One for the Record Books." Went with the territory. The higher you flew, the farther you had to fall. And fall she did.

Didn't help that her mother was a judge who God and everyone else appeared to hold in highest regard. Cue the potential for longer staying power in the news and broader humiliation.

"You are correct, Detective Graves; I am not practicing right now. But that status doesn't change the fact that I understand my rights and have the ability to judge my own needs."

He held up both hands. "I meant no offense," he hastened to assure her. "Like all the persons of interest in this case, your background has been thoroughly reviewed." He shrugged. "To tell you the truth, I'm just a little worried. There was that . . ." He shrugged again. "What did they call it in the reports?"

He asked the question aloud when it was clearly not meant for her to answer.

He already had the answer.

"A psychotic breakdown I believe was the term." He nodded, answering himself. "You had a nervous breakdown last year. In the middle of the trial of the decade." His expression turned to one of sympathy. "They say you came back to work too soon after your husband's murder."

The lump that instantly rose in her throat at the mention of her husband belied the unshakable confidence she pretended to possess. Whenever her careful facade dared to crack, it invariably made her angry. Primarily at herself. The breakdown had left her with a slight glitch related to impulse control. She was still working on the issue.

"What does that have to do with your investigation?" She bit her lips together, annoyed she had allowed the question to slip out in an irritated tone. Appearing angry or defensive was a bad sign in a witness. It almost always meant they were hiding something.

She was angry, of course, but the goal was to not tip her hand.

Graves carried on as if she hadn't said a word. "I read the reports." He shook his head. "It must have been horrifying for you. You were right next to your husband when he was murdered and yet you couldn't identify the man who killed him."

She blocked the images that attempted to break past the barrier she'd built all those months ago. "This is not about what happened to my husband last year, Detective. This is about *your* investigation into a crime that occurred just five days ago, and as we both know, I identified the armed man who attempted to rob the store in *your* case." The would-be shooter's face flashed in her head, followed immediately by the sound of a blast. She resisted the urge to flinch.

"You mean the dead guy," Graves suggested. "The one the store clerk shot in the head?"

"Yes." Really, it sounded worse than it was—in a manner of speaking.

"Both you and the clerk stated that the victim—"

"The perpetrator," she corrected. The man walked into the Shop Easy convenience store carrying a loaded Glock with the intent of robbing the place and potentially leaving no witnesses. He had not been a victim by even the most remote definition of the word.

"The perp," Graves allowed, "had his weapon aimed at the clerk and was threatening to shoot. When he shifted his attention to you, the clerk pulled a gun from beneath the counter and fired."

"Yes." A smart witness never said more than necessary to answer a question. It was the first rule defense lawyers taught their clients. It was also the principal focus of an ADA when questioning a witness for the defense—make them say more than they intended.

"Were you aware the store was equipped with video surveillance?"

She couldn't stop her outward reaction quickly enough to prevent his seeing her surprise. Not that she should have been. Just because the Shop Easy was run down and in the worst part of town didn't mean the owner couldn't afford the best in security measures. "I'm certain the video footage confirmed our statements."

Graves held her gaze a moment before responding.

She held her breath.

"It did." He nodded. "But it also showed something else."

Finley said nothing. This was his dance; she had no problem allowing him to lead.

"You baited the perp," he accused.

"I believe the word you're looking for is *distracted*," she argued.

"Really?" he tossed back.

"I *distracted* the perp," she explained, "preventing him from shooting the store clerk and most likely me as well." Finley felt confident a jury would see it the same way.

Graves reached for the laptop he'd placed on the table when he'd first entered the room. "Why don't we review those thirty-eight seconds that elapsed before the clerk drew his weapon from under the counter?"

He hit play, and she looked away. Didn't need to see the rerun. Repetitiveness got on her nerves like nothing else.

The clipped, tense words captured electronically floated in the air. The perp demanding the money from the register. Threatening to shoot. The clerk pleading for his life. And then, *her* voice . . .

If you want to shoot someone, why not me?

The perp had swung his attention to Finley. She'd met his gaze, daring him to act . . . emboldening him. He, of course, shouted for her to shut up. She, of course, did not, and on it went for a few more seconds before he . . . *recognized* her.

That instant clicked like a gun blast in her brain. She blinked.

"You stepped toward him," Graves said as he paused the video. "That's when he turned his gun on you."

She met the detective's accusing gaze. "Allowing the clerk to save both our lives."

Graves started the video again.

Shut up! Stay back!

But she hadn't. She had stepped even closer, allowing the muzzle of his weapon to press against her.

Go ahead. You want to shoot someone, shoot me.

Wait . . . I know—

The would-be shooter's words ended abruptly when the clerk pulled the trigger of the weapon he'd snatched from beneath the counter.

The bullet plowed through the perp's head, splattering his blood and other matter across Finley's face, effectively obliterating the word he would have said next.

The brief flutter of disappointment she'd felt when he failed to fire his own weapon rushed through her now. It was the oddest, most unexpected reaction. Some small part of her had felt relief, but mostly she'd experienced a sort of regret.

She was still alive.

Her therapist would be disheartened by her momentary lapse, which was why she had no intention of telling him. What the man didn't know couldn't hurt him; however, if he were to find out, it would certainly cause a pain in Finley's ass.

"I'm guessing," Graves said, "he was going to say *you*. What do you think?"

Finley stared at the detective and said what any good prosecutor would. "He walked into the store, a loaded weapon in hand, with the intent to commit robbery and possibly murder. Whatever he was going to say is irrelevant, Detective. His actions spoke loudly and clearly."

"What about *your* actions?"

"Are we finished here?"

The silence lagged for a beat too long. A cliché tactic to say the least.

"Almost." His gaze searched hers as if he expected to see guilt or maybe fear. "You're certain you didn't know this man?"

"As I've told you already, I did not know this man." There was a distinct difference between knowing a person and having met him before. The detective hadn't asked the right question.

"Very well." He exhaled a breath loaded with frustration. "I felt an obligation to send a copy of the report to your therapist—particularly since he refused to answer any of my questions."

Fury whipped through Finley. "That's crossing the line, Detective, and you know it."

"Under the circumstances . . ." He shrugged. "I didn't think so."

She had to give him credit: the move was one she hadn't anticipated.

Finley pushed back her chair and stood. "You have my number if you feel the need to repeat any more of the questions I've already answered."

He followed suit, moving more quickly than she would have believed him capable of to open the door. Before stepping aside for her to exit, he spoke once more. "Like I said, I read the file on your husband's murder."

The anger still simmering inside her burst into outrage, but she knew better than to open her mouth when she was this furious. Courtroom battles were lost when emotion was allowed to make an untimely appearance.

"What the perp did to you after he killed your husband was unspeakable." Graves shook his head. "I have a daughter, and I can't even imagine."

Could he not just step aside and let her go? Feelings she'd buried as deep as her psyche would allow threatened to surface. She forced them back.

She would not go there again.

"It's a damned shame he hasn't been caught." He made a tsking sound. "Hard to do when the bastard left no evidence." He shook his head. "Not one damned speck."

The silent standoff lasted another five or so seconds before Graves finally moved.

Finley walked out.

What had he expected her to say?

No one wanted to get the person responsible for Derrick's murder more than she did. In fact, no one had believed her when she named him. The ones—and there had been more than one—who carried out the execution had been following orders. Giving them up to the police would not have prompted the desired result. They would get theirs, just like the asshole who'd bled out on the floor of that convenience store on Saturday.

One down, two to go.

Three, actually. But she was saving the one who gave the order for last.

Not until she exited the building did her lungs fill fully with air. The scent of wisteria mingled with the thick humidity of July in the South was as familiar as the smell of her own skin. Heat wrapped around her like a wool coat, and instantly the sparse dab of makeup she'd bothered with felt ready to slip down her cheeks.

In the cross-body messenger-style bag draped against her side, her cell phone vibrated. Before she could reach for it, her attention snagged on the man propped against her car. *Matt.* She paused. He grinned and gave her a little wave.

Finley waved back as she closed the remaining space between them. "I'm thinking your timing isn't coincidental, Mr. Quinn."

Another of those broad grins split his face. The way that grin made his eyes sparkle never ceased to catch her off guard. Blue eyes, sandy-blond hair, tall, inordinately handsome. Had she mentioned smart? Like uber intelligent. She and Matthew Quinn had been best friends since they were children. Lived on the same street in Belle Meade growing up. Matt graduated from law school one year ahead of her and was promptly invited to clerk for one of the state's premiere justices. Three years ago, he was handpicked to serve as the liaison between Metro, the DA's office, and the mayor's office. Sort of like a mediator of the unholy trinity. And he was good. Very good.

The man would be governor one day.

He pushed away from her car and gave her a hug. "I had a meeting with the three in the chief's office, then a briefing with the commander here." He hitched his head toward her decade-old Subaru. "Saw your Outback as I was leaving and decided to hang around. See if you had plans tonight."

"No plans."

She never had plans beyond work. Not the kind he meant. Not anymore. Except when Matt decided she needed to get out or when her dad persuaded her to attend some family function that just wouldn't be the same without her. Saying no to her dad was something she'd never learned to do well.

"Good." Matt opened the driver's side door for her. "Then I'll swing by at seven. You pick the place."

She pulled the strap of her bag over her head and tossed the worn, comfortable leather into the passenger seat. "What's the occasion?"

Had he finally met someone and decided to settle down? *He's not getting any younger*, her mother, the Judge, would say. She certainly had pointed out Finley's advanced age—at least until she'd met Derrick, and suddenly Finley was moving too fast. *You scarcely know him. He's not in your league, dear. You'll never be happy together. Is he the father you want for your children? For my grandchildren?*

Finley forced the echo away. The concept of the Judge and grandchildren was completely incongruent. Judge Ruth O'Sullivan wouldn't think of taking time from her prestigious career for anyone. Just ask Finley's dad. He'd retired last year to help Finley with physical rehab after . . . what happened. The idea wouldn't have crossed the Judge's mind. But Barton O'Sullivan, a mere director of community and social services, was expendable. His career had always come a distant second to her mother's.

Finley turned to Matt. "Are you sure the Judge didn't put you up to this? I know how you love staying on her good side."

He braced his arm on her door. "You know better, Fin. I'll see you at seven."

A little salute, and he was off.

She watched him walk away. Yes, they were friends. In truth, he was her only real friend. It wasn't that he didn't invite her to dinner fairly regularly, actually.

It was the timing.

He must have heard about her follow-up interview with Detective Graves.

Which meant tonight wasn't just two old friends getting together to catch up.

Matt had gotten a heads-up on something that concerned her . . . something related to the shooter at the Shop Easy, maybe. The thought unsettled her more than it should have.

Apparently, she really was a suspect.

Oh well. It wouldn't be the first time.

3

3:00 p.m.

Finnegan Law Firm
Tenth Avenue
Nashville

The law office where Finley worked as an investigator wasn't really an office. Not in the traditional sense, at any rate. It was an old church in a forgotten neighborhood only blocks from downtown. Some years back Jack Finnegan had taken it as payment from a client who'd been real estate poor at the time. With his law career's resurrection, Jack had decided that working out of a church was fitting. He'd turned the former house of God into a well-laid-out suite of offices for himself and his staff. Trees lined the parking area, providing a barrier between the former church and its neighbors, a mixture of early-twentieth-century homes and small low-rent businesses.

Inside, Finley paused at the reception desk to pick up her messages. "The boss is MIA."

Finley looked from the cluster of messages to the lady who'd spoken. Actually, Nita Borelli was more of a drill sergeant than a lady. She kept the firm and its handful of employees on their toes. Jack was the boss in name only. Everyone understood Nita was the real boss.

"He didn't call?" Worry stirred in Finley. Jack was always the first one to arrive and the last one to leave . . . except when he was fighting a relapse—as he called it.

"He did not, and I've called his cell a dozen times." She paused in her typing and looked over her glasses at Finley. "The last time this happened, we didn't find him for three days."

Finley groaned inwardly. The high-profile wrongful death case he'd been working on for months had closed yesterday with the kind of settlement attorneys lived for. If Jack had decided to celebrate, he may have fallen off the wagon. It hadn't happened in years, but once an alcoholic, always an alcoholic.

"I'll find him," Finley assured the other woman. Though Finley had worked with Jack only since leaving the DA's office last year, she knew him better than anyone else on staff.

Nita returned to her furious typing. "Wallace went to the Drake after court, around noon, and Jack wasn't there."

The Drake was one of Music City's oldest motels. In its heyday it had been a popular place. Now it was just another old icon that had lost its luster. For Jack, it was home.

"Did Wallace go inside?" Finley asked.

Adan Wallace was the other attorney on staff. He handled most of the firm's smaller cases. Helped out wherever Jack needed him. He was a good attorney but lacking the ruthless aggression required to take on the bigger cases. Jack called him a kitten in a lion's territory. Not a bad thing—in legal battles it took all kinds.

"He did," Nita said as her fingers flew over the keyboard. "Wherever Jack slept last night, it wasn't there."

"Did you call—"

"I called all hospitals and the morgue. If he's hurt or dead, no one's found him yet."

That was a good thing. Possibly. "He's probably at his cabin. I'll head there now and bring him in."

Nita grunted an affirmative without taking her eyes off the computer screen.

Finley shuffled through her messages as she headed back to her car. Nothing that couldn't wait. Percy Priest Lake was only about twenty-five minutes away. She would try Jack's cell on the way, but chances were it was dead by now. The man never remembered his charger.

Afternoon traffic slowed her exodus from the city. She frowned at her reflection in the rearview mirror. Her ever-present ponytail needed refreshing; strands of stray black hair hung around her cheeks. Way too many lines furrowed her brow. Frowning had become her customary expression. These days smiles took effort. Large, dark sunglasses hid the circles under her eyes.

Derrick would have said she needed sleep, worked too hard. He would have insisted she needed a break. She should have appreciated more the way he'd tried to take care of her. But she hadn't, and now it was too late.

"What I need," she grumbled at herself for even going down that path, "is to find Jack."

The traffic vanished as the woods crowded in on the two-lane road that led to the rustic cabin Jack considered his getaway. He swore he'd won the place in a poker game way back when he was working his way through law school. This might or might not be accurate. Jack wasn't always completely straightforward. Particularly if whatever he was hiding involved stretching or otherwise manipulating the boundaries of the law.

Jackson "Jack" Finnegan was the sweetest, most caring person—besides her father—Finley had ever known. He worked extra hard to take care of those who needed him most. A real-life hero for the underdog.

If not for the drinking, he would be the top attorney in the Southeast. He had an incredible legal mind. The Judge used to tell stories about Jack Finnegan's legal prowess. The two of them had been good friends—like Finley and Matt. They'd grown up in the same neighborhood and attended school together. Jack was Finley's godfather. He'd been a part of the family until five years ago during her final year at law school. But something had happened between him and the Judge, and even Jack wouldn't talk about it. Whatever it was, the two of them were no longer on speaking terms.

Jack had been sober for twenty-five years when the falling-out and his dive off the wagon happened. Finley had no idea if one had anything to do with the other, since he'd quit the law office where he'd been a senior partner for decades and disappeared for six months. Finley had graduated and taken a position with the Davidson County District Attorney's Office by then. In true Jack fashion, he'd reappeared one day and started renovating that church. He'd sold his bungalow over on the West Side and moved into the Drake. The resurrection of his career appeared to have come with a mission: to represent the people no one else wanted to bother with. The Judge had been appalled. Finley, on the other hand, had considered his decision quite selfless. Much to the Judge's dismay, Finley and Jack had remained close as if nothing had happened. And why wouldn't they? He was her godfather. He'd always been a part of her life.

Every time he won a case, Finley ensured her mother heard about it. Not that he ever lost. He always won. It drove the Judge and lots of other people quite mad that Jack had rebounded so brilliantly. There had been something different about him when he returned. Finley called it his "no more Mr. Nice Guy" attitude.

He was as cutthroat as they came. Winning was his only goal. Well, that and making money. Most in the profession would call him ruthless. They would speculate that he would do anything—make a deal with the devil himself—to win. Which made his decision to buy the old church and turn it into his firm all the more ironic. Society didn't exactly consider lawyers virtuous. "A necessary evil" was the more prevalent classification. But Jack Finnegan was a legend twice over in Davidson County. No one liked squaring off with him in a courtroom.

Despite his ruthless reputation, Finley was well aware that deep down Jack remained first and foremost a champion of the small and vulnerable. He was the quintessential good guy when no one was looking. All his testing of the boundaries was always for the right reason.

She took the next left onto a gravel-and-dirt road. The tree canopy over the road was so thick it blocked the sun entirely, plunging the narrow road into darkness. A half mile after the turnoff, the trees opened up into a clearing. The rustic cabin sat back against the tree line on the other side of the clearing. A path through those trees led to the lake. Everyone assumed Jack came here to fish, but he didn't. Other than the johnboat left behind by a previous owner, he didn't even own a boat, much less a fishing pole. This was where he came to clear his head or, if he felt on the verge of relapse, to battle his demons.

Since his vintage Land Rover sat in front of the cabin, she assumed he was here.

She parked and collapsed back against her seat for a moment. She and Jack were a lot alike. They were both broken to some degree. Few people understood them. For the first time she wondered if this was all there was for people like her . . . and Jack. People who had given everything to their work and then ended up alone for one reason or another. Alone and in pieces.

Her cell chimed, and she dug it from her bag. She had a voice mail and new emails. The voice mail was from Detective Wellman. Her pulse thumped at the idea that maybe, finally, he'd caught a break on Derrick's case. His message asked her to call him back when she could. She did immediately, and the call went straight to voice mail.

She left him a message. "Hey, sorry I missed your call. Call me back."

Finley ended the call and checked the emails. A notification of her upcoming appointment from her therapist's office. An official complaint from yet another Metro detective she'd rubbed the wrong way. She rolled her eyes. The primary issue the detective had was that she didn't play by his rules. This was actually one of the perks of being an investigator for the firm. She wasn't a cop, so she wasn't bound by the same rules. She didn't need a warrant for cell phone records. She had *other* sources. This, more often than not, ticked off the law enforcement folks working a case.

A year ago she would have been appalled at the idea of not playing by the rules. But things were different now.

She was different.

As Jack would say, *You gotta do what you gotta do.*

She climbed out of the car and tucked her phone into her back pocket. Watching her step, on the lookout for snakes, she trudged through the ankle-deep grass to reach the porch. Jack's lawn service must have taken a couple of weeks off. She banged on the door. Listened to the silence on the other side for about ten seconds, then banged again.

When no response came, she went to the pot of dead flowers that sat next to the steps and dug around for the spare key. She wiggled it out, unlocked and opened the door, then tossed the key back into the pot and dusted off her hands.

The instant she crossed the threshold, the odor of fresh paint assaulted her senses. Bright-white walls and ceilings gave the old cabin a cottagey look. The too-quiet stillness and warm temperature set her on edge. Why wasn't the air-conditioning on? Then she noticed all the windows were open. Maybe for the painting. She relaxed the slightest bit and wandered deeper into the space.

On the coffee table in front of the ancient sofa sat an open bottle of bourbon and a tumbler. The good news was the bottle remained full.

Finley relaxed a little more. Maybe he hadn't jumped off the wagon. Then again, there was heart attack, stroke. She shuddered. He may have fallen off the ladder while painting.

"Just find him," she muttered.

Heading into the short hall, she noted the bathroom was clear, as was the first of the two bedrooms. Jack's was the one at the end. Door was open, but the room was dark.

"Jack?" She walked in, flipped on the light switch—and there he was in all his glory, stretched across the bed, facedown, wearing nothing but paisley boxers. She watched for a moment to see if he was breathing.

Oh yeah. He was breathing. Relief rushed through her, but it was short lived. Why the hell was he in bed at this hour of the afternoon?

She scanned the room for one or more empty bottles. None to be seen. The walls and ceiling, like the rest of the house, had been painted. She checked under the bed. Only dust bunnies.

"Jack." She leaned down closer to his head and shouted loud enough to wake the dead. "Jack, what the hell?"

He didn't move. "Keep it down," he murmured, his voice muffled by the pillow.

"It's after four o'clock in the afternoon, Jack," she said a little quieter. "Nita sent me looking for you."

A couple of swear words disappeared into his pillow. "I was up all night."

She sat on the edge of the bed. Bringing her voice down a couple of decibels, she asked, "What the hell happened?"

He raised his head and shoved his long hair out of his face. He flopped onto his back and glanced up at her, his eyes seriously bloodshot. "The place needed painting."

Okay. "You need coffee," she suggested.

His eyes closed. "Yes. Please."

"I'll make coffee," she said as she pushed up from the bed. "I expect you to join me in the kitchen, which means you have to get up and get dressed."

"Give me five minutes."

"Right. Five minutes." Finley was guessing it would be at least ten.

After rummaging through the cupboards, she located the tin of coffee and a couple of mugs. The process of brewing coffee took a while, since she couldn't quite bring herself to use the machine until she'd thoroughly washed it. Clearly Jack had not been here in a while. By the time the scent of coffee filled the room, he'd shuffled slowly in from the hall. His shirt wasn't buttoned, but he was wearing pants and he'd fastened his long hair into place at the nape of his neck. His blond ponytail, now streaked with gray, had been his trademark hairstyle since he graduated from high school. He plopped down in the nearest chair, propped his elbows on the table, and rested his chin in his hands.

Even with no sleep, his long hair a little messy, and his face unshaven, he was still a good-looking guy. He remained fit, was mostly charming. The ladies liked him, maybe a little too much. His colleagues, on the other hand, did not. They called him clever and cunning and other things that didn't bear repeating.

For Finley, he was her mentor and her friend. He was family. Always would be. She was named after him. The Fin in Finley was from Finnegan. How could she possibly cut him out of her life? Finley wasn't like her mother; she couldn't pretend he no longer existed.

Eight months ago when she'd taken the job with Jack's small firm, the Judge had basically disowned her. It wasn't like they had been on good terms anyway. The most noteworthy trouble had started when Finley met Derrick. Marrying him had made things worse. Apparently going to work for Jack had been the straw that broke the camel's back, the cardinal sin.

The fact that her own mother hadn't attended Derrick's funeral or come to see Finley in the hospital had been the true cardinal sins. That too-familiar combination of outrage and hurt seared through her. How her father managed to continue living with the Judge was beyond Finley.

She placed a hot cup of coffee in front of Jack and took the seat next to him. This close, it was impossible to miss the lines around his eyes that spoke of years of sleepless nights and high-pressure courtroom battles. But, unlike hers, his lines only added character.

He breathed in the coffee's aroma and sighed. "I may live after all."

Finley rolled her eyes and asked the $64,000 question. "What had you contemplating a dive into the bottle?" The evidence was just across the room.

He sipped his coffee. Ran a hand over his stubble. "Who knows?" He drank more coffee. "Yesterday was a big day. I decided to come here to get away for the night."

"And you brought your old friend Jim Beam?"

He downed a bigger swallow of coffee, made a face at the burn. "No, he was already here. I knew he was. It's a little game he and I play."

She understood now. For whatever reason, he'd wanted a drink. He threw down the gauntlet by putting the goods front and center, even going so far as to open the bottle. Then the battle began.

"I painted one wall and then another," he explained. "Every time I moved on to the next wall without taking a drink, it was another win for me. I painted until I was physically exhausted, and then I crashed."

"How about coming to my place the next time this happens?" Her entire house needed painting—inside and out.

He chuckled and reached for his coffee. "It works better if I do this alone."

She figured.

"Nita's pissed," Finley warned.

He threw back more of the coffee. "I work all week and most weekends. Can't a guy take a break now and then?"

"Sure." Finley rose, crossed to the counter, and poured herself a cup of coffee. "All you have to do is tell someone. You can't just disappear. You have obligations and people who depend on you."

"Everything and everyone was fine," he argued. "I had the situation under control."

Only an alcoholic could rationalize skating that close to the edge so reasonably. "You're a grown man; you can risk screwing up if you want to. It's just not your usual MO, which is why I'm guessing something disturbing happened." Wasn't his case because he'd aced it.

"I met with a new client yesterday afternoon."

"So you didn't come here immediately after the hearing?"

"No. We had lunch together."

Good. At least he'd eaten at some point in the past twenty-four hours. "Tell me about this client."

"The media will be all over this one." He sat his cup on the table. "Look, I know your father was hoping you'd go to the lake house with him for a few days, but I need you with me on this one. Right now."

Finley felt guilty for being relieved. She'd hoped for an excuse to avoid the lake trip her father had planned for next week. It wasn't a matter of avoiding her father's company, but she simply wasn't ready for a stay at the lake house. The last time she'd gone had been with Derrick. Knots tightened in her belly.

Derrick Reed. Her husband. Her *murdered* husband. The one whose name she'd chosen not to take for career reasons. An ache pierced her at the memory of how confused he'd been when she first told him.

It's very common for career women, she'd assured him.

He'd pretended not to mind, but deep down he had. He never said anything, but she recognized the hurt later . . . too late to make it right.

She should have compromised on that one. The name thing had been far more personal than the damned prenup Matt had prodded her into.

"Not a problem." Finley pushed the memories away. "Tell me about the case." Maybe this crappy week could be salvaged after all. She was off the hook with her dad, and there was a new case.

"Charles Holmes," he said. "Five years ago, he murdered Lance Legard."

"*The* Lance Legard who owned the music label?" Finley remembered the name and the tragedy. The Legard label had and still carried some of the biggest stars in the country music industry.

"That's the one. Holmes claimed he killed Legard for his Jag. Was halfway to Mexico when he was caught. He let the investigation and trial play out like some sort of chess game before confessing."

"Holmes was a repeat offender who hadn't been caught," she said, recalling more details of the case. "The Legard case ended up connecting him to several others."

"Exactly." Jack stood and walked back to the coffee pot. He refilled his cup. "Mr. Holmes has allegedly found Jesus and decided to confess the whole truth about what he claims actually happened." Jack leaned against the counter. "He insists his other victims deserved what they got, but not Legard."

"His decision to murder Legard and steal his car was outside his usual MO." Finley recognized the dissimilarity. Legard's murder had been a random act of violence, according to the statements Holmes had made at trial.

"That particular murder is supposedly weighing on his conscience."

"Since he found Jesus," Finley suggested.

Jack nodded. "In fact, he now claims he didn't murder Legard. He only cleaned up the mess for his girlfriend—the man's daughter."

Now there was a hell of a one-eighty. Parricide was one of those things people didn't like to think about, but it happened. "Too late for any sort of appeal," Finley noted. "Does he have evidence to support this new claim? Was his confession coerced?"

"Apparently he has evidence of some sort. The timing of the confession coincided with his previous crimes coming to light during the trial, but he now maintains it was a lie."

Not all clients of the firm were saints, but Holmes was a new low altogether. "Are you planning to represent him?"

Jack laughed. "Not in this lifetime. Sophia Legard—"

"The widow," Finley offered.

Jack's gaze sidled away. "Yes."

Finley wondered about the abrupt eye shift. Jack was typically very straightforward when discussing their work. No beating around the bush. No dodging scrutiny.

"She asked me to represent her daughters."

"*Daughters?* Holmes didn't name which daughter supposedly lured him into this arrangement?" Legard had two daughters, his only children to Finley's knowledge.

"According to Holmes it was Cecelia. The problem is the daughters are twins," Jack explained. "*Identical* twins. Both deny the accusation. Sophia—Mrs. Legard—feels they will both need representation."

"I see." This could be interesting. Particularly since Jack appeared to have some sort of stake in the case beyond the usual "do whatever it takes to win."

"We need to understand what sort of evidence—if any—Holmes has."

Jack rubbed his temples. "His attorney has agreed to a meeting. We should know what we're up against by the end of the day tomorrow. Meanwhile—"

"Meanwhile," she interjected, "you'd like me to interview the twins for you."

"I'll be there, but I want you right beside me. No one is better at reading people than you, kiddo. If one or both of these girls—ladies—are lying, we need to know. I don't like taking cases I can't feel good about winning."

But he would take this one, Finley wagered. This one was not just a case. That much was pretty clear.

"If one of them actually hired Holmes to murder the father," she suggested, "we need a motive the jury will see as an act of self-defense." There was murder, and then there was *murder*. If the father was abusing one or both daughters, then it wasn't *murder* in the eyes of most anyone with a child of their own.

"Sophia stands by her daughters." He frowned. "She also insists her husband was a devoted father."

Her husband was dead—there was no changing that. Would she change her claims about her late husband if it meant saving one or both daughters? Definitely interesting. "Did you find her convincing?"

"For the most part. She's rich, white, and well educated. She'll need work to come off as sympathetic to a jury. But I'm convinced she's telling what she believes to be the truth."

"What about the daughters?"

"I didn't talk to them." He shrugged. "We have a meeting with the mother and both daughters at nine tomorrow morning in the Legard home. Olivia is flying in from San Diego. She moved away for college shortly after the trial, and she's lived in California since. Single, no children. Cecelia, on the other hand, has remained at home, living with her mother. Didn't attend college. She's also single. No kids. I've got Nita digging up whatever she can find on the two. Friends, work and school history. Criminal records, if any."

It was possible Cecelia had been closer to her mother and felt she needed to take care of her rather than flying the coop. Olivia may have simply wanted her freedom. Just because they were twins on the outside didn't mean their inner hopes and dreams were in any way similar.

"The files from the original investigation," Jack said, drawing her attention back to him, "should have been delivered to the office today."

She would check with Nita, then stop back by the office and pick them up if they'd been delivered. "Do we know who's representing Holmes?"

"That's the icing on the cake. Theodore Siniard." Jack grimaced. "There's something about that guy. He gets under my skin. I wouldn't trust him as far as I could throw him. He's a snake in the grass."

Finley opted not to point out that plenty of his colleagues considered Jack a snake. But he was right about Siniard. He was a little oilier than most. How the hell had Holmes managed to land Siniard? The Legard name, she supposed.

"When you speak to your father, don't mention this case. I'd like to see how this shakes down before the news that I'm representing the Legards gets out."

Finley eyed her boss speculatively. Well, well . . . the stakes had just risen to the next level. "So, my mother is the judge who drew the case."

"I'm hoping she'll recuse herself," Jack offered.

Not a chance. Her mother would die first. "I won't hold my breath on that one."

"When there's nothing else, Fin, there's always hope."

She wasn't holding her breath on that either.

This felt like the perfect opportunity. She went for it. "Are you ever going to tell me what happened between you and the Judge?"

His silver eyes narrowed to slits. "You kick a guy when he's vulnerable, do ya?" He grunted. "And they call *me* ruthless."

"I should get to work," she said rather than waste time arguing an unwinnable case. "You need to go by the office on your way home and take your penance."

He groaned. "I haven't had a drink in nearly five years. Don't I get credit for not screwing up my record?"

"Sure. It's the disappearing act that has you on Nita's bad side. You should have called."

He growled. "We've worked together for a lot of years—this is the first time I have failed to call."

"Even if you're a model citizen your whole life," Finley reminded him, "and then you kill someone, you're still a murderer."

Which begged a question: Why did having lunch with Sophia Legard push Jack so close to falling off the edge?

4

9:20 p.m.

Finley sat in the darkness of her car. She'd begged off Matt's dinner invitation. Worse, she'd done it via text and then turned off her phone. He would forgive her. Work was his obsession too. He was just a little better at appearing to balance work and his personal life. She'd never quite refined that skill.

Derrick hadn't minded. He'd respected her dedication.

So, like most evenings, tonight she had spent hours going through the Legard case file. She'd read every single report. The interviews. The autopsy. And she'd done some research into what the daughters and the mother had been up to for the past five years.

Sophia Legard, the mother, had taken the reins of her husband's company. As it turned out, he'd been involved in far more than the music label. He had dabbled in property development and the stock market. The Legards' current worth was several times more now than before the murder. Part of that, of course, could be ascribed to the recent real estate boom. The majority, however, was related to far wiser investing in the market. The wife had a knack, it seemed, for choosing well.

Did that include her friends? At fifty-nine she was two years younger than Jack. It was conceivable they knew each other. Nashville wasn't that large. Both were high-profile people. It was certainly even possible they were friends. She thought of how her boss had felt the need for his first drink in years after a single meeting with Sophia Legard and how he'd averted his eyes when they'd talked about her. Finley made a mental note to look into the possibility the two had a personal history.

The daughter Cecelia was suspected of being agoraphobic. According to social media and various style and social bloggers, she had left the house less and less over time. She had no assets of her own that Finley could locate. No driver's license. She looked basically the same—at least in the most recent photo available on the World Wide Web. Her hair was short now, in one of those neck-hugging shaggy styles considered to be cute and sexy. Dark-brown eyes, like Finley's. If anything, Cecelia was thinner than before.

Olivia, on the other hand, had gone blonde and wore her hair around shoulder length—the way the twins had five years ago. According to her essentially inactive social media page, she had graduated from USC and worked at a small advertising firm. Her apartment was in a more modest area of San Diego. No record, not even a parking ticket. According to what Jack had learned from the mother, Olivia was headed to Nashville but wouldn't arrive until late tonight. She'd wanted to do her interviews via Skype, but Jack nixed the idea. Not only did he want to interview the twins in person; he was well aware Judge Ruth O'Sullivan would never allow a remote deposition in a murder case unless there was simply no way around it.

Finley considered the Legard home. Elegant. European style situated on a large treed estate lot in one of the city's grandest communities. The twins had attended a premier private school. A deeper search of social media prior to the father's murder showed glamorous trips abroad and huge parties. In the many photos still available on the net, the two had been photographed more often with their doting father than with their mother.

Finley had studied the way the father looked at his daughters. Where his hands rested whenever he touched one or the other. Nothing overtly sexual. Cecelia and Olivia appeared as fond of him as he was of them. There were slightly more pics of Olivia with her father than of Cecelia. But not enough of a difference to represent any significant relevance.

The media snapshots taken during the trial had showed three women, mother and daughters, all seemingly equally devastated. Once the trial was over, the surviving Legards seemed to fade into the sunset. Olivia moved away, and Cecelia withdrew into the massive mansion. Sophia worked primarily behind the scenes, leaving the day-to-day operations of the family businesses to trusted staff. She was rarely mentioned in news released about the company. Her charity involvements landed her an occasional appearance in the Inside Nashville section of the *Tennessean* or a mention in the *Nashville Lifestyles* magazine.

Lance Legard had no history of noteworthy issues, personally or professionally, that had attracted unwanted attention. No lawsuits. No nasty rumors. He had either been very discreet or incredibly careful.

Finley started her car and eased away from the curb. Going from this neighborhood to her fixer-upper on Shelby Avenue was like moving from Neiman Marcus to Walmart. Not that she cared. She'd grown up in a house not unlike the Legard residence. More a museum than a home. When she and Derrick met, he'd been working on a fixer-upper on the East Side, and she'd felt more at home there than she'd ever felt in her condo on Woodmont Boulevard or her childhood home in Belle Meade.

A mere two weeks after they met, she had been spending more time at his place than her own. Barely a month later she'd leased her condo and moved in with Derrick. After what happened—in that very house—most who knew her didn't understand why she kept staying in the fixer-upper that remained *unfixed*. Her husband had died there. She didn't know a single one of her neighbors. People had come by after her release from the hospital to offer their support and/or sympathy. She didn't recall their names. In all probability most were more curious about the murder in their neighborhood than in her well-being.

Over the past year, many of the houses along her block had been completely renovated, while hers remained a bit of an eyesore with its ragged siding and sagging front porch. Roof still leaked. A bucket to catch the rain was a fixture in the dinky hall. Inside, the walls were only partially done. Electrical wiring and plumbing remained exposed in some areas. The original floors were in great shape, comparatively speaking. Derrick had said those floors had been the main draw for him.

Finley nosed her car into her cracked driveway. Grass had sprouted in the gaps of concrete. Walking to the front door, she ignored the fact that the tiny yard desperately needed a good mowing. She should hire someone. The neighbors' Fourth of July decor finally coordinated again with the stuff that had been hanging on her porch since July of last year. She'd meant to take it down, but each time she started, her mind played a nasty trick on her by replaying the night she and Derrick had hung those lights and the red, white, and blue decorations. Laughing. Lighting sparklers. She shook off the memories and unlocked the door.

As much as she loved those memories, they remained too tender to touch with any regularity.

After wrestling the box of files in from the front passenger seat, she shoved the door closed with one hip and hauled the unwieldy package into her living room.

For about ten seconds she stood still, eyes closed in the darkness. She allowed the memory of *his* voice to echo through her.

You're home late. Have you eaten?

She was always late. Work consumed her life then and now. Of course she hadn't eaten. More often than not she had to remind herself to eat. As hungry as she was when she finally made it home, seeing him had made her forget. Her shoes came off; her clothes followed. They would make love and then drink wine and eat cold pizza or peanut butter sandwiches.

Finley collapsed against the door and ordered the memories away.

He was gone.

No matter that his clothes still hung on one side of the miniscule closet they'd shared in the unfinished bedroom.

He wouldn't be coming back.

Even now she sometimes caught herself thinking "when Derrick gets home."

She should donate his clothes. She could use the space.

His old pickup was still in the garage. When she'd moved in, they had joked about how the right-leaning structure would never make it through the year. But it was still here, creaking when the wind got up and groaning when the rain was heavy.

The memories, his clothes, his truck . . . all those things were the reasons she couldn't move from this house. Parts of him were here, and she wanted to be near any part of him she could reach.

She switched on the light and blinked to hasten her eyes to adjust.

Despite all the work still to be done, the walls, the windows and doors—every part of this house had been touched in some way by him.

Just as every part of her had been.

"Enough." She rarely allowed the memories to overwhelm her. Doing so only led to bouts of severe depression and overmedicating with alcohol. Not a good thing.

Pushing away from the wall, she tossed her bag aside and went in search of wine. She would sit on her favorite end of the sofa and study the case file some more while she drank herself to sleep. If she was lucky, she wouldn't dream of *that* night. She'd relived it far too many times already.

For days after . . . *that* night . . . she'd lain in a coma. Bones broken, her body bruised and battered. Eventually she'd come around, and then the real pain had begun. The physical pain of healing and the emotional pain of facing the fact that Derrick was dead—and she wasn't.

All the while, there was the investigation into what had happened, with its "one step forward and two steps back" pattern. Her pain turned to anger and bitterness. By the time she was out of physical rehabilitation, nearly two months had passed and the case had gone nowhere.

Her life on a sort of blurry autopilot, she had returned to work at the DA's office. As if fate intended to finish the job started the night of the murder and, for added effect, right in the middle of her first big postrecovery case, she fell apart.

A psychotic episode, they had called it. Complete breakdown. Another month of a different kind of hospitalization and rehab followed. Bordering on violent, her episode in the courtroom garnered her probation from the bar. In a fit of outrage, she'd quit her job. To her way of thinking, she had lost everything anyway.

But she hadn't cared.

She hadn't cared about anything for a while. She'd holed up here—in *the murder house*, the news articles had called it—and tried to disappear.

Then Jack had pounded on her door and insisted she come work for him. He didn't give a damn whether she cared about living or not, he'd claimed. He just wanted her to try. He promised Finley that if she couldn't find her way back, he'd personally put her out of her misery.

How could she ignore the challenge?

Now, eight months later, she didn't think about giving up or dying very often. Only when an in-your-face opportunity arose, like the one during the attempted robbery at the Shop Easy. What she hadn't told Detective Graves was that she hadn't been trying to get the guy with the gun killed. Not really. In that fractured, twisted moment, she was hoping he would take her out the way he should have done before. Then she wouldn't have to keep trying to have a real life, and Jack wouldn't have to worry about holding up his end of their bargain.

In any event, she was still breathing. The ordeal had been nothing more than a momentary lapse in courage. No big deal. If Graves would get off her back, she could move on.

Lapse. Ha. With Jack it was relapse, because he'd fallen off the wagon before. For her it was lapse, because so far she hadn't actually killed herself. Just thought about it from time to time. But she couldn't. At least not yet. There was work she had to do first. Obviously no one else was going to do it. Didn't matter. It was her responsibility anyway. She was the reason Derrick was dead.

At first she'd tried to pretend it wasn't true. There had been no evidence. No witnesses. The police seemed more inclined to consider the event a random home invasion with a casualty. In the beginning she tried to believe this explanation herself. But then whispers and images from that night had started to invade her dreams, and she'd slowly realized what it all meant.

The case. The one she'd closed only a few weeks before Derrick's murder. That win was the reason he was dead. The bastard had even been so brazen as to ensure she knew the reason her husband was dead.

You take something from me. I take something from you.

The memory of those words whispered in her ear by the man raping her that night had put everything in perspective.

Except no one had believed her. Even Jack wasn't convinced her two and two were adding up to four.

But she knew. And she would prove it . . . in time. Until then she would take it one step at a time.

Really, she should be celebrating. The fact was, the police were wrong about the intruder that night. There had been three—not one.

But only two remained.

She had wiped the blood of the other one from her face in that Shop Easy. He had recently lost favor with his employer and was desperate—or so she'd heard through her sources. In any event, he'd decided to rob a convenience store for enough cash to get out of town or move on, whatever. Finley had been watching him for weeks before she'd followed him to the Shop Easy. She couldn't possibly have known his intentions.

But the situation had presented an opportunity. She'd taken it.

One down, two to go. For now, wine bottle in hand, she settled in next to the case file to engross herself in work. This Legard case wasn't nearly as simple as it might seem. There was something else here—something more than a murder for hire or a con man trying to get right with Jesus.

Finley opened the folder that interested her the most.

No one loved a good mystery better than her. Putting the pieces of the puzzle together would distract her for a while.

This one piece was especially enticing.

She read the name on the folder. *Olivia Legard.*

5

Olivia

10:05 p.m.

Legard Residence
Lealand Lane
Nashville

I never wanted to come back here again.

Never.

It makes me sick to stand in the street just looking at the house. The prospect of going inside is inconceivable.

I hate this place.

I blink back the burn of tears.

The two of them are in there . . . waiting. Waiting to stare at me and make me feel like I'm the one who did this.

It wasn't me. I have no idea how I will prove my innocence, but somehow I must.

They—my own mother and sister—will do all within their collective power to see that I'm the one to pay.

The route they will choose is easy to anticipate. I'm not completely innocent. I did things that will come back to haunt me now. In truth, they have haunted me all these years. No matter that I stayed away. You see, the things you do are the things you do. Nothing can change the facts. Others might lie or distort those things, but they never go away. Your choices, your actions are forever. You leave a footprint that can be followed if someone is determined to look closely enough.

The worst part is the idea that someone knows. Either someone saw you, or you slipped up at some emotional point and told someone.

They never forget.

Oh, they will claim not to remember. They will act as if they don't recall. But they do. They always do.

And that is how they will attempt to blame me.

Fury tightens my lips.

But it won't work.

My mouth relaxes into a smile. You see, I'm no longer the naive, sweet girl I once was. I've learned a great deal since I left this house of horrors.

They're going to be very, very sorry I was forced to come back.

6

Thursday, July 7

8:05 a.m.

The Murder House
Shelby Avenue
Nashville

Today's interview required that Finley dress the part. Professional. Unaffected. Black dress slacks, simple pale-gray blouse, and leather flats. The leftover parts of her life before. Except for the jacket. She'd almost always worn a jacket back then. But it was too damned hot to bother with a jacket today even if she'd felt the urge. A rainy spring had kept June relatively cool, but July so far was determined to make up for the unseasonably cool temperatures of the previous month.

Three cups of coffee and a slice of toast, and Finley was good to go. She tucked her toothbrush into the holder next to the sink and then rinsed her mouth. Derrick's Superman toothbrush still stood in the holder next to hers. The only bathroom in the house was too small for his-and-hers sinks.

Finley dried her hands and stared at her reflection in the mirror. Despite how carefully she'd slicked back her hair into a ponytail, her budding blonde roots peeked out here and there. She blinked. Considered shaving her head but decided she didn't want to deal with her father's fretting and questions. He had overreacted enough when Finley dyed her hair black. At the time it had seemed fitting. Her husband had been murdered. She was grieving. Black fit perfectly. The carefree blonde hair she'd been born with wasn't appropriate for her new, dark existence. She blinked again. Studied her brown eyes. Decided eye drops were in order to help with the redness left behind by lack of sleep. She'd ended up reading the Legard file twice last night. Hadn't fallen asleep until sometime after two.

Not a problem. She had survived on little or no sleep since law school. Enough caffeine prevented the lack of rest from affecting her performance. At least that was what she told herself. So far, Jack had no complaints. Then again, he might not tell her if he did. Just like he wouldn't care if she shaved her head as long as it didn't put off clients.

She walked through the house, grabbed the cross-body messenger bag she used for everything—purse, briefcase, what have you—and walked out the front door, locking it before moving on to her car. In the beginning she hadn't bothered to lock the door whether or not she was home. Nothing had mattered. What difference did it make if someone got in? She supposed the fact that she locked it now was a step in the right direction. An indication that she cared in some way.

Maybe. Survival was a primal instinct after all.

Besides, she did have unfinished business. Leaving things undone was poor form—assuming you had a say in the matter.

Finley ignored the pair of joggers who trotted past on the sidewalk as she climbed into her car. She had learned if she didn't acknowledge others with eye contact, she was less likely to be dragged into a conversation in which she had no interest. People couldn't help themselves. They possessed an innate curiosity that prompted questions: *Have they found your husband's killer yet? How are you doing? How's the house coming along?*

Attention focused straight ahead, she rolled through her neighborhood and merged onto Main Street. She would pick up Jack at the Drake and head to their destination. Her cell rang, and she fumbled in her bag for it. A glance at the screen and she cringed.

Dad.

Finley loved her father, but she didn't love his hovering. The man worried too much. Asked too many questions. And he was persistent. If Finley ignored his call, he would only call again. He would worry until he heard her voice. She accepted the call. "Hey, Dad, what's up?"

"Well, sweetheart, your mother is what's up."

Finley suppressed a groan. "What's the Judge done now?"

"As you know, it's her birthday on Sunday. I need you to be here, Fin. A person doesn't turn sixty every day. I want the day to be special. Can I count on you?"

Yes, Finley was well aware that Sunday was her mother's birthday. Her father had mentioned it several times in the past two weeks. There would be a grand party. Everyone would be there.

How could she say no? After all the man had done for her when she couldn't do a thing for herself? Impossible. Despite the fact the Judge no doubt couldn't care less if Finley showed up, her father would care.

"Are you certain she wants me there?" This was a reasonable question considering it had been months since Finley and the Judge had spoken.

The Judge hadn't approved of Derrick. She had done all within her power to make him disappear. Even going so far as to try paying him to leave Nashville. Things had gotten more than a little ugly. Finley wasn't sure she could ever forgive her. There were moments when, deep down, she couldn't help wondering if her mother had something to do with . . . what happened. She flinched at the idea. As much as she hated the way the Judge had treated Derrick, she couldn't bring herself to actually believe she'd go that far, or at least Jack had convinced her the idea was preposterous. Frankly, Jack had as much reason as anyone to throw the Judge under the bus, yet he'd marched Finley through the facts that her mother couldn't possibly have been the one responsible for the nightmare that had invaded her life.

The temporary obsession with the possibility had only been a way to try to relieve her own guilt. Finley knew who had killed her husband. She also understood that her actions were the reason he was dead.

She pushed the painful thoughts aside.

The Judge might not be guilty of murder, but she was guilty of a charge equally malicious: betrayal. She had betrayed Finley's trust. Pretending it hadn't happened wasn't an option. Nothing her mother did now was going to fix what she had done.

Their relationship could not be repaired.

"Of course she wants you there," her father insisted, dragging her back to the conversation. "And it would mean a great deal to me if you were there. To our friends as well. Everyone will want to see you."

Ah, the old "for appearances' sake" excuse. Judge O'Sullivan was a revered woman in the community. A *god*. To have her only child not show up for her birthday party would be blasphemy. It would be all the buzz in social media and on the news.

"After all that's happened this past year," he implored, "can't we have just one day of peace? You can go back to hating her after the party."

"A temporary truce." Finley almost laughed. "Historically speaking, I'm not sure this is going to achieve the effect you're looking for."

"Just do this for me," he urged. "Even if you only stay a short time."

There were many reasons the Judge didn't deserve Finley's father, and this was a perfect example. Barton O'Sullivan was far too kind and compassionate for her.

"For you I will put in a brief appearance." Agreeing didn't make Finley feel any better. The next couple of days would be sheer misery. The dread would overshadow all else. She slowed for the turn into the parking lot of the Drake. "I have to go now. Love you." She made that smooching sound she and her father had used since Finley was a toddler and ended the call.

She sent Jack a text letting him know she was waiting. His room was on the first floor at the end of the building. It was actually two rooms that connected. He'd made a living room and home office in one and a bedroom suite in the other. Everything he needed was provided for in the room costs. Cleaning and laundry services ensured he was taken care of. Takeout and delivery kept him in hot meals.

What else did a single guy need?

He walked out of his room sporting his signature ponytail and wearing the navy suit that deepened the pale gray of his eyes—not that you could see them behind those dark sunglasses. He opened the passenger-side door and slid into the seat.

"Morning."

Clean shaven and smelling good too. "New aftershave?"

"Same thing I always wear," he argued as he tightened the knot of the tie at his throat. The red-paisley pattern looked good against the lighter blue of his shirt. "You don't usually pick me up. By the time you show up at the office, the cheap stuff is worn off."

She was no cologne aficionado, but it smelled damned expensive to her.

"You read the file?" He fastened his seat belt.

"Twice."

"Thoughts?"

She eased out of the parking lot and merged into traffic. "Holmes has an agenda that has nothing to do with Jesus."

Any fool could see that.

"What about the other players?"

"There's a list of them for sure." Finley navigated traffic as she ticked off the names in her head. "The two detectives involved, Jones and Montrose, interviewed everyone even remotely associated with Legard. They couldn't find a link between Holmes and the Legard family. It feels like they pretty much stopped looking after their first round of questioning garnered nothing useful to the investigation."

"That's exactly what they did," Jack agreed. "They had their guy, eventually he confessed, and that was that."

"Saved the taxpayers a few dollars."

"That's what they tell themselves."

As Finley made the turn onto Lealand Lane, she noted the three protesters, handmade signs held high, at the corner. **JUST TELL THE TRUTH** and **CHARLIE HOLMES IS INNOCENT**. Not protesters, she decided. His followers. Holmes had spent a few years searching for fame and fortune in Music City. Like loads of others, he'd decided playing the low-rent club circuit would get him noticed and maybe make him a star. Except it hadn't. Eventually he'd given up and settled for being a session musician. He'd only managed a gig with a high-profile artist once, but he had found work often enough to survive. The rest of the time he mooched off the adoration of others. His life on the fringes of the industry, combined with his dark good looks, had garnered him a small but faithful following.

"You have to wonder about people who worship a killer." Jack turned to Finley. "What the hell is this world coming to?"

"Don't ask me," she warned. Though she wholeheartedly agreed with him, some part of her understood she was in no position to judge anyone.

At the gate to the Legard residence, she pressed the call button, then provided their names. The towering iron gates slowly swung inward. She silenced her phone and focused on the primary questions that stood out after reading the file. Why would Holmes come forward half a decade later with this earthshaking news? Had he decided spending the rest of his natural life in prison was not as much fun as he'd first thought? Not that overturning this one murder conviction would change his sentence. Maybe he was merely looking for a little more media attention? Maybe he was bored. Wanted a book deal.

Or revenge.

If a member of the family had paid him to clean up the mess, was there supposed to have been more money? Possibly some other promise had not been kept. Money wasn't necessarily a surefire way to guarantee a successful prison break. What did he have to gain? Nothing, as far as Finley could see.

Revenge. Had to be.

How was Jack connected to the family?

She glanced at her boss as they readied to exit the vehicle. Something about this case had shaken him to the core. More importantly, why was it—whatever it was—a secret?

Finley studied him over the top of her Subaru as she closed her door. "Anything else I should know, Jack?"

He straightened his jacket. Tugged at his tie one last time. "That's what we're here to find out."

Just what she'd expected. A nonanswer.

They walked side by side across the cobblestones and up the wide steps. "I hope you were able to sleep last night after sleeping all day."

"Like a rock." He removed his sunglasses and tucked them into a pocket. "That's what Ambien is for."

A frown needled at her. "Wasn't Ambien blamed in a sleepwalking murder once?" she asked. "Wait, no—it was like a whole crop of cases."

He rolled his eyes. "We're not having this conversation."

She moistened her lips to hide a smile. No man liked admitting he needed assistance for anything. Jack was no exception.

A press of the doorbell, and a tune of double notes echoed through the house. "When you wake up on the roof of the Drake or in the middle of the freeway naked, don't say I didn't warn you."

The door opened before he could fire off a comeback. Finley had anticipated a member of the household staff would greet them, but she had guessed wrong.

Sophia Legard, looking as regal as ever, stood before them. Her dark hair was cut and styled in an elegant blown-back bob, revealing smooth skin highlighted with just the right amount of makeup. As in her media photos, it was her green eyes that grabbed your attention. Wide, watchful. Cautious, maybe. She wore a sophisticated black formfitting dress.

"Good morning," Finley offered, propping a smile in place. "I'm Finley O'Sullivan."

Sophia blinked at Finley and immediately turned her attention to the boss. "Jack, we're so glad you're here." She opened the door wider and ushered Jack inside, her arm entwining with his.

First-name basis. Touchy feely. Note to self: What the hell, Jack?

Finley followed, closing the door behind her.

The vast foyer was exactly what Finley had expected. Lavish. Museum-like. She should have felt right at home, except she hadn't felt at home where she'd grown up in a long time now.

Derrick had changed everything. Her heart skipped a beat.

She blinked away the painful distraction.

"Knowing you would be here is the only reason I slept at all last night," Sophia said as she glided along the marble floor like an otherworldly being in a wisp of black silky smoke curling around Jack in his handsome navy suit.

At a towering set of french doors, they entered a grand parlor decorated in the same untouchable luxury. Perched on a long white sofa was Cecelia Legard with her shaggy dark hair. She didn't look up. Her attention remained transfixed on her fingers where they lay knotted in her lap. Her dress was a charcoal gray, almost black as well. Unlike her mother, who wore designer shoes with daggerlike heels, Cecelia's feet were bare; her toenails, like her fingernails, were short and unpainted.

"Cecelia, you remember Jack," Sophia said to her daughter.

Cecelia glanced up at Jack and gave a vague nod.

"Cecelia," he said.

"This is his associate, Finley O'Sullivan." Sophia gestured to Finley.

Cecelia gave Finley the same sort of acknowledgment.

Finley returned the gesture.

"Sit wherever you like." Sophia announced this as she settled on the sofa near her daughter.

Jack waited for Finley, who chose the chair directly across from Cecelia. Finley asked, "Olivia will be joining us as well?"

Cecelia flinched at her sister's name.

Jack took the chair neighboring Finley's while Sophia sat in silence, apparently grappling for a response to the question.

"Olivia prefers to meet with you . . . privately," Sophia said with only one stumble. "At her hotel. It's still difficult for her to be here."

Jack nodded. "Whatever works best for her. I'm sure she's feeling a bit jet-lagged this morning."

"We could reschedule," Finley offered, "if you prefer to do this together."

Cecelia looked up, her gaze locking with Finley's. "She won't come here. She hates this house. Hates us."

Her voice was oddly rusty, as if she rarely used it. She looked away as suddenly as she'd spoken. The hope for an honest and revealing response was the reason Finley had made the suggestion.

"She doesn't hate us, Cecelia." Sophia rolled her eyes and gave her head a little shake. "She's lived away for years now. This doesn't feel like home anymore. She's more comfortable in her own space."

Cecelia's fingers tightened so hard around each other they turned a bright white blotched with red. "I'm sure you're right, Mother."

"I'm certain," Finley offered in an effort to lessen the tension, "this is a very painful time for all of you."

"Having this nightmare ripped open again can't be easy," Jack added. "It was painful enough the first time."

Finley barely kept the frown off her face. How would he know how painful it had been for the family? Was his comment only a sympathetic gesture?

"It is unconscionable, and yet, here we are." Sophia pressed Finley with a stern glare as if she were the one who'd spoken. "Jack assures me you are the very best investigator on his staff. He's quite convinced you'll be able to get to the bottom of whatever this horrible man is up to."

Finley wasn't surprised that Jack had presented her in this way. Particularly since she was his only investigator. Besides, he couldn't exactly tell the woman that part of Finley's job was to determine whether or not one or more of the three Legard women was lying.

She glanced at him now. "He trusts my instincts, yes. We'll do all we can to resolve this matter quickly for you and your family."

"I'm astonished this charade has gotten this far." Sophia executed another of those brisk shakes of her head. "It's ludicrous."

"As I explained yesterday," Jack said, "there are protections built into the law to shelter those who are in fact innocent. Occasionally those protections are taken advantage of. Rest assured, if Mr. Holmes is lying, we will find out."

Cecelia flinched once more. This time at the sound of the man's name.

"Of course he's lying," Sophia said sharply. "You know as well as I do, he's a monster. You remember what it was like last time."

Jack definitely had some explaining to do. Since Sophia was so focused on Jack, Finley kept her attention on the daughter.

More knotting of Cecelia's fingers. Her nails were chewed to nothing more than nubs. She wore no makeup. Had scarcely brushed her hair. Finley suspected her mother had chosen the dress. Cecelia seemed more like a twelve-year-old than a woman of twenty-three.

"I remember it all too well," Jack agreed. "Our goal is to disprove his every assertion and to discredit whatever evidence he presents."

"Has his attorney provided this so-called evidence?" Sophia demanded.

"We'll have more on the evidence later today," Jack promised, charm oozing from him. "For now, let's go over some of the assertions he's made."

Both women waited for him to go on. Sophia watching Jack closely; Cecelia studying her own hands.

Jack generally preferred Finley do the preliminary questioning, so she began. "Cecelia, did you have any sort of contact with Charles Holmes before or after your father's death?"

All three women had insisted in testimony at trial that they had not known Holmes. There had been no motivation for investigating their claims. Holmes had confessed, and not once had he mentioned having been associated with anyone in the family. The act had been a random, spur-of-the-moment event. An impulse.

Except now he had changed his story.

"The police," Sophia said before her daughter could answer, "have already asked us these types of questions. Why is it necessary to go through this again?" She turned to Jack. "I'm sure you have access to the reports."

"Reports are typically not as reliable as hearing the account first-hand," Finley explained. "Forming opinions and permitting that opinion to show in a report is, unfortunately, human nature. I'd much prefer to hear your version of events rather than the detective's interpretation of your statements."

"This is important," Jack tacked on. "Believe me, we wouldn't put you through this if it wasn't necessary."

This seemed to satisfy her. "Very well," Sophia allowed. She looked to her daughter. "Cecelia, please answer Ms. O'Sullivan's question."

Cecelia shook her head before meeting Finley's gaze. "Never. I'd never heard of him before he killed my father." The last words were croakier than the others, and her voice noticeably shook.

"To your knowledge, did your sister Olivia know him?" Finley pressed.

Cecelia hesitated for a long moment, glanced at Finley before looking down again. "Not as far as I know."

"At the time of your father's death," Finley asked next, "were there any problems between the two of you?"

More twisting of fingers during a lingering pause. Finally, Cecelia shook her head once more. "Not with me. We never fought."

"What about Olivia?"

Cecelia shrugged, gaze on her twisting fingers. "I have no idea."

Finley took the opportunity to watch Sophia's face as her daughter spoke—particularly since Cecelia more often than not kept her head down, preventing Finley from assessing her expressions. Sophia's countenance remained utterly emotionless. Not the slightest change. Practiced, Finley decided. Sophia Legard kept her emotions to herself on a regular basis. Except when she wanted Jack to hear the worry and hope in her tone.

"Were there any business issues during that time?" This question Finley directed at Sophia. The subject hadn't really come up at trial since they'd already had their killer.

"This is an avenue that should have been investigated more thoroughly," Jack put in.

Sophia drew in a deep breath. "At the time I was not aware of any issues with his work. With these new and ludicrous allegations, I've taken it upon myself to speak with some of his close colleagues, and I do believe there is a matter worthy of reevaluation."

"That was a good decision," Jack offered. "These are people who are more likely to speak openly with you."

The ghost of a smile touched Sophia's painted lips. "I can't take credit for this information. A dear friend actually came to me last night. God knows our painful tragedy is suddenly all over the news again."

This was true. The Legard murder was in the top ten again. Finley estimated it would rise to the top of the headlines and remain there for the duration. "We'll need the name and contact information of your friend."

"Certainly. Alexander Collins. He goes by Alex. He was my husband's assistant at the time of the . . ." Sophia cleared her throat delicately. "At the time of his death. I'll text Jack his contact information."

"Finley will leave her number with you," Jack said. "It will be best if you provide the information to her."

Sophia nodded.

"What sort of matter does Mr. Collins recall?" Finley prodded.

"Lance had a number of private investors." Sophia angled her head slightly. "Those who prefer to stay out of the limelight but who want to be a part of the industry."

No surprise. Most large corporations had private or silent investors. Finley was familiar with the strategy.

"Seth Henderson was one of those investors. He had been friends with my husband for decades. When the label was started, Seth was the first one to throw in his support, which makes what happened all the more egregious."

"What is it you believe Mr. Henderson did?" Finley asked. It wasn't unheard of for long-term business relationships to end badly. In fact, it happened more often all the time. The world changed too fast for some to keep up. Emotions often filled the gap. Rarely a good thing in business.

"Alex didn't think much of it at the time," Sophia explained, "but with this latest drama, he believed it best that he mention what happened. Seth was having an affair with a younger woman. She really wanted to work for our label. She was . . ." Sophia exhaled an impatient breath. "A wannabe singer and thought perhaps Seth could be her ticket in. To make her happy, he asked Lance to give her a job that would expose her to the artists. Lance didn't like doing that sort of thing, but for Seth he made an exception."

The entertainment business was full of stories exactly like this one. There were those who would do anything for a chance at their fifteen minutes of fame. Finley refrained from commenting, waiting for Sophia to go on instead.

"Turns out she was a spy for a competitive label. Lance lost one of his biggest artists because of her."

"He never mentioned this to you?" Seemed like a rather big deal for him not to tell his wife about the loss.

"Not a word. Those things happened in the business. Still do. Social media is filled with what this or that celebrity did. Though my husband never spoke of this betrayal to me, I did notice Seth was no longer invited to business dinners. Lance made some excuse about the divorce that followed the affair having torn Seth apart and that he had withdrawn from everyone."

"I'll need Mr. Henderson's contact information as well." Finley removed a card from her bag and placed it on the coffee table between them.

"Unfortunately, he passed away year before last."

"What about his wife?" Jack asked. "What was her name?"

From time to time, Finley glanced at Cecelia. She kept her head down, picked at her cuticles. She hadn't once changed position. Not the first squirm. Perhaps there was something to the rumor of agoraphobia.

"Gloria," Sophia said in answer to Jack's question. "I can provide her information as well. I'm not sure how much help she can be. Neither of us were involved with the business at the time. My girls were in their senior year of high school, and Gloria was struggling with a new career of her own."

Silence held the conversation on a sort of pause for several seconds.

"There is one other question I'd like to ask," Finley said.

Sophia met her gaze and waited, her face still an unreadable mask.

Finley shifted her attention to the daughter. "Cecelia, is it true that you don't leave the house?"

Her fidgeting fingers stilled. Five beats passed before Cecelia looked up. "I never leave the house."

"It's another aspect of this tragedy," Sophia said. "I lost one daughter to geography and the other to an illness I can't understand. She has no friends. Never talks on the phone or has visitors. It's so sad for her."

Cecelia had already gone back to studying her hands.

Strange as it was, Finley completely understood.

Jack offered another assurance that he and Finley would find the answers they needed. He tossed in that there would likely be more questions. Sophia thanked him repeatedly as she showed them to the door.

The walk to the car was rife with tension, but Finley wasn't saying a word until they were out of there.

As she slid behind the wheel of her car, she glanced back at the house. Cecelia stood at a window staring out at her. Finley waved, and the curtain fell in front of the other woman, blocking her from view.

Since she'd been overwhelmed with her final year at law school, Finley remembered very little about the Legard sisters . . . or the murder, for that matter. But, for now, it was the mother who intrigued her most.

Sophia didn't appear nearly as upset about the accusations against her daughter as Finley would have expected. She was calm and businesslike. Stated the facts. Offered opinions.

Sophia Legard was either incredibly confident or lying through her perfect teeth.

But she wasn't the only one.

When the gates opened and Finley drove away from the property, she shot her boss a look. "What the hell, Jack?"

"Don't start," he warned as he shoved his sunglasses back into place. "It was five years ago."

Holy shit. "You had an affair with her."

"I wouldn't call it an affair."

"Oh my God." Finley's fingers tightened on the steering wheel. "You should not be representing this family."

She drove several blocks before he summoned a response.

"Give me a break on this one, Fin. I gotta do what I gotta do, all right?"

She braked for a light, faced him, and stared into those dark glasses. Of course she understood. Maybe better than anyone else, considering her own circumstances. "All right." The light changed, and she drove on. "Just remember that when you get another complaint about my tactics."

Jack laughed. "Deal."

7

10:30 a.m.

Margaritaville Hotel
John Lewis Way South
Nashville

Finley and Jack were instructed by the lady behind the reception desk to wait at a table in the bar by the pool. As it turned out, Sophia Legard had known only the hotel her daughter had chosen, not the room number. Finley surveyed the outdoor dining area that surrounded them. The wait was definitely not a hardship. Nice view, and they had the space to themselves save for the bartender behind the gleaming bar.

Apparently, geography wasn't the only distance between Olivia and the rest of the family.

Not that Finley was judging. She hadn't spoken to her mother in more than six months. Their last exchange had been a heated shouting match that brought tears to her father's eyes. Not Finley's finest hour. Her father didn't deserve the pain the rift between Finley and her mother had caused. After Derrick's death, her mother had attempted to negotiate with Finley through her father, but she'd refused to listen. Wellman, the detective in charge of the case, had assured Finley that

Judge O'Sullivan had called the chief of police personally and urged him to put his best on Finley's case.

"Just look how that turned out," she mumbled.

The case had gone ice cold. Not a single lead or even the first clue.

Maybe the Judge had gotten what she wanted after all. Derrick was out of her life for good.

"Did you say something?"

Finley glanced at Jack and the sparkling water he'd been nursing since they arrived. She reached for her own glass of the same. "Nothing. I was just thinking about—"

"Mr. Finnegan?"

Finley blinked, focused on the woman who now stood at their table. Olivia Legard. The spitting image of Cecelia Legard except for the blonde hair and bloodred nails. She wore a sleek cream-colored wide-legged jumpsuit that looked somehow casual and elegant at the same time.

Jack stood. "Olivia, thank you for meeting us."

"Ms. Legard." Finley offered her hand. "I hope your trip was unremarkable."

Olivia barely grazed Finley's palm with her own. "Most unremarkable."

She sat down, and Jack resumed his seat. The waiter immediately reappeared.

"Coffee," Olivia said with a smile for the older man, who obviously thought she was some sort of celebrity.

The younger-by-five-minutes twin certainly dressed the part. Not flashy or glittery, just stylish and quietly elegant. Her makeup was flawless, making her seem far more mature than her sister. The red on her lips created an illusion of lushness missing from Cecelia's. The muted color on her cheeks gave her pale skin a healthy glow.

Finley's mother used to remind her frequently that a little touch of this and that went a long way. Finley couldn't remember the last time she'd bothered to go the distance and really make up her face. She was content with her naked lips and clean-lashed dark eyes. She'd never been especially fond of cosmetics. Her one concession was a little blush on her cheeks; otherwise, she appeared as white as a freshly drained corpse in a morgue.

"We spoke with your mother and your sister this morning," Finley began, kicking off the interview.

"I suppose they told you how disappointed in me they are." She shrugged. "I can't be a part of that anymore. I had to get away. Start my own life." She turned to Jack. "You understand. Mother is the most suffocating person on the planet."

Just how well did Jack know this family? Finley continued to be amazed.

"She worries," he offered, staying neutral on the subject.

Finley picked up her sweating glass. "I can understand the need to escape. Family is not always everything it's cracked up to be."

Olivia assessed her for a long moment. "I did a little research on you, Ms. O'Sullivan."

"Finley," she countered before sipping her water.

"Finley." Olivia nodded. "You're an outstanding attorney."

Most people qualified that statement with *were*. "I had my moments."

"*I* can understand how what happened shattered who you once were. Life is never the same after . . ." She drew in a deep breath. "Murder."

"You wanted," Finley offered, "to put it behind you."

"I had to. I was very close to my father."

The waiter reappeared and set a coffee before Olivia, then disappeared once more.

"He and I were . . ." She smiled. "So much alike. I really never had much in common with my sister beyond what you see when you look at me. We're nothing alike. She was the social butterfly. Always at one party or another. Hanging with friends. Getting into trouble."

"Trouble?" Finley's eyebrows rose. No one interviewed five years ago had mentioned either of the twins being in trouble or causing trouble.

"Skipping class at school. Sneaking out of the house in the middle of the night. Going to clubs." She sighed. "To say she was a wild one would be putting it mildly."

"She kept her grades up," Finley noted. "Graduated with honors."

"I did her homework. Took the big tests for her. The teachers were never able to tell us apart. I had no social life, so I didn't mind. I was happier at home or at a library with my head stuck in a book."

The good daughter. "Were your parents aware of Cecelia's adventures?"

"Father was onto her constantly. Mother pretended not to notice. In her eyes, Cecelia could never do anything wrong. She still protects her. Coddles her rather than getting her the help she needs."

"Sounds as if Cecelia and your father didn't get along," Jack suggested gently.

"Not at all."

"Is that why she wanted him out of the way?" Jack asked, not so gently.

He was particularly good at shifting gears and even sides at just the right juncture. Pouncing like a cat on an unsuspecting mouse.

For one long moment, Olivia stared directly at Jack. Then she blinked. "If you're asking me if Cecelia was glad when he was gone, I suppose on some level she was. Mother let her get away with anything. Without him to run interference, you can imagine Cecelia was much happier."

"Except she turned into someone else." Finley set her water glass aside, waiting for the other woman to meet her gaze. "She withdrew from life. Stopped leaving the house. She was suddenly free to do as she pleased, and she chose not to have a life."

"I left. I have no idea what my sister does or doesn't do." Olivia poured creamer into her coffee and stirred. "It's better that way."

"Did you know or have any interactions with Charles Holmes before your father's murder?" Finley asked.

"I had never heard of him. Certainly never met him."

Unlike her sister, Olivia maintained steady eye contact. No flinches, no winces. Not even a twitch.

Finley pursed her lips a moment. "Why do you suppose Holmes came up with this story about Cecelia?"

Olivia lifted her cup. "Maybe he's telling the truth." She shrugged. "How would I know what makes a psychopath do what he does?" She tasted her coffee, then placed her cup back into its saucer.

Finley couldn't argue the last point. The man wasn't a psychopath, but he was a sociopath. No question.

"Do you think he read about the two of you?" Jack asked. "Watched you on the news? Did some sort of eeny, meeny, miney, mo? Something like that for picking one of you to blame?"

"It's possible, I suppose. There was a lot of coverage about us after what happened. It's conceivable he somehow learned about Cecelia's escapades, but I believe there's more to it than some game of 'which daughter shall I pick.'" She made a face. "I just don't understand why he waited until now."

This was the part that made the least sense in all of this. "You were closer to your father. Is it possible he knew Holmes in some capacity? Is it possible Holmes worked with one of the label's artists? Or maybe one of your father's associates was involved with Holmes somehow." It certainly sounded as if Olivia believed someone close to her father knew him.

"None of the Legard Records artists would have been involved with the likes of Charles Holmes. If my father was involved with him, it was to help him. His companies made it a priority to help people who wanted to better themselves." She rolled her eyes. "Mother put a stop to that outreach when she took over. My father was a good, kind man, Finley. He loved helping others."

"What about his associates? Investors? Close friends? Was there anyone with a reason to want to hurt your father?" Jack asked, drawing her attention to himself once more.

"On the numerous occasions that I visited my father's office, it was abundantly clear that everyone loved him. I honestly do not believe he had a single enemy." She gave an adamant shake of her head. "I can't believe he did."

Finley was reasonably confident at this point that the man had at least one.

"Your mother feels one of his associates may have been involved," Jack pointed out.

"I'm sure she does." Olivia sipped her coffee again, leaving a red lipstick smudge on the rim this time. "Anything would be better than the truth."

Finley studied her for a moment. Like her mother, Olivia was quite adept at keeping her face clear of emotion. "What truth?"

"The truth about Cecelia. I can't prove it, but I'm convinced he—Charles Holmes—is telling the truth. Cecelia must have hooked up with him somehow. As I look back, it makes complete sense. She virtually hated our father. She was running wild. She could have met Holmes, and we would never have known."

"You have no doubt Cecelia was capable of this sort of thing?" Finley was surprised the woman would throw her sister under the bus so early in the game.

"None at all."

"Like you," Jack challenged, "Cecelia says she never met him. Didn't know him."

"There's something you should know about my sister, Mr. Finnegan."

"What would that be?" he asked.

"She lies. All the time. About everything."

8

1:00 p.m.

Finnegan Law Firm
Tenth Avenue
Nashville

Finley spread the pages across the picnic table, then placed borrowed mugs from the break room on the stacks. She dropped the printer-paper box on the grass and propped her elbows on the table to survey the first pages of each stack. This was how she spent her lunch whenever she was at the office—weather permitting, of course.

Being outside—alone—cleared her head, allowed her to concentrate.

Not that eating was on her mind. It was the case. Always the case. She flipped open her spiral and scanned the notes she'd made on the interviews of the Legard family. Jack was catching up on calls and kissing up to Nita to make amends. He was still keeping mum about his former relationship with Sophia Legard. They'd barely dug into this case, and already there was enough conflict of interest to gracefully bow out. Finley had a feeling that was not going to happen.

In the parking lot behind her a car door closed, drawing her gaze there.

"I figured I'd find you here," Matt called out as he walked toward her, a white lunch-size box in each hand.

"My fav work spot." She reorganized her stacks to make room for him and the boxes she recognized from the Hole in the Wall deli over on Main. Her stomach rumbled, warning that she was hungry whether she bothered to acknowledge it or not. She should have taken Jack up on his offer to buy her lunch after the meeting with Olivia. But she hadn't wanted to eat. She'd wanted to dissect the conversation.

Matt settled on the opposite side of the picnic table and started removing butcher paper–wrapped goodies from the boxes. "Since we missed dinner together last night, I decided I'd surprise you with lunch."

Oh yeah. He definitely had something on his mind. Something he really didn't want to tell her but had no choice. Something outside the boundaries of their friendship.

"How do you know I didn't already have lunch?" she countered. She'd known him her whole life. He was many things, but he was not psychic.

"I called Nita and asked her."

She grinned. Nope, Matt wasn't psychic, but he was very good at finding the answers he needed.

"So who did I piss off this time?" Probably the mayor. Or the chief of police. She may have mentioned something to a reporter about needing better police presence in light of the attempted robbery and shooting at the convenience store. "If it's the chief, he can get over it. I have a constitutional right to my opinion."

"Eat," he ordered. "Then we'll talk."

If they hadn't practically grown up as brother and sister, she would have told him to bug off. But they had, and Matt was a good friend. He'd visited her every week in rehab, on both occasions—the physical one and the mental one as well. Besides, he was also an excellent source of information for her. Good sources were scarce.

So, she ate. Turkey and swiss on wheat with mayo and tomato, just the way she liked it. And sweet iced tea. A slight breeze fluttered the pages of her stacks. The picnic tables sat beneath big old trees with wide canopies for shade. She imagined many church picnics had been held beneath these trees on hot summer days like this one. Being stuck inside four walls had always been a sore spot for her. She'd hated her windowless office downtown. At least her office here had a window. Still, outside was better.

Matt finished off his sandwich and wadded the paper. "You're working on the Legard case."

The word was out, was it? She shouldn't be surprised the unholy trinity would be paying close attention to this one. The Legard case would make the national news. Preserving Nashville's reputation would be of singular importance to the city's most powerful threesome.

"I am. Jack is representing the family."

"Briggs is concerned that this one—being inordinately high profile— might be a problem. He's worried that if your history is brought into media focus, it could jeopardize the case."

The direct hit from the Davidson County district attorney Arthur Briggs, her former boss, wasn't easy to swallow. But Finley sipped her tea, then placed the paper cup carefully on the table before responding.

She shrugged. "I'm not surprised. Not really. Our esteemed DA and his buddy the chief of police are worried I'll find something one or both missed."

Matt chuckled. "No question. It's a big case. Everyone involved the first go-round will be holding their collective breath to see how it shakes out this time." He turned his cup around and around between his fingers.

Finley's instincts stirred. It wasn't like her friend to hesitate once he started down a particular path. "What is it you're not saying, Matt?"

She didn't miss the flash of indecision in his eyes before he spoke.

"You're certain you're up to this?" he asked.

It wasn't necessary for her to demand if he was serious. She felt confident her face reflected precisely that. Even as the shock rattled through her, she couldn't deny the question was a valid one. Didn't mean she liked it. Appetite gone, Finley rewrapped the remainder of her sandwich and tossed it into the box.

The truth was, that day in the courtroom last year had been a catastrophe. One that had defined her short career despite all her prior successes. Her mind had gone blank for several seconds, and then the room had come back into focus with a brightness that had hurt her eyes. Pain followed by anger had blazed through her skull. When the judge reminded her that the witness was waiting for her next question, Finley had lost it. All attempts to calm her down had only resulted in fanning the flames. She'd thrown her notes—anything she could grab—at opposing council. The only saving grace was that not a single person present had the wherewithal to video the episode.

Thank God.

"Hey." Matt placed a hand on hers.

She didn't draw away. He'd grabbed her hand a thousand times growing up. Whether it was running through the woods or wandering the fairgrounds to scope out the shortest lines at their favorite rides. His touch was familiar and calming. Maybe not so calming just now considering the question he'd felt compelled to ask.

"I'm here for you, not for them," he said as if he'd read her mind. Probably had. "We shouldn't even be having this conversation, but I can't *not* tell you, Fin."

"Tell me what specifically? That my dependability in a stressful situation is unreliable?" He needed to spell it out.

He released her hand, scrubbed his own over his smooth jaw. "This is more than concern for whether you can handle the stress. It feels like they're using what happened to mount some sort of distraction." He shrugged. "One designed to pull you away from your work with Jack. With the Legard case, I mean."

This gave her pause. Matt was far too logical and too pragmatic to contrive conspiracy theories. "What kind of distraction?"

"You may not have heard, but Detective Wellman shot himself yesterday afternoon. The official cause of death hasn't been released—"

"Shot himself?" The news jarred her. She gave her head a shake. "As in accidentally?" Why on earth would he have done so otherwise? Wait. No. Either way, this didn't make sense. She had to be missing something.

"As in, he stuck his service revolver in his mouth and pulled the trigger."

Finley blinked at the violent image his words conjured. "Why?"

"Don't know. The chief pointed out that his wife died a couple years ago."

"Two years is a long time to wait to join your partner in death," Finley argued. Wellman had talked about his wife often. "Besides, he has—had—two sons who have kids. They visit him all the time. Why would he check out like that? Did he leave a note?"

"If he did, it hasn't been found yet."

It wasn't like this sort of thing didn't happen. Cops weren't immune. But . . . Finley thought of the voice mail. "He called me yesterday, but I missed him. I tried calling him back and got his voice mail."

Why would he call her if he'd planned to take his life? To apologize for not solving Derrick's case? Had he learned something new he wanted to share before . . . ? She doubted he would take the time to update her if he was contemplating suicide.

"He called you?" Matt frowned, took a moment to absorb her news. "I don't have any idea why he would have called you, or any other details about his death." He searched her gaze a moment. "It's the chief's reaction to Wellman's death that has me worried. He reassigned Derrick's case first thing this morning."

Now Finley was even more confused. Wouldn't all Wellman's cases be reassigned? Chief of Police Lawrence's personal interest in the reassignment was likely because he and the DA were friends of the Judge, and she wanted the case closed. Wellman had told Finley how her mother pushed him about the case.

"You've lost me. What does Wellman's death and the new case assignment have to do with the chief and my involvement in the Legard case?"

"Lawrence gave specific instructions regarding Derrick's case. He wants it dissected," Matt explained, "starting with any role you played in what happened that night. He wants this new detective to get deep under your skin. His words, Fin. He wants you pressured."

"Wait." Finley held up her hands. She had to have heard that one part wrong. "What the hell does that mean, *the role I played*?"

"He didn't clarify the statement." Matt leaned slightly forward as if what he had to say next was particularly important. "But given the two cases—Derrick's and Legard's—came up in the same conversation as did the emphasis on your supposed role, there must be a connection. I don't recall all this concern for how Derrick's case was being handled months ago or even last week. Do you?"

When she moved her head side to side in a no, he went on. "There's a motive here, Fin, and I think it's about keeping you in check."

Anger fired in her, burning away the confusion. "You're right. The chief didn't just wake up this morning with a one-year-old unsolved homicide on his mind. This is unquestionably about the Legard case."

"Whatever the goal, you need to watch your back," Matt warned. "You may want to consider speaking to the Judge. Maybe she knows what's going on, maybe she doesn't, but she needs to know that *you* know."

The Judge would be fully informed. Finley had no doubt about that part. Not to mention, the Judge and Detective Wellman had attended church together when they were kids. According to Finley's dad, the Judge considered Wellman a stellar detective. She would already be aware of all this.

Had the chief expressed his concerns to the Judge and briefed her on his plan for Derrick's case? Or . . . was this *her* plan?

Who the hell knew?

"As grateful as I am for the heads-up," Finley said, "I can't have that conversation with the Judge. Our relationship doesn't work that way anymore." Before he could counter, she asked, "Who's the new detective on the case?"

If the chief wanted the case dissected, the new guy would want to repeat all the interviews. Go over all the reports and lack of evidence. Finley wasn't looking forward to walking that road again, but if it helped prove the truth, she would walk across broken glass. But it wouldn't. Throwing her story at another detective wasn't going to change the steps he or she chose to take either. Especially a new detective who would want to impress the boss.

The chief and the DA were convinced Finley's theory about the man who had her husband killed was just another facet of her breakdown. So she'd stopped trying to convince them.

"Eric Houser," Matt said. "He's new to Metro. Word is, he's top notch."

"Fresh eyes can't hurt," she offered less than enthusiastically.

"We both know what they're doing, Fin."

They wanted her off the Legard case. What better way than to attack her credibility?

"The shooting at the convenience store was mentioned as well," Matt went on.

Of course it was. She took a breath, thought through her response. Whatever else Briggs and Lawrence suspected, they couldn't know the parts she had kept to herself.

No one did. Not even Matt.

"I'll try really hard not to give them any more ammunition," she said, annoyed the words were even necessary. She was not the bad guy here! Damn it.

But was she still one of the good guys?

Finley squeezed her eyes shut for a second to force the idea away.

"I want you to tread very carefully going forward, Fin," Matt said softly—too softly. "Something is out of bounds here, and I'm not privy to whatever the hell it is. What I can say is that I don't like it. I don't trust it."

Trust in the system was something she had lost after Derrick's murder. When she'd finally started to recall parts of that night, her statements had been dismissed. It hadn't taken her long to understand what was happening. No one wanted her conclusions to be the truth. So Finley had stopped trying.

She suspected the DA, the chief, maybe even the mayor wanted her to fade quietly into the sunset. She was a thorn of some sort in their collective sides.

"I'm not asking you to walk around on eggshells forever," Matt urged. "Just until I have a handle on what's going down."

"I can do that," she agreed without actually agreeing at all. The truth was, she could do it . . . but would she? This was her life, and her husband who had been murdered. She wasn't going to play disinterested or oblivious. Never in a million years would she pretend to not understand the big picture.

Matt searched her eyes as if he desperately wanted to see what she was thinking. "Briggs made a mistake. He should have recognized your vulnerability."

There he went, talking too softly again. As if she were too fragile for what needed to be said. "I was the one who had something to prove. That I was fine. Derrick was dead, but I was fine."

Her friend shook his head. "He didn't care. Briggs only wanted to win, no matter the cost, and he knew you could do it."

Except she hadn't.

"Then he let you take the fall."

"I didn't leave him a lot of choice. I flipped out." She wasn't going to lie to herself or to Matt on the subject. In the end, her former boss had done what he had to do to save face—to protect his organization.

"Say what you will," Matt countered, "but he should never have put you on that high-pressure case after what happened. It was too soon. He knew better."

"Whatever." She shook off the memories. "I'm on *this* case. End of story."

Matt exhaled a big breath. "You will be under scrutiny. More so than ever. You have your own way of doing things, Fin, and I've always appreciated your abilities. What's more, you're very, very good at what you do. But between Derrick's murder case and this Legard thing . . ." He shook his head. "That's a lot of pressure and a hell of a lot of eyes on you."

She smiled despite her frustration. Couldn't help herself. He was the kind of friend who came along once in a lifetime if a person was lucky. Trustworthy, dependable, and caring. The Judge had expected Finley and Matt to end up together. She'd had the wedding and their whole lives planned before they hit puberty. But it never happened. Best friends. They'd never been anything else. Not a kiss, not even a close encounter. Certainly, being married to Matt would have been easy. They were exactly alike. All work and very little play. Focused. Content to be so.

Honestly, she had expected to be alone for the rest of her life . . . until Derrick.

Why in the world was Matt alone?

Good question. She frowned, stared at her friend. "Why aren't you married? If I could fall in love and end up in matrimonial bliss, why haven't you?"

"Is that what we're doing now? Shifting the focus to me?" He tossed his drink cup into the lunch box and studied her as if she'd just punched him.

"I'm serious. You're handsome, charming—you have money and a prestigious job. I know you date. Why are you still single?"

He laughed. "You may not know everything you think you know."

She was the one shaking her head now. "Don't you dare try that with me. If you'd met someone, I would know. You need to slow down and let yourself have a life. We're not getting any younger, you know."

Oh God. She sounded like the Judge.

Matt propped his elbow on the table and sat his chin in his hand. "I can't believe you don't know."

Her frown deepened. "Don't know what?"

"You're the only girl for me, Fin. Since you said no back in fifth grade, I'm doomed to spend the rest of my life alone."

Sweet Jesus, she'd forgotten about his proposal—contract, actually. He'd written up a very detailed contract regarding their futures. They would always be best friends. They would get married after college and law school because that was what people were supposed to do. And if necessary, they would have children to keep their parents happy. But no kissing or any of that other weird stuff.

Finley couldn't help herself. She laughed out loud. "You're right. You're doomed."

He glanced at his watch and grunted. "I have to go."

She pointed a finger at him. "I want more details, Matt. ASAP. Whatever is going on with Derrick's case, I have a right to know." Technically that wasn't accurate, but it sounded good.

"Count on it." He got up, grabbed their lunch remains. "Remember what I said—be careful."

"Don't worry, Jack and I have got this."

As he walked away, she couldn't help wondering if he was thinking the same thing she was thinking.

Famous last words.

9

3:00 p.m.

Collins Residence
Laurel Street
Nashville

Finley was glad Jack had been tied up the rest of the day. With yesterday's cancelled appointments as well as today's schedule, the boss was playing catch-up. She hoped Collins would be more open with her. Jack could be intimidating by just being in the same room.

Alexander "Alex" Collins might have been a mere assistant to the boss five years ago, but he'd apparently done well for himself since. His address was a stylish condo in a downtown Nashville high-rise with a city view that loudly proclaimed he had arrived. There was only street parking, but she lucked out and found a spot right away.

A doorman—of course there was a doorman; this was the lap of luxury, after all—had checked that her name was on his list before allowing her into the building. He had then directed her to the bank of elevators.

The elevator car zoomed up to the proper floor and opened into a lushly carpeted corridor. Discreet lighting and tasteful paintings lined the walls. Up ahead, the door to Collins's residence opened as she approached. The doorman had obviously informed Collins that she was on her way up.

"Ms. O'Sullivan." He gave her a brisk nod and opened his door wider in invitation.

She stepped inside and surveyed the place. Mostly what she'd expected. Elegant furnishings with just enough leather and wood to lend a masculine appeal. What she hadn't anticipated were the endless framed portraits of nude people. Women and men, old and young. Then there was the stream that flowed beneath glass and cut right through the floor of the room. Interesting.

"Thank you for making the time to see me." She didn't offer her hand since he'd kept his close to his person. Some people still preferred to avoid unnecessary touching, particularly with strangers.

He closed the door and gestured for her to precede him deeper into the massive room that was the pinnacle of open concept. From this room one could see into every part of the condo, including the bathroom. She decided the glass walls of that private space surely had some sort of darkening technology. One could hope.

"Of course. Lance Legard was the person who made my career in the industry. Anything I can do for his memory is not only my pleasure but my duty."

Good to know.

"Would you like a refreshment?" he asked, indicating the bar a few feet away.

"No thanks."

"I always have a scotch and soda in the afternoon." He walked to the glass bar that formed a waterfall at one end and disappeared into the stream beneath the glass. "Something I learned from Lance. Unpleasant things are always more tolerable after a good drink." He motioned to the sofa behind her. "Sit. Please."

Finley settled on the sofa and studied the man as he prepared his drink. Medium height, black hair with the slightest sprinkle of gray.

Deep suntan. The body-hugging henley and the snug trousers revealed his dedication to a serious workout routine. She'd been a runner once. But that had been before Derrick . . . before she couldn't possibly waste a moment of her time away from the office doing anything but being with the husband she'd been certain she would never have.

Did that make her like her mother? She'd often wondered why the Judge had bothered with marriage and motherhood. One Christmas during law school Finley had asked. She'd gotten an answer all right. *When I was young, it was expected. Women weren't considered legitimate without a husband and family.*

Well, that explained everything. Her mother had graduated from law school at the top of her class. Promptly married and popped out the requisite kid quickly and efficiently so she could get on with her career. Nothing like knowing you were wanted for all the *expected* reasons. The gospel according to the Judge.

Collins padded barefoot across the gleaming marble floor and sat down directly across from her. "How can I help?"

"Mrs. Legard mentioned you recalled some trouble between her husband and a Seth Henderson."

He sipped his scotch, then nodded. "Oh yes. Cherry Prescott. The P-trap, we called it. Three guesses what the *P* stood for," he said with a knowing look, "and the first two don't count."

Men could be such assholes. Then again, she might have dubbed the incident the same way. Men could also be incredibly stupid. She thought of Derrick . . . and Matt, and her dad. Not all men, but a good many.

"There was an affair," she suggested.

"It was far more than an affair," he contended. "Lance gave Seth's *friend* Cherry a coveted position, and it cost him dearly."

"Mr. Legard lost a major star because of Henderson's *mistake*," Finley began. "Do you believe the incident was in any way related to his murder?"

He shrugged, made a "Who knows?" face. "I certainly can't say for sure, but there was a lot of bad blood between the two after. Lance made it his mission to ruin Henderson. Not that anyone could blame him. This was a multimillion-dollar loss at the time. Considering the star in question and the heights his career has reached, perhaps well into the billions."

"If you would, explain how Legard ruined Henderson." It was fairly easy to guess, but she wanted the facts.

"Oh, it was very simple. He shared the disgrace with everyone who was anyone in the business." Collins leaned forward. "Discreetly, of course. Henderson was eventually edged out of the business. He retired early. Became a recluse until his death." He knocked back a slug of scotch. "Most believe he got exactly what he deserved."

Talk about motive for murder. From her research into Henderson's background, he had once been a very wealthy man. Yet his last-known personal net worth was scarcely above the poverty level. Whatever had remained of his wealth after the Prescott trap, his wife had taken. The two never divorced, but they lived apart for the final years of his life. She took what she wanted, and he'd let her.

"Do you have reason to believe Seth Henderson had anything to do with Legard's murder?"

Silence expanded in the air for a beat or two as Collins visibly considered the question.

Drama, Finley decided. Mr. Collins liked drama. It was the reason he lived in this exotic and elaborate downtown condo and the impetus for his "look at me" manner. He adored being the center of attention and, more importantly, in the know. Several of his so-called friends had plugged him similarly on social media.

"I really don't believe so. Seth didn't have the stomach for that sort of thing. His wife, Gloria—now there's a different story. She would eat her own children alive if it meant surviving."

"One last question," Finley said, deciding to leave the seeds of uncertainty she'd sown to germinate. "Why didn't you mention this incident to the police at the time of the murder?"

He nodded solemnly. "I've asked myself that question many times. As you can imagine, I've wondered if his death was a mere random act of violence. How does such an important and influential life end so randomly?" He closed his eyes a moment for effect. "Such a waste. Anyway . . ." He drew in a breath and met Finley's gaze. "I suppose I was in a sort of shock. They found Holmes almost immediately with his Jag. The story seemed clear cut. Eventually, the man confessed. The P-trap thing felt trivial at that point."

"What exactly did Ms. Prescott do for Legard Records?" Sophia hadn't gone into detail as to what she did.

Alex smiled patiently as if she were a child who simply didn't understand. "Well, I was his *professional* assistant. His right hand, so to speak. Cherry was his *personal* assistant and all that it implies."

Plain enough. "Cherry Prescott, is she still around?"

"Oh ho ho, yes." He snorted. "The way I hear it, she had a bad row to hoe for a few years after the murder, but she never gave up. A few months ago, she won the lottery. She is now the wife of Elton Inglewood."

Local movie producer. Not exactly Hollywood royalty but a big shot in the business. "Do you have her contact information?"

His smile was smug. "I have the contact info on everyone who's anyone in this town, dear girl. I'll text you her info."

Finley pulled a business card from her bag. She placed it on the glass coffee table that stood between them. "I appreciate it. If you think of anything else at all that might be useful in finding the truth, please call me."

He produced another of those smug smiles, his right forefinger roving up and down his nearly empty glass. "Do you want the truth, or do you want evidence that protects your client?"

Finley produced a fake smile of her own. "Isn't that the same thing?"

This was why she would never be a good defense attorney. The truth was what mattered to a prosecutor. Justice. The Judge had drilled that concept into Finley's head her entire life. This was also why even when her probation was lifted, Jack would never have her work for him as an attorney.

Finley liked sending guilty people to prison.

Sometimes defense attorneys had to defend guilty people. Not something she would do well.

When she stepped out of the building, the heat pressed in on her. She pushed her sunglasses into place and drew in a deep, humid breath. Temps would only get worse next month. August was always hotter than hell in the South.

Next stop—Cherry Prescott Inglewood's house.

She wouldn't call. Surprise visits were always the best.

At her car Finley paused. A note had been stuck beneath the driver's side windshield wiper. She pulled it free and opened the single fold in the piece of paper.

You are ice cold. Not even close.

She surveyed the parking lot. Spotted a man leaning against the streetlamp post watching her. He grinned, gave her a two-fingered salute.

A follower of Mr. Holmes, she surmised.

When he pushed away from the streetlamp and turned to walk away, her guess was confirmed.

Charlie is innocent! was emblazoned across the back of the T-shirt he wore.

Henderson Residence
Canterbury Rise
Franklin, 5:00 p.m.

Since Cherry Prescott Inglewood was currently unavailable according to her personal assistant, the widow Henderson was next on Finley's list. Henderson's personal assistant had assured Finley that she would inform the duty guard at the gate to allow her entrance.

The gated neighborhood was located in the Franklin community, where life was purportedly quieter and slower paced. Like Belle Meade, Franklin was one of those areas where the rich and glamorous flocked to avoid the commercial downside of Nashville. A good many young families who could afford the cost of living settled in Franklin to send their kids to the premier schools.

Gloria Henderson had sold their prestigious family home in Belle Meade right after her husband's fall from grace and built this home, leaving him to waste away in a cheap apartment on the less desirable end of Nashville's West Side.

Finley paused at the gate and showed her ID before moving on to her destination. The Henderson home was stately like the rest in the neighborhood, with pristine landscaping and the requisite luxury automobile in the garage. Finley had checked. Gloria Henderson drove a one-year-old Bentley she'd purchased with part of the proceeds of her husband's insurance. No wonder she'd never bothered with a divorce. A two-million-dollar policy was nothing to sneeze at.

The door opened as Finley crossed the veranda. A twentysomething woman with hair in a painfully tight bun and wearing what looked like a yoga outfit smiled in greeting.

"Welcome, Ms. O'Sullivan. I'm Donna. Mrs. Henderson is waiting for you in the library."

Finley followed Donna across the marbled entry hall and deeper into the home. The library was on the right beyond the main living area. No wood paneling or heavy furniture here. The room was decorated in pastels, and walls of bookcases were filled with books. Several sat face out, the revealing covers suggesting romance novels. The lady of the house appeared to adore one author in particular.

"Aurora Reynolds."

Finley turned to Gloria Henderson, who'd spoken. "She must be your favorite," Finley suggested.

"In a manner of speaking. Join me." Henderson waved a hand to the floral sofa. "Would you like tea, or perhaps something stronger?"

"Water would be great." Finley settled on the comfy sofa. Down filled, she decided.

"I'll have the same," Gloria announced.

Donna nodded and rushed away. Finley considered that next time, instead of a husband, she'd have herself a Donna. A personal assistant who could bring her tea or coffee or whatever. Do the laundry and shopping. The problem was, she doubted she could afford a Donna.

Mrs. Henderson snuggled onto the end of the sofa opposite Finley. "You're here about the P-trap. Alex called me."

Finley was grateful the lady didn't want to beat around the bush. "I'm specifically interested in how the incident affected Mr. Henderson's relationship with Mr. Legard."

Gloria Henderson was your usual high-society matron. She was closer to seventy than sixty but had the smooth skin of a woman half her age. If that was what made her happy, Finley had no issue with her life choices.

The lady had a fetish for pink. Soft pastel-pink trousers, pink blouse. Pink cheeks and lips and ice-blonde hair. Her manicurist had ensured her nails matched her fav shade of pink. Pastels had never been Finley's thing, much to the Judge's dismay. In her opinion all refined ladies wore something pink in their wardrobe every day. Maybe it was that age group.

"I'm sure Alex explained the dirty details." Henderson rolled her eyes. "It was all quite ugly, but I bowed out early. Seth's disgrace was biblical. The people in the music industry work hard for what they attain. Anyone who threatens or undermines that hard work suffers the consequences."

Donna reappeared with a tray and glasses of water embellished with lemon wedges.

"Mr. Henderson was aware of the woman's intent when he introduced her to Legard?" Finley sipped her water.

Gloria shrugged. "Who knows? Doesn't matter. What happened was his fault. Period."

"Do you believe he had anything to do with what happened to Legard?"

"Knowing what a coward my husband was, I doubt it."

"What about you? Your husband isn't the only one who suffered."

Gloria laughed. "I would have done something far more creative." Her eyebrows arched with knowing. "Prescott is the one you should be talking to."

"Really?" Finley studied the woman's contented expression. "She seems to have gotten her happily ever after in spite of the kerfuffle."

"In time, yes," Gloria agreed, "but she was dragged through the mud first. No one would hire her." She smiled. "Her life was a living hell for quite some time. Maybe you hadn't noticed, but the twit had the same dark hair and eyes as those daughters—the twins. Could have been her who hired Charlie Holmes. She may have passed herself off as one of his daughters."

The images Finley had pulled up on the net showed a blonde Cherry Prescott. But hair color could be changed, especially when a person wanted to hide. Finley knew this firsthand. Olivia Legard had done the same thing. Definitely a lead worth following up.

"But *you* didn't know him—Holmes, I mean—or have any dealings with him at any time," Finley clarified.

"Absolutely not." Gloria's face contorted in distaste.

"You never met him?" Finley pressed. "Never heard of him?"

"No."

"You called him Charlie," Finley pointed out. "A moment ago, you said Charlie. Why would you call someone you don't know by a nickname?"

Gloria's smug expression vanished. Face blanked. She blinked. "Did I?" Another shrug, this one a little jerky. "I must have heard him called that on the news. I don't know him, and I've certainly never met him."

Finley placed her glass on the tray Donna had left on the table in front of the sofa. She slipped a card from her bag and left it next to the tray. "I hope you'll call me if you remember anything else that might be useful in finding all the facts surrounding Mr. Legard's murder."

"I will," Gloria confirmed as she rose to her feet. "Here, let me send one of my favorite books with you."

Finley started to tell her she didn't have a lot of time to read, but the woman thrust a book in her hand too quickly for her to beg off.

"I've already autographed it. Enjoy."

Finley looked from the book to the woman. "This is your book? As in . . . you wrote it?"

Gloria waved a hand at the bookcases. "I wrote all these books. Using a pen name, of course. Seth's money was good for a while, but I had my own money. Still do." She looked directly at Finley then. "If you're thinking I wanted some sort of revenge against Legard for ruining Seth in the industry, think again. I didn't need his money, and as far as I'm concerned, Legard did me a favor. In truth, Cherry did as well."

Finley surveyed the quiet neighborhood as she walked back to her car. Other than calling Holmes by his nickname, which may very well have been because she'd heard it on the news, Gloria Henderson presented herself as frank and forthcoming. Finley's instincts told her that she was telling the truth.

She glanced one last time at Gloria Henderson's home. It was strange, really, when one thought about it. Life happened like a stage play, all the characters fulfilling their roles—surviving tragedy and reveling in success. Trudging through the paces required of the roles. Was the success sweeter if preceded by tragedy? Certainly seemed that way for Gloria Henderson.

10

7:00 p.m.

The Murder House
Shelby Avenue
Nashville

Finley tossed the burger wrapper into the bag as she slowed for the turn onto her street. She'd gone over the Collins and Henderson interviews with Jack. The P-trap business had intrigued him. His orders were for Finley to track the woman down one way or the other. Not a problem. Finley knew where she lived.

Jack had an update as well. Siniard had shared the evidence that supposedly supported the claim by Holmes. A handwritten letter from Cecelia Legard. Cecelia, of course, denied writing it. However, analysis showed it was her handwriting. That said, lots of teenagers wished their parents dead. Plenty talked about it, but that didn't mean they really intended to do it. Not to mention, the note stated Cecelia wanted *it*— and, for the record, *it* was not elaborated on—done as soon as possible. The trouble was, there was no actual mention of the victim. Holmes couldn't prove Cecelia asked him to murder her father. The letter only showed she had contacted him and wanted something done. Siniard was obviously hoping to raise enough doubt to win.

Finley braked to turn into her drive, and the gray sedan parked at the curb had her frowning. She wasn't expecting anyone, and street parking was par for the course in the neighborhood. Could be a visitor for any house on her block. She parked. Washed down the last bite of burger with a slug of water. She crumpled the fast-food bag and grabbed her water bottle, all the while watching the rearview mirror.

The driver exited the vehicle. Tall, male. He strode around his trunk and started up her drive. So not a visitor for one of her neighbors.

Older. Sixties, maybe. He adjusted his jacket.

Cop.

The instinctive adjustment that allowed for the comforting feel of the badge and the holstered weapon was unmistakable.

Maybe this was the new detective—something Houser—assigned to Derrick's case.

Finley got out, tossed the bag into the trash receptacle that sat at the corner of her driveway, and headed for the front door, which was apparently the visitor's destination as well.

"Can I help you?" she asked since he hadn't spoken yet.

He paused before reaching the steps, allowing her to go up to the porch first. "I think I might be able to help *you*."

She'd heard that line before. "How about some ID?" She paused and turned back to him. The two steps up to the porch separating their positions gave her the perception of an advantage.

He reached beneath his lapel.

"Easy," she reminded him.

His eyes tapered with impatience, but he obligingly displayed both hands palm out, then pulled back his lapel to show he wasn't wearing a weapon. Or a badge.

So maybe not a cop? Private investigator?

He reached into an interior jacket pocket and removed a credentials case, which he held in front of her face.

Richard Montrose. Retired Metro PD.

The face, the eyes, and the hair she hadn't recognized. Montrose had sported black hair five years ago. Still tall and fit, he couldn't have been retired long, though she hadn't run into him during her four-year stint as a Davidson County ADA.

The name, however, she recalled from the Legard investigation reports. Detective Richard "Dick" Montrose was one of the two detectives involved in the investigation.

"Finley O'Sullivan," she said, turning to her door. "But then I guess you knew that." She unlocked the door but didn't open it.

Montrose had joined her on the narrow porch, making it feel all the more restrictive.

"I hear you're looking into the Legard case."

On the street a dark sedan rolled slowly past. She watched. The driver, whose face was concealed with dark glasses and a beard, glanced her way. As if in slow motion, his mouth spread into a grin.

Finley didn't have to wonder who he was. She recognized him instantly.

He'd been watching her more closely since the shooting at the convenience store.

She smiled back. *You'd better be watching, asshole.*

She blinked and he was gone.

"The Legard case," the man next to her repeated.

Finley drew back to the here and now. "Sorry. What?"

"You're looking into the Legard case."

His voice was smoother than she'd expected. Inordinately deep. He probably sang in his church choir. Had a wife who had been his childhood sweetheart and a couple of kids in college. He looked exactly like the type.

"I am. My firm is representing the Legard family."

He nodded. "There are things you need to know," he said more quietly.

"I have the case file." Like that always gave the whole story.

He took a long breath as if the exchange had exhausted him. "I only want to help, Ms. O'Sullivan."

The exasperation that made a brief appearance on his face didn't show up in his voice. It seemed he really needed to get something off his chest but wasn't prepared to simply blurt it out.

She pulled her cell from her bag and held it up to photograph him. "You don't mind, do you?"

"By all means."

She snapped the pic. Sent it to Nita with the hashtag #visitor.

Then she reached for the door. "Come on in, but I warn you my place is a mess."

She switched on the overhead light to chase away the gloom. Didn't help that much. One of the bulbs had blown. Derrick always took care of those things. *Not anymore.*

She closed the door behind her visitor. "We were in the middle of renovating."

Derrick would have laughed and said, *The middle might be optimistic.*

An ache pierced her. "Have a seat if you'd like." She gestured to the one empty chair. Took her a moment to clear a spot on the sofa for herself. "I may have a couple of bottles of beer in the fridge if you're interested."

He shook his head. "Don't go to any trouble for me."

She placed her bag at her feet. "So, what is it I need to know?"

"My partner and I were the investigators on the case."

She made an agreeable sound. Leaned back into the sofa to prevent sitting awkwardly on the edge and crossed her arms over her chest.

"He was senior."

"Detective Raymond Jones," she said for clarification.

"Yes."

He shrugged, his whole body seeming to be a part of the movement. "I couldn't get right with the confession Holmes gave. The Jag was too clean except for all the blood and the perp's prints. There wasn't even any of the victim's prints, or a member of the family's. It was like someone cleaned the car very carefully, then tossed the dead guy and a bucket of blood inside. Then Holmes made it a point to touch everything."

That part was definitely not in the reports. "Why was that aspect of your observations kept out of the reports?"

"The word was, we had the killer. No need to muddy the water by asking unnecessary questions. Close the case."

"Did you voice your objections to anyone other than your partner?" His partner was deceased. Montrose would be in the clear if the shit hit the fan over whatever he said now. Lay it on the dead guy.

"I went to the chief," he said. "I told him I was concerned with the way the case was being handled."

"You spoke to Chief Andrew Lawrence?" Not really a question. Lawrence had been the Metro chief of police for the past fourteen years.

Montrose nodded. "He reminded me what a good, dedicated detective my partner was and that I should take a lesson from him and maybe I'd be looking at a promotion in the near future."

"Were you up for promotion?" Finley held back the fire that ignited. She didn't know this man. Jumping to a particular conclusion based solely on his word wouldn't be a smart move. But the chief was an easy target for her. She didn't like him at all. He was more politician than police chief. It was, she admitted, part of the territory. Yet, somehow it still felt wrong.

Montrose shook his head. "No, and I never received one. I did get suspended. After that my wife begged me to suck it up and stick with the job until I could retire, and that's what I did. At the end of my suspension, I transferred out of homicide and put in the rest of my time."

"Why were you suspended?"

"Because I blew up in a meeting with the chief, the DA, and Jones. I made my concerns known again, and I paid the price."

"This meeting included DA Briggs." That fire began to build. Her right knee started to bounce a little.

"It did."

Finley shot to her feet. "I'll get those beers."

Deep breath. Another. She had to be calm until she could verify this man's statements. Although, she wasn't sure how the hell she would manage that feat. She thought of Briggs's personal assistant—she and Finley used to have lunch occasionally—but that was likely a no-go. Most of the friends—she used the term loosely—and sources she'd made while an ADA had dropped out of her life after her courtroom debacle.

She snagged the last two beers from the basically empty fridge and squared her shoulders before returning to the living room. She handed one to Montrose and resumed her seat on the sofa. A quick twist of the bottle top and she downed half the contents.

Slow, deep breath. "You were saying."

Montrose sipped his beer. "That's it." Another swallow of beer, this one more substantial. "I said my piece, and that was that."

"Why bring this information to me now?"

Another quick slug. "Because I believe it was a setup and maybe finally someone will do something about it."

"You believe Charles Holmes is innocent?" Quite possibly *innocent* was a poor choice of words.

"Innocent?" He laughed. "The man is pure evil. He's not innocent by any stretch of the imagination. But I don't believe he killed Lance Legard. I believe he was hired by someone, or maybe he was covering for them. Either way, that someone needs to be behind bars with Holmes."

Finley sipped her beer again, took her time, relished the distinct fizz. "The scenario doesn't fit with his known MO, is that what you're saying?"

At the time of Legard's murder, Charles Holmes didn't have a known MO. It wasn't until all the evidence came back—connecting his

DNA to five other crimes, two of which included murder—that he was labeled a repeat, nonserial homicide offender. He hadn't sought out his victims. One victim had tried to rob him. The other was a man who'd attempted to have sex with Holmes's then girlfriend. He confessed to all once the evidence was put in front of him.

That said, Charles Holmes had all the earmarks of a sociopath. He even had the traumatic childhood to blame for his antisocial personality disorder.

"That's exactly what I'm saying," Montrose confirmed. "The chances of him out of the blue deciding to take a joyride with the dead guy he'd just killed—it doesn't work for me. He was too careful about protecting himself in his previous crimes. Why the sudden lapse in judgment with the Legard murder?"

As careful as Holmes had been about not getting caught in the past, he had left DNA at those previous crime scenes. A hair at one. A couple of blood droplets at another. Prints at three others. No big deal in his opinion. Since he hadn't been caught, he wasn't in the system. No witnesses. Nothing to fear.

"You're suggesting he wanted to get caught that last time," she offered.

"It's the only reasonable explanation," Montrose insisted. "If he wanted a joyride in a Jag, why not steal the car while the owner was asleep or at work? When he was pulled over by that state trooper, he hadn't taken a single step to cover up what he'd done. The body, the blood . . . his prints. All right there. He wasn't high or inebriated. He was stone-cold sober. Why? Unless he was covering for someone else or paid to take the fall?"

Finley couldn't argue with his assessment. "You weren't allowed to put this scenario into the file?"

Montrose moved his head side to side. "No."

Finley moved on to her next question. "Do you have suspicions as to who the actual murderer was?"

"Sophia Legard. She would have done anything to get rid of her husband to protect her daughters."

Finley leaned forward, her anticipation getting the better of her. "Did Mrs. Legard say something to you or your partner to suggest she felt her husband posed some threat to their daughters?"

Montrose stared at her for a long moment before he spoke. "She said she thought her husband was sexually abusing their daughters."

Finley sat back again, absorbed the impact of his words. "Your partner, the chief, the DA—no one believed this information required additional investigation?"

"Passing along that information is why I was suspended."

Finley's fresh outrage petered out a little as confusion took the lead. "Why would you be suspended for relaying potentially direction-changing information provided by a person of interest in a case?"

He stared at his nearly empty bottle. "Because it was my word against hers, and Sophia Legard said I was lying."

Well, hell. He said, she said was never a winnable situation. "Why would she share this information and then call you a liar?"

"I don't know. Maybe she lost her nerve." He shrugged. "Decided she didn't want to drag her daughters through the mess of it. Or maybe she thought I was getting too close to the real truth. I was the only one Olivia had opened up to even a little. The kid seemed afraid of her mother and her twin. I think the mother was worried her daughter might tell me more than she should. Could be she was confident Holmes was going down and adding another layer of ugliness to the situation seemed unnecessary. Whatever the case, Sophia Legard swore I was lying, and I almost lost my job. The chief let it slide with a suspension as long as I never repeated my story. So I didn't."

"Until now."

He nodded.

The chief couldn't fire Montrose because he was retired. She supposed it was possible he could lose his pension. "Why now?"

"I lost my wife to a stroke three months ago, and last week I found out I have terminal cancer. There's nothing that matters they can take from me at this point."

It was a long while after Montrose left before Finley stopped staring out the window. It was dusk by then. Streetlights had flickered on, and the children who'd been playing in yards had gone in for the night. The air was oddly still, the humidity too thick for it to move.

Detectives were not that different from prosecutors when you got right down to the basics. Both wanted to come out the winner in the end. Solve the case. Bring the perp to justice. Deals were made. Compromises. Even in light of what Montrose had told her, Finley could see how the right course had appeared to be clear cut. They had overwhelming evidence. It was all there. Motive, of sorts. Opportunity. Means. Why borrow trouble by deviating down some other path and diluting the case?

Renewed fury tightened her lips. Because it was the right thing to do.

What kind of decisions and deals had been made in Derrick's case? Don't look at this. Do look at that. What counted and what didn't?

These types of compromises were the reason she would never go back to this DA's office. She couldn't. Not after what she'd been through. Like most students of the law, she'd come out of school thinking she would conquer evil and injustice. Be a hero to those in need. But that wasn't how it turned out. There were the deals and the compromises—for the greater good. Some DAs took it further than others, and Briggs was one of those. He chose the easier route.

Maybe Lance Legard prompted his own murder by setting out to destroy Seth Henderson. Maybe Henderson caused the whole thing by falling for the damned P-trap and cheating on his wife.

Could have been exactly the way Holmes stated. He'd wanted what Legard had and in the heat of the moment decided to take it. Although that scenario was not nearly as likely. Humans were creatures of habit. Habits weren't abruptly changed without some sort of prompt.

But what if Lance Legard had been sexually abusing his daughters?

Maybe Sophia decided to take care of the problem. Or it could have been Cecelia as Holmes now claimed.

But what if it was none of the above and Cherry Prescott had decided to make Legard pay for damaging her plans?

Henderson's wife had insisted the other woman looked enough like the Legard daughters to pass herself off as one of them. In the end the woman had landed on her feet, but she'd gone through some bad times first. It would have been difficult to see any sort of good ending during those hard times.

The biggest question in Finley's mind was, Why would Charles Holmes take the rap for anyone? What was in it for him? He had no wife or children. No siblings or parents still alive.

What did he hope to gain? Notoriety? A name in the country music industry one way or another?

There had to be an endgame.

The pieces will come together. They always do.

Derrick would have said that if he were here. He had told her so many times that no one was better at figuring out puzzling cases than her.

But that was before she lost him and then lost her mind. Who knew if her brain would ever function as well as it once had? She had worked numerous cases for Jack already without any slips. This one was different, though. There were far more missing pieces. Far more pieces, period.

Not to mention lots of possible suspects beyond the confessed killer.

She needed a hot shower. A good stiff drink and a long mindless movie before bed. But that would never happen. No matter how interesting the movie, she wouldn't be able to keep her mind from wandering back to this case, or to the one that stayed close to the edges of her thoughts day and night.

Derrick's case.

In the bedroom she reached beneath the mattress on her side of the bed and removed the folder she kept there. She eased onto the rumpled quilt and opened the folder. The image of Carson Dempsey stared back at her. One of the wealthiest people in the country. He'd created a pharmaceutical empire. There were rumors that he was utterly ruthless and his tactics with the competition could be lethal, but there was no proof of any of those rumors. His support to this city made him a hero. Dempsey's influence was formidable and far reaching.

His one and only son, on the other hand, was a drug-addicted piece of shit. Finley couldn't prove it, but she was certain he had raped more than one woman and gotten away with it. But that last time, he'd made a mistake. His victim had scratched him. He hadn't noticed or hadn't cared. Either way, she'd had the intelligence and the wherewithal to protect her hands until she was at the hospital having the evidence collected. The other women who'd come forward couldn't prove their allegations, but this one could, and Finley had only needed one.

For months—before and during the trial—she had been under tremendous pressure to watch her step. Taking down the son of Carson Dempsey was simply unthinkable. There had to be a mistake. The evidence was tested and retested. Every aspect of the investigation had been gone over and over. But there had been no cracks. No mistakes. And Finley took him down. It was a huge win. National headlines spouted how money couldn't buy everything. Finley was suddenly a celebrated hero.

Then the obscure threats had begun. Eyes watching her. Little warnings, like a flattened tire and coming home to an open door. She'd talked to Briggs about the incidents, and he'd blown her off. She was overreacting. He was busy. To tell the truth, she had gotten the impression he hadn't liked sharing so much of the limelight with her. He was probably secretly pleased that she was dealing with the blowback.

Mere days after the trial was over, as if the Fates had decided to up the ante, the son ended up dead. Someone inside the prison—another prisoner? A guard? Who knew?—killed him. Two weeks later Derrick had been murdered, and miraculously, Finley had survived.

She was relatively certain that had been a mistake.

Once she'd been back home, it hadn't been long before she spotted the eyes watching her again. Like tonight when she'd been on the porch with Montrose and that sedan had driven by. Slowly but surely, she had recalled those eyes from that night. Dempsey's lackeys. No question. Then, when she was well enough, she had turned the tables on them.

Now she watched them. The same way they watched her. She knew their names, who they worked for, where they lived.

Not every day, particularly during a case like this one, but she watched. And they understood.

One down, two to go.

She put the folder away and went through the motions of preparing for bed, though she probably wouldn't sleep for hours yet. The tiny bathroom, like the rest of the little bungalow, was a work in progress. The toilet worked, and so did the sink, as long as you only wanted cold water. The hot water side had stopped functioning months ago. She could call a plumber, but the idea of someone else touching any part of Derrick's work in progress was more than she could bear. Still.

She turned on the shower, which still had both cold and hot water. Stripped off her clothes and stared at herself for a moment in the mirror. There wasn't a mirror over the sink, but they'd bought a cheap plastic one that was supposed to be full length but was actually only about two-thirds her height. It stood in the same corner next to the shower, where Derrick had placed it, the price sticker still on the glass.

She was too skinny. Her dad had fussed at her again and again about working to put some weight back on. Dark circles were permanent residents under her eyes. She seriously needed to take care of those roots. Why bother? She could just let the black grow off and go back to her old look. Be her old self again.

Finley dismissed the thought. The person she used to be was gone. Too damaged to resurrect.

The best she hoped for these days was simply to be. Dr. Mengesha, her ever-patient therapist, wouldn't be happy when he received that report and the video from the convenience store shooting. If she were lucky, Detective Graves was bluffing. He'd damn well overstepped his bounds if he hadn't been bluffing.

Speaking of lapses and relapses, when she'd spoken to Jack, he hadn't sounded like himself. Finley didn't like how this case seemed to be leaching more deeply into his personal life. She had a bad feeling about where that leak was headed.

For the past year in particular Jack had been her rock. Her anchor. If something about these clients shook him, they were both in trouble.

Big trouble.

Finley stepped under the hot, steamy water and closed out all the worrisome thoughts that haunted her. It would take more than a long hot shower to keep them away, but she would take whatever relief she could rally.

Tomorrow she would visit the prison where Holmes was incarcerated. Jack had contacted one of his resources at the prison and set up an opportunity for Finley. She needed whatever information she could get her hands on about any visitors he'd had over the years, and if she was really lucky, she might get an opportunity to chat with his pal who'd purportedly brought him to Jesus. The trick would be not getting caught.

To cover for her true agenda, she had a legit visit with Jack's favorite snitch.

Funny. It was almost like she worked on the opposite side of the law now, but that wasn't the case. She was just on the opposite side of the aisle fighting for truth by whatever means necessary.

She considered the idea again.

Wasn't that really the same thing?

Only the rules of play were different.

11

Cecelia

10:55 p.m.

Legard Residence
Lealand Lane
Nashville

They want everyone to believe it was me.

I know they do.

I know *she* does.

After all this time, how dare she come back and act as if she did nothing wrong. It was her. She loved making everyone believe I was the bad daughter. She was no angel. She just never got caught.

Even now she is fearless. She realizes this new person investigating the case will find her out, and still she dares to pretend she is innocent.

I smile. I hope Finley O'Sullivan finds the truth. Then it will all be over. I never have to be afraid of my sister again. Ever.

Look at her. She acts as if she is too clever to be caught. Slipping in, slipping out. If she makes a mistake, they will find a way to blame me. I am all too familiar with how her mind works. How they work together.

Finley O'Sullivan lies asleep in her bed. Did she not lock the door? She seemed so much smarter. She knows things. Sees things. I watched her when she wasn't looking at me. She's more than simply smart . . . she feels things deeply.

The cell phone camera focuses on her face. Her wide mouth. I like her lips. It's too bad ours aren't fuller. Olivia and I always hated our lips. Maybe if things had been different, one or both of us would have had some augmentation done. My wicked sister is thinking about the same thing. That's why she has the camera so focused on this investigator's lips.

Finley sleeps in an oversize tee. Probably belonged to her dead husband. I find it ironic that she lives in that house after her husband was murdered there. The killer did things to her too. The news articles I found on the net didn't spell out all the details, but I read between the lines. Her husband was murdered right in front of her. Then she was knocked unconscious. When she woke, she was restrained. Then she was raped. Beaten. The articles said she almost died.

I wonder if she realizes how close to death she is at this very moment with my evil twin looming over her. The soft flutter of her pulse at the base of her throat could be stopped with little effort.

My heart beats more quickly. I don't want her to go away. I like her.

The camera scans over Finley's room. It's too dark to make out the details of the interior of the house. Quite shabby. The visual moves through the back door and into the yard. It's too dark to see. Then the video sent to me via text ends.

What would my sister do if I called the police and told them what she had done?

She would only find a way to blame me.

It wouldn't matter that I'm a prisoner in this house. Or that my nightmare has never ended and likely never will.

This is my sentence for the part I played in what happened.

I close my eyes and throw my phone across the bed.

Someone else will die.

There is no way to stop what is happening. Not now. Not with the cat out of the bag.

I can only brace for what is coming next.

And hope it won't be me who ends up dead.

12

Friday, July 8

7:00 a.m.

The Murder House
Shelby Avenue
Nashville

Two cups of coffee down, Finley checked her bag once more to ensure she had everything she would need. Spiral with her notes. Relying on her memory was something she'd learned the hard way didn't always work out. Two pens, one pencil. ID, wallet, dental floss, and breath mints. Along with a fresh stack of business cards.

She'd gone over today's plan with Jack, and he'd signed off on it. Her actions reflected on him, so she attempted to be cautious, particularly when her intent was to bend the rules by bribing prison personnel and basically trampling all over the rules of evidence.

Nothing more than a typical day's work, and nothing like the "color only within the lines" work she used to do.

When she'd awakened this morning, her first thought was of Detective Wellman. Usually Derrick was her first thought. In that moment before fully waking up, her mind would bring him into focus and she could almost feel him next to her, hear him breathing. But then her mind moved into full consciousness and reality rammed its way deep inside her like a knife.

But today she hadn't suffered that sharp, piercing pain of personal loss because she'd thought of Wellman and his death. Why would he commit suicide? Why had he called her that same day? It made no sense at all. She'd picked up nothing that suggested he felt at his wit's end or despondent during their last conversation. She should ask Matt the name of the detective investigating his death. There had to be something more. Maybe like Montrose, Wellman had learned he was dying. Still didn't make sense.

A tap on her front door drew her thoughts away from the idea and announced her father had decided to pay an unscheduled visit. He was the only visitor who tapped. Jack banged. The man didn't like to wait. Impatience exuded from him. Matt had a rapid staccato knock that reflected his optimistic attitude and utter certainty that whomever he was visiting would be happy to see him. Anyone else, usually a door-to-door salesperson or religious advocate, used the doorbell—which thankfully didn't work.

Finley checked the time on her cell. She loved her dad, but this would have to be a short visit. Her trip to Riverbend was all about timing.

She opened the door and smiled. Seeing her father nearly always made her happy—even when she was on a tight schedule. The only exception was when the Judge had sent him to plead on her behalf.

He held up a small paper bag. "I have bagels."

She hugged him. "Come on in. I'll make coffee." She loved the person who'd created single-serving coffee pods. Fast and close enough to brewed to keep her taste buds happy.

When they were settled at the small metal table that had been in the backyard when Derrick bought the house and was given new life as their dining table, her dad passed around the bagels and condiments.

"Your mother says you're working on the Legard case." He said this while spreading cream cheese on his bagel. A packet of strawberry jam waited close by to join the cream cheese. Her dad never ate cream cheese without strawberry jam. Routine was his middle name.

Finley dipped a finger into her little tub of cream cheese, licked it off, and then took a bite of bagel. She no longer had a routine. Go with the flow, or fight against it—anything else was basically irrelevant. That was her current motto. "Jack is representing the daughters."

Her dad nodded slowly, then bit into his bagel.

He and the Judge had discussed the news. Not that Finley was surprised. They'd been married more than half their lives—they talked about everything. The question was, Why had he shown up this morning, bagels in hand? Not that she actually needed to ask. The answer was easy. The Judge had something to say about the case and Finley's involvement.

"She doesn't want me on the case," Finley said, going straight to the most likely point. No doubt the Judge had been privy to the discussion between the unholy trinity.

He frowned innocently. "She didn't say anything to suggest as much to me."

Maybe she hadn't. Then again, her dad worked particularly hard not to take sides. "She probably thinks the case will be too stressful."

"She does worry about you," he agreed. "We both do. Especially . . ." One shoulder lifted in a hesitant shrug. "When things happen."

Aha, the Judge had heard about the convenience store shooting. "It could have happened to anyone," Finley said without preface. "Nashville is a big city. Robberies happen on a regular basis. It was just my turn to be in the wrong place at the wrong time." Statistics. No one could avoid them unless they stayed home twenty-four seven, and even then, criminals broke into private homes all the time. A perfectly logical explanation.

The thought of her missing hairbrush poked at her. She remembered using it last night. But it was nowhere to be found this morning. The towel she'd thrown on the floor after her shower was spread across the rim of the tub. Her discarded clothes were in the hamper. Maybe she'd done those things and forgotten. She'd been tired and distracted last night. Wouldn't be the first time she'd forgotten something.

Yet, it felt wrong. As if muscle memory were denying any such activities.

Her dad placed his half-eaten bagel on the napkin in front of him and sat silent for a moment. Finley's senses went on high alert.

"She saw the security video, Fin. She—we—were terrified by what happened."

Not good. "You saw it, too, I guess." Great. Graves was at the top of her shit list now for sure.

Her dad nodded. Emotion shining in his eyes. "She showed it to me."

Appetite gone, Finley pushed the remainder of her bagel away. "It was a snap decision," she said, going for gentle but not quite making it. "It was an attempt to distract the guy, and it worked. Most likely saved my life as well as the clerk's."

Relief flashed in his eyes. "I told her you probably knew exactly what you were doing."

She reached across the table and grasped his hand. "I knew exactly what I was doing. Trust me." Did that make her a killer? Maybe. No guilt. The memory of the bastard's face so close to hers as he growled cruel words flashed. She blinked it away.

Her dad smiled. It was a bit wobbly, but the expression made her heart lighten. She assured him, "The Judge always thinks the worst."

He chuckled. "She worries."

They talked awhile longer and finished their coffee before her dad announced he had an appointment and should be going. Finley was thankful not to have to usher him away with her tight schedule.

"Don't forget your mother's birthday," he called out as he loaded himself into his electric-powered Prius.

How could she forget when he kept reminding her?

Finley promised she wouldn't and waved as he drove away. Before heading to Riverbend, she walked through the house once more and tried to recall moving her towel and clothes. And where the hell was her brush?

She would find it later. Had to be here somewhere.

Less than an hour later she was turning onto Cockrill Bend Boulevard. The maximum-security prison was located on well over a hundred acres and divided up into about twenty buildings. Riverbend housed nearly a thousand inmates, including all the state's death row convicts. Finley was to meet her contact at the loading docks behind the commissary. Mickey Kruger, a kitchen manager with ten years at the prison under his belt, knew his way around the place. Knew the personnel, including guards, who would look the other way for the right price.

Jack had an endless list of contacts, any one of which he could name without thinking twice. He refused to have the names and contact info written down anywhere. He always tapped his temple and said the safest place was right there.

At the security gate Finley showed her ID and was allowed to enter the property. Her name was on the list for visiting Arlo Gates, one of Jack's favorite jailhouse snitches. Jack took care of Arlo's elderly mother, and Arlo took care of Jack's needs inside the prison walls. A mutually beneficial arrangement.

Today Finley needed two things: a look at the visitors roster for Holmes and a conversation with the inmate he appeared to consider his buddy—Rudy Davis, the one who'd helped him find Jesus. Having a chat with Holmes would be the ultimate coup, but she wasn't sure even Jack would agree with that level of risk. There was bending the rules, and there was flat-out breaking them—like witness tampering.

She parked in an empty spot, powered her window down, and waited.

Two minutes later her contact, wearing scrubs and an apron, exited onto the dock and hustled down the steps. He surveyed the parking area and walked straight to her car. He opened the passenger door and dropped into the seat.

"Hey," he said with a nod.

He looked nervous, but that was understandable. She would be concerned if he wasn't nervous. Overconfidence was rarely a good thing.

"Hey." She waited for him to make the next move. This was his show; she was just here for the party favors.

"We'll go through the kitchen." He reached into his apron pocket, removed a visitor's badge, and passed it to her. "There's an office just off the dining room that the guards use sometimes. I can show you what you need to see on the computer in there."

She clipped the badge onto her tee. Mickey had suggested she dress casually. Jeans and a plain white tee. Worked for her. She preferred casual any day of the week. "What about Rudy Davis? Will I be able to speak with him?"

"Let's not get ahead of ourselves," Mickey suggested. "One thing at a time. The Preacher has his days where he isn't approachable."

"Got it." She'd been told Davis—a.k.a. the Preacher—was somewhat eccentric.

She followed Kruger into the kitchen and through the hubbub of activity. Feeding hundreds of inmates kept the staff hustling. Once she and Mickey were beyond the dining room, they entered a long corridor with doors on either side. Their destination turned out to be door number three on the left. The space was small with a narrow table outfitted with a computer and two chairs. No windows. No decor on the bland white walls. Nothing to stir or inspire emotions.

"Click the mouse," Mickey said. "What you're looking for is already loaded on the screen. I took care of that first to make sure it was up and running when you came in."

"Thanks." She settled into one of the chairs. The sooner she was finished and on her way, the better for both of them.

Navigating the application was easy enough. She located the name of the inmate she was looking for, and up popped the calendar for the current month. This was going to take some time. More than four years multiplied by twelve months.

She tapped the mouse and got to it. When she reached a date with a visitor listed, she used her phone to snap a photo of the screen.

There was a single name that didn't belong to an attorney or a detective associated with the case. *Alisha Arrington*. She was listed as the inmate's sister.

The thing was, Holmes didn't have any siblings. Parents were deceased. No known next of kin.

"I need an image of this visitor." Finley tapped the screen and stated the date.

Mickey leaned in close to the monitor. "I can get that for you. Maybe not today. I'll send it to your email as soon as I can."

"That would be great."

Scrolling in reverse-chronological order, she spotted that same visitor's name once each month all the way back to barely a month after Holmes was delivered to Riverbend. The woman—his alleged sister—had abruptly ended her monthly visits in February of this year.

Finley had a new mission for the day: find Alisha Arrington.

Mickey escorted Finley back to the docks. "I'll keep working on the Preacher. You'll hear from me if seeing him today is possible." He hitched his head. "Stay against the building. I adjusted the angle of the security camera away from it. Once you reach the end of the building, walk beyond the pavement, on the grass, until you get to your car."

"Good deal." She passed the badge back to him. "Thanks, Mickey. I'll be looking for that image."

He nodded and headed back inside.

Finley made the trek as directed, then settled into her Subaru. She checked the time. She still had a few minutes to drive over to unit one of the complex and visit Arlo. Getting an opportunity to speak with the Preacher would be great, but she would take what she could get. Arlo was very good at finding information. Every piece of info, no matter how small, helped fill in the blanks. Sometimes it was the most unexpected tidbit that made all the difference.

Arlo wasn't one of the worst offenders at Riverbend, which allowed him to meet face to face with visitors in a supervised visitation area. Finley parked and headed into the building. She signed in and waited for the next visitation time. Other visitors were there to see their friends or loved ones. A few minutes elapsed before the bell rang and the current group of inmates said their goodbyes and left the area. Maybe two minutes later the next group was allowed entrance. Arlo was at the front of the line of inmates. He walked straight over to Finley's table. The thing she didn't get about Arlo was that he was smart. Really smart. She hoped when he'd served his time he would go to college or do something worthwhile with his life. At thirty, he was still young enough to start over and have a long and full life.

"You're looking good, Fin." He grinned.

"You don't look so bad yourself, Arlo."

He laughed. Any compliment she paid him made him smile.

"So, Charlie Holmes." He scanned the visiting area, ever watchful. "He's the talk of the house these days."

"Is this whole 'found Jesus' claim legit?" She had her doubts, but it happened. There were inmates who found religion, decided to educate themselves or learn a trade. Being incarcerated gave one time to reflect and to change life for the better. It also provided an opportunity to go down a darker path. Prisons had their societal hierarchies and their secrets. There was more than one world within these walls. There were numerous kings and lords. The secret to staying alive was often as simple as keeping your mouth shut and your eyes forward. Other times it was a battle of wills or sheer luck.

"The guy Rudy, Rudy Davis," Arlo explained, "Charlie's best friend since like three months ago, is a serious Bible thumper. Walks around with the Bible in his hand all the time. Quoting scripture and shit, which is why they call him the Preacher."

"Three months." Didn't seem like much time for a lifelong criminal to become a changed man.

Arlo leaned forward. "Story is, old Charlie is making preparations for taking care of his family."

"Family?" He'd had one female visitor in all this time, and she hadn't visited recently. "Are you talking about his followers?"

Holmes had a small cult following related to his short-lived attempt at fame in the country music industry. Dozens wrote to him. Women and men. Some claimed to be in love with him; others wanted to be him. It wasn't unusual for a high-profile criminal to have followers. For a while there was some trouble in Nashville. Mostly private-property damage. Names of jurors were leaked and their homes vandalized. From time to time billboards were painted over with phrases proclaiming his innocence. Until recently, the group had basically faded into history. Now there was a social media page and protestors showing up on street corners who passed along warnings about the leads she was following. Finley expected to find them at her door any day now.

"I think it's someone more personal than that," Arlo suggested.

"An Alisha Arrington visited him once a month from shortly after he arrived at Riverbend until a few months ago. She signed the log as his sister. You heard anything about her?"

He considered the name for a moment. "Doesn't ring a bell, but I'll ask around. If this is right, I'm guessing the woman has more to do with Charlie's sudden change of heart than the Preacher, since he claims he has a family."

Finley agreed. It made a certain sense in terms of the timing. Holmes had been silent all this time, and suddenly he was ready to tell the whole story. If the notoriety garnered him a book deal or something on that order, he could certainly support a family. Especially if this sister got tired of visiting him in prison, as it appeared she had. Maybe he needed to make an impression for her. Or, more likely, money.

"I need anything you can find on this family. Whatever you can get." Anticipation burned across her nerve endings. This could be a significant break.

"I'll see what I can do."

"Any other rumors going around about Holmes?" she asked. "Maybe speculation about the Legard case?"

"Not so far, but I've got my ear to the ground."

They talked about how he was doing, and he asked Finley to check in on his mother. Then the bell signaling the end of visitation sounded.

"See you soon," he said as he got up to leave.

"Thanks, Arlo."

That familiar urgency she felt when she was onto something was pulsing through her veins on a burst of adrenaline. This female visitor was important. Finley felt it all the way to her bones.

She checked in with Mickey via text. He'd had no luck hooking her up with the Preacher. Maybe tomorrow. At least she wasn't leaving empty handed.

Beyond the exit doors the humidity met her like a wall of Jell-O. The parking lot was all but empty now. The shiny red sports car parked next to her dusty Subaru stood out like a sore thumb. As she hurried to her car, the driver's door of the red car—a Porsche no less—opened. A man sporting dark sunglasses emerged.

"Ms. O'Sullivan, I've been waiting for you."

Thirtyish. Dark skinned. Maybe Hispanic. Tall, dressed like a businessman. The sort who made an impression. Not someone she'd met before. She would remember.

She leveled a long look at him across the top of her car. "I'm afraid you have me at a disadvantage."

"My name is Xavier Stratford. Like you, I'm an investigator for a law firm."

Now she got it. "You work for Siniard."

"I do."

"Then I suppose you're here for the same reason as me."

"I don't think so." He removed his sunglasses and leaned on her car. "You see, you can't interview our client without our express permission. I certainly hope that's not why you're here."

"Of course not. Why would I break the law? Have a nice day, Mr. Stratford." With that she climbed into her car. Started the engine, turned the air-conditioning to full blast, and sped out of the parking spot, sending Mr. Stratford reeling back against his own car. She so disliked arrogance.

Siniard had eyes on the competition. No surprise there. He hadn't achieved the reputation he had by sitting back and allowing the other side to get one or more steps ahead of him.

Siniard wouldn't want Jack or his people anywhere near Riverbend.

Nothing he could do about her visiting the firm's own client. If their client passed along some sort of info about Holmes, there was nothing Siniard could do about that either.

For now, Finley's top priority was finding the mystery woman—Alisha Arrington.

13

1:28 p.m.

Inglewood Residence
Morning Glory Court
Brentwood

An invitation from Mrs. Elton Inglewood, formerly Cherry Prescott, waylaid Finley's hunt for Alisha Arrington. Braking to a stop at the towering iron gates, Finley pressed the intercom button and provided her name. The gates slowly glided open, and she rolled forward. The Inglewood home defined the term *modern mansion*. Twelve or fifteen thousand feet at least. Two acres on a cul-de-sac in an exclusive neighborhood. The hand-cut-limestone house was more palace than home.

"My, my. You've come a long way, baby." This was Finley's first up-close look at the place. Last time she hadn't gotten past the gate. The dense landscape made seeing the house from the street all but impossible.

Her cell buzzed deep in her bag. She shifted into park and dug for it.

Boss. She accepted the call. "Hey, Jack."

"You headed back to the office?"

"I was, but I got a call from Prescott's personal assistant saying she was available to meet with me. I just pulled into her drive." Finley made a long, low whistle. "Talk about moving up in the world."

Jack grunted. "Gotta give the girl credit. She didn't give up on what she wanted."

This was true. "I'm surprised she bothered to call me back."

"Technically she didn't. Her assistant did."

"You've got me there. So what's up?"

"Look, Fin . . ."

His hesitation had her bracing for bad news.

"You remember Lori Ann—she's been a clerk at city hall since God was a baby?"

"And God and everybody knows her," Finley said in answer to his question.

"She called and passed along a rumor she overheard."

"About?" Finley prodded.

"You."

She was certainly Miss Popular lately.

"Some sort of issue has cropped up in Derrick's murder investigation, and your name was mentioned."

"Yeah. I heard." A cold feeling slinked through her insides. "I am—was—his wife. My name coming up in a discussion about him isn't surprising." No need to mention Matt's visit. Jack worried too much as it was.

"I don't know, kid. Lori Ann didn't hear the details, but it sounded to her as if the thinking is that you're not giving the whole story. We both know that's not the case, but it sounds like someone is determined to cast you in a bad light, Fin. We need to find out what the hell is going on. You should talk to the Judge and demand to know what she knows."

Finley took a breath. "First, we both know this is some sort of witch hunt. Briggs has a bug up his ass about me, and evidently he's determined to take me down for . . ." She shrugged. "For whatever.

Fin

Particularly since I'm working on this case with you. As for talking to the Judge—"

"I'd be at her door now if she'd speak to me, but you know she won't. It has to be you."

"I'll see what I can find out, but no promises where the Judge is concerned." Finley swallowed the lump that rose in her throat. It was only a matter of time before someone figured out there was more to the story than what she'd provided. Or maybe Dempsey was behind this turn of events. He was no fool. One of his former lackeys was dead, and Finley had been at the scene. A reaction was to be expected.

"We can't let this slip through the cracks, Fin, or we'll be playing catch-up when the shit hits the fan, and it's smelling like that's about to happen."

"I'll call you after my meeting." She ended the connection before she said too much. She hated keeping things from Jack, but she refused to drag him into this. He'd worked hard to make his comeback. She would not be the reason he went down again.

Before exiting the car, she put through a call to Matt. If something more than what he'd already shared was brewing, he had to have heard. The call went to his voice mail. Matt spent most of his time in meetings, and callbacks were the norm. She left a message.

Shoving her phone into her bag, she took a big breath, then climbed out and headed for the front door. She pressed the doorbell and listened to the chime echoing inside. A few seconds later the door opened. Cherry Prescott Inglewood stood in the open doorway, dressed to the nines in a designer sheath with super-high-heeled shoes. Her makeup was flawless, her smile picture perfect, and her blonde shoulder-length hair impeccably coiffed.

"Please come in, Ms. O'Sullivan."

"Thank you for seeing me."

Cherry showed her to the second room on the right, a generous-size sitting room. Like the woman, the furnishings and decor were elegant.

The difference between Cherry's house and the Legard mansion was a subtle sense of hominess. The lived-in feeling. The people who lived here actually *lived* here.

"My husband left for LA late this morning and won't be back until Monday. I'd like to get whatever it is you need from me over while he's away."

Of course she did.

"I can't guarantee I won't have more questions as this case unfolds, but I can assure you that I will be as discreet as the law allows."

This seemed to satisfy her for the moment. She visibly relaxed. "What is it you want to discuss with me?" She glanced toward the door as if to check one last time that they were alone.

Finley said, "You can start with your side of the story regarding the falling-out between Lance Legard and Seth Henderson."

"I've already been interviewed by Mr. Siniard and the new detectives working on the case. I told them the same thing I told the detectives five years ago. I was young and ambitious, and I made mistakes. But I have no idea what happened to Mr. Legard or if Mr. Henderson played a role in what happened."

"I appreciate that you feel you've done all you can, but it's so often the smallest of things that change the course of a case." Finley removed her spiral from her bag and readied a pen. "I haven't found any information on how you and Mr. Henderson met. Can you tell me how you came to be acquainted?"

To her credit, Cherry took Finley's persistence in stride. "I was delivering documents for a local service. I delivered to Seth's office at least a couple of times a week. He was always nice. Complimentary. Just a pleasant man." She shook her head. "To this day his wife believes we had an affair, but we didn't. We were only friends. He wanted to help me make it in the business. He saw me as the daughter he never had. He and his wife had two sons, but they're both in Los Angeles and never seemed to have time for calls, much less visits."

Mrs. Henderson certainly didn't possess any warm and fuzzy feelings about her husband's relationship with Cherry. This was precisely why it was always best to go straight to the source if possible. Not that Cherry's was the final word. She could be making up her story as she went along, but her version carried as much weight as anyone else's until proven otherwise.

"You had aspirations of making it in the entertainment business?"

"Doesn't everyone? I worked off and on with a nobody band," she went on. "I even did a couple of commercials. I really believed I could be the next big thing. Another Taylor Swift or a Jennifer Lawrence. But that was a long time ago."

Five years wasn't so long, but it probably felt like a lifetime to the woman trapped in the viciousness of the event.

"According to others involved, you were a spy for a competitor," Finley said. "You lured a big star away from Legard Records, creating a chain reaction of bad things."

"Sammy Bryant." Cherry's lips tightened. "I took the fall for his leaving, but he's the one who chose to make the change. He'd been unhappy with Lance for a long time. Sammy and I were friends. Nothing else. In fact, he's the one who introduced me to Elton." She smiled in spite of the frustration she clearly felt. "Sammy is a good friend."

"Seth Henderson's reputation took a beating over Bryant's move."

"Check the case file, Ms. O'Sullivan. You won't find any interview where Seth said I was the reason Sammy left the label. That hurtful rumor came from Lance. I was his scapegoat to his investors."

"For the record," Finley said, shifting the conversation, "you're stating there was no sexual relationship between you and Seth Henderson."

"There was not," she practically hissed. "As I said, Seth was like a father figure. You don't get a lot of that in the business. I cherished our relationship."

Her story was convincing enough. "What persuaded or led Mr. Legard to believe you were the reason Bryant left the label?"

She drew in a deep breath. "What happened was never about Sammy. It was because Elton and I became involved, but . . ."

Finley waited patiently for her to go on.

"Lance wouldn't let me go. Elton warned Lance to back off, and Sammy took Elton's side in the matter. He was outraged by Lance's behavior. Lance terminated his contract and then told everyone that Sammy had left. There was an out-of-court settlement with a gag clause, so no one ever heard the truth."

Finley was still mulling over the first part of her statement. "Can you be more specific when you say Lance wouldn't let you go?"

"Lance and I were having an affair." She closed her eyes, shook her head. "I was a different person then. I made a mistake."

This was certainly a new twist. No one had suggested Legard and Cherry the P-trap were having an affair. There had been nothing in the case file along those lines either. Considering all Finley had discovered so far, the entire situation could have led to several seasons of *Real-Life Celebrity Scandals*.

Jack had been screwing Sophia Legard. Cherry here was screwing both Lance Legard and Elton Inglewood. Finley couldn't wait to find out who else was involved.

How was it Lance Legard's assistant, Alex Collins, and Seth Henderson's wife, Gloria, could have gotten it so wrong? Maybe Alex had been backing up his boss and Gloria had seen the situation as a way to kick her husband out of the house.

"Did you tell the detectives investigating his murder about the affair?"

She shook her head. "No. It wasn't relevant. Our affair was over by then, and I didn't want to rekindle the ugliness. I didn't want to be involved in any of it."

"Why do you suppose Sophia never mentioned the affair? Assuming she knew. It seems to me she would have wanted the police to investigate your possible involvement."

"She knew. I don't know why she chose not to say anything. Maybe she was afraid I would tell the police the things Lance had said about her. I can't think of any other reason. I was just grateful she didn't."

Finley couldn't deny the possibility. "How long had the affair been over when he was murdered?"

"About a month." She closed her eyes and shook her head. "You don't understand. I had to hide from the world to break away from Lance," she went on, pain in her voice. "He was obsessed with me."

This was a total one-eighty from the stories Finley had heard so far. "Were his daughters aware of the relationship?"

She nodded, her lips pressed tightly together. "Those women are . . ." She shrugged. "They're ruthless. Mean. Just mean. They do terrible things. Lance told me they could never have pets because Cecelia always hurt them. She was mean to Olivia. He really believed Cecelia was dangerous. But Sophia wouldn't hear it. Cecelia was and probably still is her favorite, and she protected her from everything and everyone. Even her own father and sister."

"Are you suggesting Lance Legard and his daughter Cecelia had issues?"

Cherry made a scoffing sound. "Lance had issues with Cecelia *and* Sophia. I'm telling you those two are nuts. Insane. Olivia seemed forgotten by all of them. She basically stayed out of the way. I felt a little sorry for her."

"You're only a few years older than his daughters." Finley decided to push the envelope. The worst that could happen was Cherry would shut down. Why not go for it? "A few have said his relationship with at least one of his daughters was something besides fatherly. Did you ever feel that his relationship with you was motivated by how much you look like his daughters?"

She blinked once, twice. "I don't know who told you such a thing." She squared her shoulders, lifted her chin. "Personally, I never thought I looked at all like his daughters."

But she did. Even with the blonde hair, particularly since Olivia had gone blonde. "Is that a no?" Finley pressed.

"I can't imagine." Cherry looked away, shook her head. "Don't get me wrong. Lance had problems. He was obsessive and domineering. But he was no pedophile."

Finley supposed that depended upon one's definition. The man was having an affair with a woman barely older than his own daughters.

"What about Sophia?" Finley asked, switching gears. "Was there a confrontation with you or about you?"

"She couldn't have cared less. As long as Lance kept her financially happy, he was free to do as he pleased. They didn't even share the same bedroom. Lance mentioned more than once that she had her own playthings."

"Do you have reason to believe Sophia had anything to do with her husband's death?"

"I don't know. She certainly had the most to gain. She and the twins. But I only knew what Lance told me about his wife and Cecelia. Mean. Ruthless. I kept my distance from his family."

"What did you do to prompt him to let you go?"

"Elton had a huge fight with him and made a number of threats. It was terrifying. I couldn't take it, so, like I said, I left. I went into hiding. The next thing I knew, Lance was dead."

"You understand that what you're telling me makes your husband a suspect."

"My husband wasn't in Nashville the day Lance was killed. Check for yourself. He couldn't have hurt Lance."

"What about you?"

"I was away."

"Away?" Finley wasn't letting her off so easily.

"I couldn't be here with all that was going on. I'd just found out I was pregnant, and I wasn't doing well."

Now there was another news flash. "Pregnant?"

"Yes." She closed her eyes for a moment as if she dreaded sharing this part. "I have a son. Brantley."

Which begged the next question: "Are you willing to share the father's name?"

"Elton is his father."

So why had they only gotten together a few months ago? "Did you tell him you were pregnant when you found out?"

"I didn't tell anyone for a very long time." She drew in a deep breath. "I kept a low profile for years. The rumors and social media were too much. Then Brantley and I were in town shopping, and we ran into Elton. This was last fall. Elton recognized himself as a kid. He was angry with me at first, but eventually we worked through it all and fell in love again." She smiled. "We became a family."

The perfect Hallmark movie.

"I'm very sad," Cherry went on, "that this nightmare has resurfaced. I will tell you what I thought then and I believe now: whatever happened to Lance, Cecelia or Sophia was involved. Whatever this Charles Holmes says about that family is probably true. You don't know them. They'll never let you see that side. I wouldn't have known if Lance hadn't told me." She shrugged. "And, if I'm being brutally honest, maybe he deserved what he got."

Surprised at the comment, Finley asked, "Now that you've said it, can you elaborate?"

Cherry stared at her for a long, tense moment. "Lance was so careful with his public persona. But behind closed doors he was a control freak, and at times, he was utterly cruel." She shuddered visibly. "Getting sucked into that relationship was the biggest mistake of my life."

Interesting that no suggestion of that sort had made its way into the police reports or the news. "Has anyone in the family been in contact with you at any time since the murder?"

"I did all within my power to avoid those women." She drew in a deep breath. "Frankly, I was terrified of them. In the beginning I couldn't be sure if my son was Lance's or not, and I didn't want to risk one of them deciding to try to hurt him if it turned out he was Lance's child."

"You didn't care that your son might be an heir to the Legard fortune?" Hard to swallow coming from a self-professed former gold digger.

"Believe me, after what I went through, no amount of money was worth diving back into that ugliness. Then last year when Elton and I ran into each other, it was obvious whose child he was. Brantley is his father's son." She laughed. "They have the same nose. The eyes are exactly the same. There's no question."

"You never noticed this before you ran into Elton again last year?" It was difficult to believe she wouldn't recognize her ex-lover's nose and eyes in her child, and she'd just stated that she avoided the Legards since she couldn't be sure which man was the father.

Cherry smiled, but the expression was strained. "Obviously you don't have children, Ms. O'Sullivan. If you did, you'd understand that they change so much as they move from being toddlers to little boys. Their features become much more pronounced. I was with Brantley every day, so I didn't really notice all the subtle changes until I was face to face with Elton. It was stunning for all involved."

"Why not just do the test and be certain?" Finley pushed.

Cherry smiled patiently. "There really was no need."

Moving on, Finley asked, "When you were involved, did Lance speak often of the issues with his daughters?"

"He was convinced Cecelia would end up dead or in prison one day. Olivia was a homebody. She never got into trouble. Cecelia was the one always getting into trouble. Those are the things I recall."

In the end, Olivia had run away from the tragedy and started her own life while Cecelia had become the homebody of sorts who had no life.

"Was there a friend Cecelia seemed particularly close to?" Whatever Finley could learn about one or both twins during that period could prove immensely useful. Particularly considering the conflicting stories of then and now.

Cherry considered the question for a time. "The only one I recall was . . ." Her forehead furrowed with concentration. "Bethany. Bethany something." She made an aha face. "Briggs. Bethany Briggs."

Whoa. Finley nearly got whiplash from the double take she did. "You're certain that was her name?"

"Yes. I'm certain."

Finley fished out her cell phone and pulled up a photo of the only Bethany Briggs she knew. "Is this the Bethany Briggs who was friends with Cecelia?"

Cherry stared at the photo for a moment, then nodded. "That's her. Definitely."

Wow. "Her father is the Davidson County district attorney," Finley explained, more than a little stunned. "You're sure about this?"

Cherry made a scoffing sound. "Oh yes. I'm certain—and I'm also certain he had no clue what his daughter was up to. Drugs, crazy sex parties. She and Cecelia were constantly trying to outdo each other with some challenge."

"What sort of challenges?"

She shrugged. "Like sneaking into stranger's homes and watching them. God only knows what all they did. I'm talking insanely wild. Once Lance said something like 'serial killers in the making.'" Cherry winced. "He was probably kidding."

But was he?

Bethany Briggs. No wonder Finley's former boss was so concerned about this case. His daughter had been best friends with one of the potential suspects.

Finley removed a card from her bag and passed it to the other woman. "Please call me if you think of anything else that might help sort out this business."

"Of course."

They were nearly to the door when a boy rushed in, sending Cherry back a step.

"Slow down, sweetie," she chided.

"Mom! Wait until you see—" He stopped. Stared at Finley.

Finley smiled as Cherry introduced her son. He did resemble the multitude of Elton Inglewood images plastered all over the net. But was that because Cherry had suggested it? Suggestion was a powerful influencer.

Checking out Inglewood's airtight alibi went on Finley's agenda. Right behind Bethany Briggs and Alisha Arrington.

14

3:05 p.m.

Inglewood Residence
Morning Glory Court
Brentwood

"Damn it." Finley gripped her cell tighter as the call to Jack went to voice mail. She needed to talk to him. "Jack, call me as soon as you get this message. We need to talk."

She tossed her cell into the passenger seat and braked outside the gate of the Inglewood home before easing onto the street. The revelation about Legard's affair with Cherry was definitely a huge twist in the optics of this case. No question. But the idea that the darling Bethany Briggs, who'd graduated from Vanderbilt with her nursing degree so she could dedicate her life to helping others, had been such a wild teenager gave Finley inordinate satisfaction.

How many times had she heard DA Briggs boast about his only child and how brilliant she was? She was going to be a doctor—a surgeon no less. But then she'd spent a summer in some third world country volunteering with Doctors Without Borders and realized what the world really needed was more nurses.

Bethany this and Bethany that.

Finley had read Bethany's engagement announcement in the *Tennessean* a couple of months ago. She hadn't become a surgeon herself, but she'd snagged herself one for a fiancé. Finley felt certain the DA was immensely proud.

Since Briggs had so loved to brag, Finley knew exactly where to look for Bethany. She worked at Vanderbilt hospital, and she lived on Acklen Park Drive in one of the glamorous condos on the corner at Long Boulevard, mere walking distance from the hospital. Finley opted to try her residence first. Finding her at the hospital would be a little more complicated in light of the increasingly tight security measures. She mentally ran through the list of her contacts in the medical field, particularly anyone who worked at Vanderbilt, in the event going to the hospital was her only option.

By the time she reached the ultramodern building where Bethany lived, Finley had come up with three good contacts employed at Vanderbilt. If the former wild child was not home, Finley would call in some markers. A good lawyer—or investigator—was always happy to do favors. When people owed you one thing or another, they were easier to manipulate. Sounded illicit, but it was the nature of the beast. Information was power.

Thankfully there were only four units in the building. She started at the top, ringing buzzers.

"It's me," Finley said, using her jolliest tone. "I'm here!"

"Who is this?" came the stern response.

"Bethany?" Finley asked, going for puzzled.

No response.

On to the next buzzer.

"Hello?"

Older voice. Definitely not Bethany's. Finley decided to go for a more direct approach this time. "Is Bethany home?"

Silence.

Well, hell.

"She is not. May I leave her a message?"

Didn't really sound like Bethany's mother. When Finley didn't immediately respond, the woman tacked on, "I'm her housekeeper. I can leave her a note for you."

Finley relaxed. She could work with this. "No need. I worked at her father's office. I'll just go catch her at the hospital." She used the past tense because that made the statement true. She hoped the housekeeper didn't notice. Finley was counting on her desire to be helpful.

"She's off this afternoon," the housekeeper explained. "Her wedding dress came in and she had to go to a fitting."

Finley smiled. There were two wedding shops the young, rich, and famous of Nashville preferred. She opted to go with the older of the two. "I'll catch her at Winnie's," Finley said.

"Yes, okay."

The sear of anticipation rushing through her, Finley made the drive to Hillsboro Pike in record time. The parking area in front of the bridal shop was fairly empty. Not surprising since appointments were required. The moment she stepped into the shop, a fleeting sense of regret washed over her. She hadn't bothered with a wedding dress or a chapel wedding. She'd grabbed something from the rack at her favorite shop, and off they'd gone to the justice of the peace. The only photos were the few on her phone a clerk had snapped.

The whole big-wedding thing was overrated, Finley had told herself. She shook off the nostalgia. An overpriced dress and a proper chapel wouldn't have changed the way things had turned out.

The shop reminded Finley of New York with its urban style and harsh lines. All the silk and lace in various shades of white stood out against the heavy concrete floors, the background walls of wood and metal. Gave the space an unexpected appeal.

A well-dressed clerk appeared. Her smile warm. "Welcome to Winnie's. Is there anything I can help you with? Perhaps you'd like to make an appointment with a consultant."

"I have a delivery for Bethany Briggs." Finley patted her messenger bag.

The woman nodded. "This way. She's just finished her fitting."

She guided Finley to a room filled with mirrors, doors, and racks of dresses. She walked to one of the doors and tapped. "Ms. Briggs, your delivery has arrived."

"Thank you," Finley said in dismissal.

The clerk nodded and disappeared.

"Come in!" came the gleeful response from the other side of the door.

Finley opened the door and stepped into the surprisingly large dressing room. Two walls were mirrored. There was a sofa, a bar, a rack holding what she suspected was Bethany's wedding dress. Bethany stood at the dressing table studying her face in a mirror surrounded by Hollywood lights.

"I'm Finley O'Sullivan. I'm here to speak with you about the accusations Charles Holmes has made against Cecelia Legard."

The brush Bethany had been holding hit the table. She whirled around. "What?"

The blonde hair was the same as her father's, only longer and without the streaks of gray. The gold eyes she'd gotten from her mother. Her father's were more brown. Bethany was tall and thin and looked as if she hadn't eaten in weeks. The wedding preparations, no doubt.

"You and Cecelia were close friends at the time of her father's murder, and we're attempting to determine if you played any part in her interactions with Holmes."

A deer-in-the-headlights expression claimed Bethany's face, then she blinked. "I . . . I . . . know you."

Oops. They'd never actually carried on a conversation, but they had passed in the hallowed corridors of her father's domain. "We've met," Finley agreed.

"At my father's office. You work for him."

Good. Finley smiled without answering. "I'm sure he has discussed the Holmes situation with you."

Bethany grabbed her bottled water and moved to the sofa. Collapsed there as if the fitting had worn her out. "He did. I'm not supposed to talk to anyone about it."

"I hope you're following that order. There will be reporters and all sorts of people trying to get a sound bite from you considering you and Cecelia were best friends at the time."

"He told me." The fear and surprise were gone, and impatience had taken its place.

Finley wandered to the sofa and settled at the opposite end. "He's trying to protect you."

"Trust me," she said, "I'm aware. I've spent most of my life listening to his lectures about what we can and cannot do in public."

"Cecelia mentioned that the two of you had a number of pretty exciting adventures your senior year in high school."

Bethany grinned. "We did some wild shit, for sure. My father would die if he knew half the stuff we did." She seemed to catch herself. "I was immature. I would never do those things now." A frown tugged at her face. "How is Cecelia? I haven't heard from her in years. She like never leaves the house."

"She doesn't, no," Finley confirmed. "Right now, she's struggling with the accusations Holmes has made."

"She liked playing with fire," Bethany said. "We both did, really. But Cecelia wasn't afraid of anything. She watched him, you know."

Finley shrugged one shoulder. She needed Bethany to say his name, but she couldn't lead the witness, and she certainly didn't want to appear overeager and trigger her suspicions. "You're curious at that age."

"But watching your father do shit is bizarre. I swear Cecelia was so jealous of him. It was weird. I was happy to go along for the ride. Her father was hot."

Father? Not the answer Finley had expected. She'd thought they were talking about Holmes. Still, the response was certainly an intriguing one.

"Was it her jealousy of her father that prompted her to start up a relationship with Holmes? It's not so unusual for a young girl to be attracted to older men."

Bethany glanced at her phone, then at Finley. "She didn't have any sort of relationship with Holmes." She looked away. "He's lying. We didn't know him. Did Cecelia say she knew him?"

Lie number one. Not only had she looked away, her voice had changed ever so slightly.

"No, she says not, but it was important to confirm her claim."

"You should talk to her mother," Bethany said. "She was the one Cecelia confided in most."

Deflection. A common tactic for shifting attention or blame.

"Maybe it was Olivia who was infatuated with Holmes. She could have pretended to be Cecelia."

Bethany scoffed. "Olivia never talked to anyone. She's a strange one."

Finley shifted her own tactic. "It's possible Cecelia may not have told you she was talking to Holmes."

Bethany shot her a look. "Trust me, whatever Cecelia was doing, I knew about it. We told each other everything. She would have bragged about it to me."

Finley decided not to push any further. She didn't want to make her suspicious. It was better to leave the door open for more questions. "I should be going." She stood. "Keep what your father told you in mind. You shouldn't talk to anyone about the Legard family. We have to control the situation. Just like last time."

"God, you sound exactly like him. He kept me under his thumb so tight last time I couldn't breathe."

"This too shall pass," Finley promised.

"I hope it passes fast. I want to be happy right now. We're planning my wedding."

"I understand."

"I can deal with it if he'll stay off my back. I get it. I can't let anyone find out I was with Cecelia that night. Especially now."

"He doesn't want you dragged into this," Finley offered, her pulse picking up speed with this new revelation. *"Especially now."*

"Well, you can tell him," she said with a knowing look, "that he doesn't have to send any more spies snooping around. I'm not telling anyone anything."

Except she had. "I'll tell him."

Before Finley could ask her to go over what happened that night, Bethany grabbed her cell.

"Speak of the devil," she announced, "that's him right now."

Briggs. "I'll get out of your way so you can speak to your father in private."

Finley started for the door.

"I'm sorry, what was your name again?"

The door opened, and a lady rushed in with a veil. "It's here!"

Finley escaped during the delighted squealing that came next. Briggs would figure out she'd had this little chat with his daughter soon enough. No use making it easy for him. If she were really lucky, the preoccupied bride would forget all about Finley's visit.

As she exited the boutique, she removed her cell from the front pocket of her messenger bag and shut off the record option. Just in case Bethany tried to walk back her statement.

Finley started her Subaru and powered the windows down to allow some of the built-up heat to escape while the air-conditioning struggled to cool things off. She strapped on her seat belt and checked her phone No missed calls.

She called Jack's cell again. Straight to voice mail. "Damn it."

Frustrated, she called the office, then merged out onto the street. Nita answered after the first ring with her practiced greeting. "Finnegan Firm. How can I help you?"

"Hey, I need to talk to Jack. Does he have a client in his office?"

"He does not. He received a call about an hour ago and rushed out of here like his house was on fire. He said I should cancel his last two appointments and he'd see me on Monday. Mumbled something about having some stuff to do at home."

"Who was the caller?"

"No clue. The call came in on his cell. But I can tell you this: All together I've worked with Jack for twenty years. He never cancels his appointments unless he's in trouble, Fin, and he won't listen to anything I say."

"I'll find him."

"I want to hear from you when you do."

Nita was right. Jack was in trouble. Since he'd painted the entire interior of his cabin already and he had mentioned home when he left the office, Finley decided to start at the Drake.

———

Drake Motel
Murfreesboro Pike
Nashville, 6:00 p.m.

Finley grabbed her bag and was almost to Jack's door when the manager rushed out of his office. Norton, Niles—whatever his name—he looked rattled. His colorful shirt and trousers always made her think of the Caribbean.

"Thank God you're here!"

A loud thump from the direction of Jack's rooms punctuated the frantic words. Her first thought was that maybe Jack was slugging it out with someone in there. But it was way too loud for that. More crash than a thump, maybe.

"What the hell was that?" She glanced around the neighboring lots. No moving trucks or construction vehicles close by.

"It's Jack," the manager cried. "He says he's renovating his rooms. Please, you have to stop him before someone complains and a city inspector shows up!"

Now she understood. "I'll see what I can do."

Another thump or thwack made her jump as she reached his door. She tried the knob—locked. She listened a second or two, then pounded on the door with her fist. "Jack, open the door!"

The door flew inward. Jack stared at her, safety glasses on his face, white dust on his gray tee, a sledgehammer in one hand. "What?"

She raised her eyebrows at his harsh bark. "We are in the middle of a huge case, and you're renovating your place?"

He removed the safety glasses, glanced over his shoulder. "Get in here and lock the door before Nelson comes back."

So that was the manager's name. She did as the boss said, and just in time—a round of knocking ensued, followed by, "Do not start making that noise again, Jack! Not today. Rooms are full! People are complaining."

Nelson had gone from terrified to pissed. Finley being here to run interference had given him a boost of courage.

Jack dropped the sledgehammer and tossed the glasses aside. He dusted off the thighs of his jeans, which were covered in that same white dust. Drywall dust, she suspected, since he'd torn down a size-able portion of the half wall that separated his living area from his office. Chunks of drywall and a few battered two-by-fours lay on the plush blue carpet. Clear plastic, the sort used when painting, had been draped along the middle of the room, protecting his office area from all the dust. On his coffee table sat an open bottle of bourbon—still full—and the requisite tumbler. Oh yeah, he was doing battle again. Not a positive sign.

"You know if you drink that, we're both in trouble."

He looked from the bottle to her. "I'm not going to drink it. I just needed to have the option available while I did some thinking."

"Nita said you received a call that sent you rushing out of the office." She glanced around at the demolition he'd started. "Was it your interior designer?"

His hands went to his waist as if he couldn't decide what to do with them. "It was the Judge."

Now there was an answer Finley hadn't seen coming. "Why did she call you?"

"She was returning my call."

"I see." Was she going to have to excavate every single word out of him? "And?"

"She claimed to know nothing about Briggs and Lawrence discussing you or Derrick's case. She warned me not to call her again."

"Sorry. She can be a bitch sometimes."

"I shouldn't have called her. I knew better."

Once again, she went to the trouble of asking *the* question despite knowing what his answer would be. "Are you ever going to tell me what happened between the two of you?"

"Maybe. But not today."

That was his stock answer whenever she asked. "Meanwhile, let me catch you up on what you've missed today."

He dusted off his shoulders. "Let's hear it."

"Cherry Prescott Inglewood's new celebrity husband went out of town for the weekend, which is why she was able to meet with me."

"She doesn't want him to find out she's involved in any way with this second rising of Holmes." Jack shrugged. "I'm not surprised." He gestured to his fridge. "You want a water?"

Finley shook her head. He grabbed one for himself and chugged half of it.

"If you can believe her claims, and I do," Finley went on, sharing the details with her boss, "she insists Henderson was an innocent bystander."

"Except *he* introduced her to Legard in the first place," Jack pointed out.

"Except for that," Finley agreed. "She's claiming she and Legard had an affair and that he was really hung up on her. Obsessed, she called it. Which makes Inglewood a suspect, but she says he has an airtight alibi. He was out of town at the time of the murder. I still need to confirm the alibi, but even if he was away, he could have hired Holmes."

Jack rubbed at his chin. "Strange that Sophia never mentioned her husband's affair." He hummed a note of surprise. "I can't see her being that naive."

"It appears they may have had a sort of open marriage," Finley offered. "Cherry said Sophia had her own playthings."

Jack's face blanked for three beats; then he shrugged. "I'm not surprised. Not really."

Except he was. Finley couldn't help thinking that Sophia had really gotten to him. She forced the issue aside and brought him up to speed on retired detective Montrose's visit.

Jack's attention sharpened. "Who suppressed his complaints? His partner? I never liked that guy anyway. A total asshole."

"Among others," Finley said cryptically.

"Meaning?"

"The chief of police *and* DA Briggs shut him down."

"Montrose had something to back up his claims, and they shut him down?"

Finley could see the wheels turning. Jack's respiration changed; his eyes grew more alert. This was exactly the sort of lead they needed.

"Just his word, since Sophia refused to substantiate his claim that she'd mentioned being worried her husband might be involved in some untoward way with one or both of their daughters."

Jack's gaze narrowed. "What's with all these delayed bombshells?"

Finley shrugged. "All the players involved last time—at least the ones still alive—are worried this time, I think. They're all focused on covering their asses. Speaking of bombshells, I unearthed another tidbit from Cherry. Since she worked with Legard closely for several months, I asked her if she knew much about the daughters, and she had plenty to say. Cecelia had a particularly wild friend, and the two were as thick as thieves at the time of Legard's murder."

Jack motioned for her to go on, dust stirring with his movement.

Finley couldn't help the grin that spread across her lips. "Bethany Briggs."

"No shit." Jack was smiling now.

"No shit. I actually interviewed Bethany a little while ago."

His smile faded. "I'm not sure I want to know how you managed that."

"I was careful, but if she mentions it to Briggs, there will be hell to pay."

"Maybe so, but the cat is out of the bag now." Jack was pleased.

"Since I know how he works, I recorded the conversation as a bit of insurance."

This time Jack laughed out loud. "God, I love you."

Finley laughed too. Couldn't help herself. But there was more, and this part wasn't at all humorous. "Cherry was pregnant when she disappeared from the limelight. She has a son."

"Legard's?"

"She says not. I don't know that the child bears any relevance to the case, but it's definitely a surprising side note."

"Certainly ups the stakes for both the kid's mother and Inglewood."

"True." Finley braced herself. "I have to ask you something, Jack, and I need the whole truth."

"Shoot."

"If there's more to whatever was going on between you and Sophia," Finley ventured, hoping the answer would not be yes, "I need to know."

Jack glanced at the tumbler and bottle of bourbon again.

Finley held her breath.

Then he shook his head. "She came to me for advice on how she might proceed with a divorce."

"But you're not a divorce attorney."

"She wanted guidance from someone who wasn't looking at how much they might gain from the case. She was unhappy. She felt she was being emotionally abused by him and her daughters. She wanted out, but she wasn't sure how to make that happen without losing everything."

Finley understood exactly where this was going. "She made you believe she needed someone. A protector and savior. That she'd never gone down that road before."

He nodded. "I fell for it hook, line, and sinker."

"How did it end?"

"Her husband was murdered, and we just kind of moved apart. She was busy putting the pieces of her life back together, and I was busy trying to rebuild my career. We had a thing, and then it was over."

A rock settled in Finley's stomach. She didn't have to tell him this sounded very much like a motive for murder.

Except this was Jack. He wasn't a murderer.

"Make sure it stays that way," Finley warned. As brilliant as Jack was, he could still be a sucker for a woman in distress.

"Since you're here," Jack said, dragging her attention back to the present, "Nita sent me the scoop on what she's dug up on Olivia Legard's life out in Cali."

"I'm guessing it's not as cut and dried as we were anticipating," Finley suggested.

"Did you really expect it would be?" He headed across the room, yanked back the plastic divider, and stepped into his office.

"That would be a no," Finley said as she followed. Nothing else about this case had been—why hold out hope now?

Focusing on the wall behind his desk, she surveyed the case board Jack had developed. Headshots of all the players were taped to the wall. He'd created a timeline much the same way a detective would. Dozens of colorful sticky notes were scattered around each photo. His notes. On his wall back at the office were certificates and photos—the artful display of his credentials for clients to see. Here, he pieced together his working scenarios and theories. Like her, Jack had a mind that didn't stop when he left the office.

He paused at the eight-by-ten of Olivia and tapped the first of about a dozen notes around her image. "We have her college room-mate." He glanced at Finley. "Nita tracked her down in record time. I think you're rubbing off on her."

Finley tugged the note from the wall. *Holly Thompson.* Her address and other pertinent info were listed beneath her name. "She lives in Seattle now?"

Jack nodded. "She's a high school teacher there."

"If she's willing to talk," Finley offered, "we could use more info on Olivia. Since Cecelia has been here all along, putting together her story has been fairly easy." Like the identity of her best friend at the time of her father's murder and the fact that she had been basically housebound right here at home since the murder.

"What we don't have," Jack said, "is a handle on Olivia's life around the time of her father's murder and in the years since."

"Other than her college transcript and a few notes from various professors who considered her delightful and bordering on brilliant." Finley considered the photo of the woman who had bleached her hair blonde so she no longer looked like her twin at first glance. "According to Bethany, Olivia was a loner. Cherry mentioned the same."

"If we're lucky," Jack suggested, "her roommate might have some details about her and her friends at the university. Who knows? Maybe Olivia talked about the murder and her family at some point over the years."

"I'll get in touch. See what she's willing to share." Face-to-face worked better in these types of interviews, but Finley could start with a phone convo.

In the end, Finley noted, the twins not only lost their father when he was murdered—they lost each other.

Or had they pushed each other away because one or the other was guilty?

15

8:30 p.m.

Drake Motel
Murfreesboro Pike
Nashville

Jack had insisted Finley stay and have dinner with him. He was actually an excellent cook. They hadn't talked about the case any further. A break was in order. He promised he would not call or visit Sophia Legard without Finley.

For now, the bourbon had stayed in the bottle.

Finley climbed into her Subaru and pulled out of the parking lot. She'd made it half a block before her cell rang.

Matt.

"Hey, thanks for getting back to me."

"Sorry it took so long. What's up?"

She switched on her blinker for the next turn. "Jack got a call from a friend who says Briggs and Lawrence are suggesting there's some issue related to me and Derrick's case. I guess word is getting around. Have you heard anything else?"

"I've been in meetings all day, so no, I haven't heard anything else. But believe me when I say I will find out."

"Thanks. This is beginning to sound a little conspiratorial." Finley had that uneasy feeling deep in her gut. This, whatever it was, was deepening, expanding.

"Damn straight it does. Anything else going on? You sound a little stressed."

"Just the case. I keep finding all these new pieces, and they don't want to fit neatly together."

"Sounds to me as if the DA and the chief should be concerned about where the Legard investigation is going."

"I don't have anything concrete yet, but it's stacking up to be a real shake-up." She thought about how she'd felt things were out of place at home. "There is something else," she confessed. "The weirdest thing happened this morning. I got up and my hairbrush was missing. The bathroom was tidied up. Not that I mind the tidying up—I just can't remember doing it. I swear it's like someone was in my house while I was asleep."

She wanted to tell him about the man with the beard and sunglasses who worked for Dempsey who'd been watching her. To suggest that maybe he'd come into her house somehow, but she couldn't without telling him the rest.

Not possible.

Not yet.

Matt was too ethical to understand her actions.

"Where are you now?"

That wasn't exactly the response she'd expected. "I'm almost home, why?"

"Just stay in the car when you get there. I'll be over as soon as I can."

The call ended, and she wanted to call him back and tell him she had plans for a long hot bath and some time to think but opted not to bother. Matt was very much like her. When he made up his mind to do something, he wasn't likely to change it.

When she turned onto her block, a silver sedan parked at the curb in front of her house had her wondering what the hell now. She turned into her drive and parked. Matt had said not to go inside. She glanced at the other car. The driver's side door had opened, and a man had exited. Not Montrose or anyone else she recognized.

Rather than sit there and wait for her visitor to walk up and knock on her window, she opened the door and got out. The man was youngish, maybe her age, tall, fit. Requisite suit. Gold shield hanging on his pocket.

Definitely a cop.

"Ms. O'Sullivan, I was hoping to catch you."

Catch her? Had he been waiting for her? For how long? She was going to have to break down and get one of those doorbell monitors.

"Well, you've caught me. What can I do for you, Detective?"

He paused a few steps from where she stood. "I'm Eric Houser. I've been assigned to your husband's case."

The new guy. Okay. She extended her hand. He shook it. Firm shake. Dry palm. Snazzy dresser. Dark hair cut military short. Nice eyes. Attractive face. She thought of one of her grandmother's sayings: *Pretty is as pretty does.*

"Let me know if I can help you in any way," she offered. "It's been a year. I'd really love to see progress on the investigation."

"I understand." He dipped his head in silent acknowledgment. "I know this is difficult for you, but at your convenience I'd like us to sit down and go over that night. Talk about the work that's been done on the case so far. That sort of thing."

"I'd invite you in," she started, "but—"

"No, no." He held up both hands, palms out. "I'm not here for that now." He gave her a kind smile. "I wouldn't ambush you by showing up out of the blue. I just wanted to introduce myself. We can talk whenever is good for you."

Interesting strategy. He was good too. She would almost believe how kind and considerate he might be if not for the fact she knew her name was being bandied about in a negative way. Then again, he was the new guy. Maybe he wasn't privy to what the old guard was up to.

"Monday sound okay to you?" she asked. "Ten o'clock?"

"Sure. That'd be great."

"Your office?"

"If that's comfortable for you."

Give me a break. "Sure."

"Well then, have a nice weekend."

"You too."

She watched him walk toward his car once more. It was probably the strangest meeting she'd had with a detective ever.

She reached back into her car for her bag.

"Oh, one thing."

His words had her rising up too quickly and bumping her head. She drew out of the car. "Excuse me?"

He stood halfway between her car and his. "Did you know your husband only bought this house two weeks before you met?"

"What?" Not possible. Derrick had been working on the house for months when they'd met.

"The previous owner . . ." Houser removed a small notepad from his jacket pocket and previewed the top page. "One Ted Walker was in the middle of flipping the place when Derrick Reed made him an offer he couldn't refuse for the place as is."

The idea was ludicrous. "Do you have evidence of what you're saying?"

"I do." He tucked away his notepad. "I'll share it with you on Monday."

Without another word, he turned and walked away.

What the hell?

He waved again as he drove off. Finley was torn between fury and shock. He had to be wrong. Derrick would never have kept something like that from her. There hadn't been any reason for him to lie to her. The story made no sense at all.

Another vehicle turned into her drive.

Matt. Relief washed over her.

He climbed out of the car, a bag in one hand.

"Hey," she said, suddenly feeling incredibly weary.

"Hey yourself. I have new locks for your doors." He held up the Walmart bag as he walked toward her.

She almost laughed despite the emotions whirling inside her. "You know how to change a lock?"

He laughed and bumped her elbow with his. "I do. I'll have you know I am a man of many talents."

The urge to lean against him and just bawl was nearly overwhelming. Finley was no crier, but she was suddenly so tired. She wanted Derrick back. She wanted the people who had destroyed their lives to pay.

She didn't want to feel so disconnected from everything and everyone anymore.

Rather than give in to those weaker emotions, she steadied herself and said, "That new detective dropped by to see me."

"Was he nice to you?" her friend asked as they reached her door.

Only Matt would ask that question. "He was nice, but . . ."

She started to tell him what the detective had said. Somehow she couldn't bring herself to repeat the words. Matt was her best friend, but she couldn't abide him thinking negatively of Derrick. She needed to figure this out first.

"But?" he prodded.

"Maybe he was too nice."

Matt laughed. "Poor guy. You'll eat him alive."

Finley mustered a grin. "I'll give him hell for sure."

"Okay." Matt set the bag down on the sofa. "We need a Phillips-head screwdriver. I'm certain Derrick has one in his toolbox."

"I'll get it."

"I'll change the locks, and then we'll both sleep better tonight."

She nodded, drew in a big breath. "Be right back."

Derrick's tools were in the garage. She felt bad for not telling Matt what Houser had said. Matt was a good and loyal friend.

The guy's in love with you. You do know that, don't you?

Finley paused at the garage door and pressed her forehead there. Derrick had teasingly made that statement to her more than once. She'd always laughed and reminded him that she and Matt were just friends. Never had been anything more and never would be.

Matt was just Matt.

16

Saturday, July 9

7:55 a.m.

The Murder House
Shelby Avenue
Nashville

Finley finished blow-drying her hair, then rounded up her favorite jeans and a tee that sported the Music City logo. Unfortunately, the new locks Matt had installed hadn't helped her sleep any better.

Houser's parting remarks kept replaying in her head. There had to be some mix-up. Maybe Derrick leased the house for a while before buying it. The whole idea was completely un-Derrick-like. He was far too nice and laid back to approach some property owner with such an aggressive offer.

I just had a feeling I could make this place a good home.

She remembered him surveying the kitchen as he said those words.

The place hadn't been taken care of in a long time.

Her chest tightened. Transforming this house had meant something to him. It wasn't just a flip for profit.

Houser had to be wrong.

Somewhere in the living room her cell rang.

She slid her feet into sandals and went in search of the annoying sound. It stopped ringing and promptly started again before she found it between the cushions of the sofa. The low-battery warning flashed on the screen.

What else was new?

"O'Sullivan," she said in greeting to the caller not registered in her contact list. California number, so she figured it was Olivia.

"I need to talk to you."

Yep. "Is everything all right, Olivia?"

"I'm worried about . . ." A sigh hissed over the line. "I'm very concerned about my sister. Can we meet somewhere? I really don't want to do this on the phone."

"Sure. Your hotel?" Where was her bag? Finley surveyed the room, instantly ticking off all the stuff that needed to be done. Vacuuming. Dusting.

Like that was going to happen.

"I think somewhere else." She hesitated. "I feel like I'm being watched here."

Finley stilled. "Have you actually seen someone, or is this just a feeling?"

"Just a feeling, I suppose. But I can't shake it."

"How about the Frothy Monkey on Twelfth? Do you know the place?"

"I do. What time works for you?"

"I'll meet you there in half an hour." She wanted to check on Jack. Give him an update.

"Thank you. I really appreciate being able to call you like this."

Finley assured her it was no problem and ended the call. She tapped Jack's name in her contact list. He answered immediately. A good sign.

"Good morning," he announced. "I am alive and sober. Thank you for checking."

Finley rolled her eyes and locked the front door on her way out. "You're a grown man, Jack. Why would I be checking on you?" she lied. "I just called to let you know I'm meeting with Olivia this morning. She has some concerns about her sister."

"Sounds like she trusts you. Make the most of it, Fin. One or all of these ladies is keeping secrets. We need to know what those secrets are."

"I'll work on the daughters," Finley said as she climbed into her car. Even this early in the morning, the heat inside was stifling. She powered the windows down and started the engine. Hot air blasted from the vents.

"I'll talk to Sophia today. See what she has to say."

"No face-to-face meeting with her without me," Finley reminded him. "A phone call will be sufficient. You got that, Jack?" Finley backed out of her driveway, noted the older lady across the street watering her plants. The woman was always watching.

She's a little nosy, but she's just lonely.

Derrick said this whenever Finley grumbled about the lady. He had made it a point to always greet her when he saw her outside. He was too nice. Nicer than Finley for sure.

"Got it," he promised.

Finley waggled her fingers at the lady as she drove away. She didn't wave back, just stood there with her water hose in hand, watching. So much for trying to be friendly.

"Good. We'll talk later," she said, ending the call.

On the way to the coffee shop, Finley called a friend who worked in the Nashville Driver's License Division. He promised to see what he could find on an Alisha Arrington. Anything would be more than she'd discovered. The only Alisha Arrington she'd found in the Nashville area was a newly graduated high schooler headed for Lipscomb this fall. She also called Holly Thompson and left a message. Nita had listed the number as the former roommate's cell. Hopefully she would call back.

Olivia was waiting at a table as deep in a corner as was possible in the small café. She'd ordered two coffees. Finley was grateful for more caffeine.

"Cecelia is out of control," Olivia said, getting straight down to business. "She's behaving erratically and ranting like a crazy person." Her shoulders sagged. "Honestly, I think she is mentally unstable. I'm certain Mother is not safe in the same house with her."

"They've been living together all this time while you were away without any trouble that was reported. Do you think it's because of what Holmes is doing? Opening up the case again?"

Olivia searched Finley's eyes, her own filled with urgency. "Yes. I think this whole thing has pushed her over the edge. I am truly worried about Mother."

"Did your mother share this information with you? It's my understanding you're not visiting the house. How do you know what's going on there?"

Olivia pushed her cell phone across the table. "Cecelia sends me bizarre text messages constantly, and she's left several ranting voice mails. Mother keeps calling to say everything is fine, but I don't believe her."

Finley skimmed the text messages from Cecelia. Most were accusations about how Olivia was the one who had worked with Holmes. Others were warnings that she'd better stay away. The voice mails were vague threats about Olivia not getting away with *it* this time. And Olivia was right—Cecelia sounded unstable. Disturbed.

"You should keep these in the event this comes up later," Finley advised. "Most of what she's saying seems aimed at you. Why do you believe your mother is in danger?"

"Because she tries to keep Cecelia calm and under control. I've seen my sister become violent with her before . . . when I lived at home."

Jack had mentioned Sophia felt mentally abused by her husband and her daughters, but that was five years ago. She certainly hadn't said anything along that line this go around.

"Why don't I drop by the house and check on your mother and your sister. If you'd like, I can talk to them about your concerns."

"That would make me feel a lot better." Olivia closed her eyes a moment. "I've worried all night."

"I'll go straight there when we're finished here."

"Thank you so much."

Finley studied the younger woman for a moment. She had been pegged as the quiet one, the homebody. Was that still true? Or had she, like Cecelia, changed over the past five years? Was she the *good* daughter? Or was she only putting up a good show for Finley's benefit? She chose not to bring up the roommate. Finley wanted to speak with Holly Thompson before giving Olivia a heads-up of her intention. The goal was to obtain straight answers from the roommate.

Bearing that in mind, Finley stuck with the subject at hand. "Olivia, why would Cecelia accuse you of having been involved with Holmes?"

Olivia pressed a hand to her chest. "I can only assume she's lost her mind, or maybe she's covering for what she did. I just don't know anymore."

Someone knew, and Finley would bet money that the mother was well aware of what had happened five years ago. Even as worried as Olivia appeared at the moment, she only allowed her emotions to show so much. She kept a tight hold beyond a certain point. When a person worked that hard to keep their deeper feelings concealed, there was a very strong motive.

The one thing Finley had pretty much concluded so far was that no one in the Legard family was completely innocent.

Legard Residence
Lealand Lane
Nashville, 10:00 a.m.

Finley had been buzzed through the gate, but so far she'd had no luck getting anyone to the door. Had to be someone in there. She pressed the bell again.

"It's Finley O'Sullivan," she called out. "Is anyone home?"

Another stretch of silence had Finley considering checking windows and doors for alternative avenues of entrance.

"Only me."

The words were barely audible, but they seemed to come from just the other side of the door.

"Cecelia, is that you?"

Extended pause, then, "Yes."

"Is your mother home?"

"No."

"May I come in? I'd really like to speak with you."

"I . . . I can't open the door."

Finley considered their options. "I understand. How about you unlock the door, then go into another room. Maybe the same room where we talked the other day. I'll join you there."

Long pause.

"Okay . . . but be sure to lock the door behind you."

"I will. I promise." The opportunity to see her alone could be useful. The mother had seemed to control the conversation during their one interview. Cecelia might open up more if it was just the two of them.

The click of the lock had Finley's anticipation mounting.

She waited a sufficient amount of time for Cecelia to have reached the living room, then opened the door and closed and locked it behind her.

"I'm inside, and I've locked the door," Finley called out.

A thin "Okay" floated back to her.

Finley found Cecelia in the living room snuggled into one corner of the sofa. This time she wore joggers and a hoodie. The hood covered her hair and shadowed her face.

"Thanks for agreeing to speak with me." Finley settled into a chair across the elegant coffee table from her.

Cecelia picked at her nails, her gaze only briefly flitting to Finley. "Sure."

"Where's your mother this morning?"

Listless shrug. "I don't know. She had stuff to do, I guess."

"Do you spend a lot of time here alone?" Seemed strange to Finley that her mother would leave her alone if she were so unstable.

"Sometimes. Mother has a lot of social obligations. I've lost count of the charity projects she supports."

"You never go with her?"

Her eyes did meet Finley's now. "I haven't left this house in like four years." She stared at her hands once more. "I can't do it."

Her words were sincere, but she averted eye contact as she said them. Then she squirmed a little as if she couldn't get comfortable.

Finley moved on to the reason she was here. "Olivia is worried that you're feeling overly upset about this Holmes situation."

Another vague shrug. "I don't like it. He's lying and making everyone think I did something wrong, and I didn't."

"I hate when people do that." Finley made a face, not that Cecelia would notice since she kept her attention cast downward. "We'll find the truth, and this time it will be over for good."

Cecelia lifted her gaze, locked it with Finley's. "Do you really think you can? The truth is hidden sometimes. Finding it isn't always easy."

"I'm very good at finding things," Finley assured her.

"But you don't always find what you're looking for, do you?"

This was the longest they'd held eye contact. Cecelia wanted to see Finley's reaction. Her mother was away, so she felt more confident.

"What do you mean?" Finley prodded. "We don't really know each other."

"I read about your husband's murder." She shifted her attention to her hands once more. "You still don't know who killed him."

Oh, Finley knew rightly enough. It was proving it that she couldn't do.

"The detectives are still working on his case."

"I'll bet you've kept everything just like it was when he was alive. At your house, I mean."

Finley felt the first prick of uneasiness. "I have. I suppose I'm not ready to let anything go yet."

"My mom had my dad's stuff packed up and taken away practically before he was in the ground." She met Finley's gaze again. "What do you think of someone who would do that? Cold, wouldn't you say?"

"Everyone grieves differently." Finley watched Cecelia's face closely as she asked the next question. "Do you know where I live?"

She nodded. "I did some research on you."

"You can visit me if you like," Finley suggested.

Her gaze narrowed. "I told you I don't leave the house. How could I visit you?"

"Then what difference did it make where I live?"

"I was curious." She studied her fingers, picked at her cuticles. "Olivia said something about being surprised you lived in such a dump."

Finley laughed, a dry sound. "It definitely qualifies as a dump. My husband was remodeling it, and I just haven't followed through. I'll get around to it."

"Do you have a therapist since the breakdown?"

Apparently, she was the one being interviewed. "I do. How about you?"

Cecelia nodded. "Mother likes her because she makes house calls. In my opinion, she's worthless. Wants to keep me medicated all the time. I hate it."

"I hated the medication too. But it was necessary for a while."

"We're alike, you know." Cecelia stared at Finley with a smugness she made no attempt to conceal.

"How so?"

"Neither of us wants anyone to know everything we think."

"What are you thinking, Cecelia?"

Tension mounted in the ensuing silence.

"That you have no idea what's coming."

Before Finley could ask what she meant, Cecelia stood. "I'll tell my mother you stopped by when she returns. Please lock the door when you leave."

She rushed out of the room without a backward glance. Finley took her time, wandered around the room, noting nothing of significance. Eventually she wandered out, locking the door behind her. She couldn't lock the dead bolt, but she was able to engage the knob lock.

Finley sat in her car for a while after the meeting, just staring at the massive house. More likely than not Cecelia was watching her.

Cecelia had thrown down the gauntlet. Whatever she and her family were hiding, she was daring Finley to find it.

Her cell vibrated with an incoming text. She dragged her attention away from the house and checked the screen. *Mickey.* Her contact at Riverbend. He'd sent the image of the woman who'd visited Holmes. Unfortunately, it was a little grainy, and the woman wasn't looking directly at the camera. The baseball cap she wore didn't help. But something about her chin and the angle of her jaw was vaguely familiar.

Finley turned her attention back to the house.

Cecelia had predicted that something was coming.

A warning? Or a game?

Maybe both.

Finley suspected that whichever it was, she and Jack weren't going to like it.

As she approached the gate, it opened, and she drove through. She braked before pulling out onto the street. She looked right and then back to the left.

A man stood outside her window.

Finley jumped. Caught her breath. Had he been walking by and she hadn't noticed? Jesus, she could have run him over.

He leaned down and stared at her through the glass. His head was clean shaven, his running suit a spiffy blue.

She powered her window down just a couple of inches. "Sorry, I didn't see you."

He grinned. There was something about the expression that set her on edge.

"Charlie said to tell you you're getting warmer, Finley."

He jogged around the hood of her car and sprinted away.

This was her second message from a follower of Holmes.

Apparently she was getting warmer.

Good to know.

17

Noon

The Murder House
Shelby Avenue
Nashville

Another ring echoed along the line.

It was Saturday. Most people were out shopping or simply doing all the things they couldn't do during the week because of work. Finley paced the length of her living room and waited through another ring.

"Hello."

Thank God. "Hey. Sandy—it's Finley."

"Oh, hey, Fin. What's up?"

Sandy Woods wasn't exactly a friend. More an acquaintance. They'd attended the same high school but never traveled in the same circles. Sandy worked in the county clerk's office. She'd been there since graduating from business college with an associate degree in administration. One of the benefits of working in the DA's office was learning about all sorts of resources within local government.

"I have a question, but if you're in the middle of something or whatever, I can call you later." Finley crossed her fingers and hoped for the right response.

Eric Houser's revelation had been steadily nagging at her. Ignoring it any longer just wasn't possible.

"I was just about to sit down for lunch."

Finley made a face. "I'll call later, then. I don't want to interrupt your lunch." She mouthed a few curse words. Resisted the urge to stamp her feet.

"No, it's all right. It's only a peanut butter sandwich. It can wait."

Finley executed an air punch. "Thank you. I really appreciate it. I'm trying to locate the previous owner of my house." She hissed out an exaggerated sigh. "Since my husband's death I haven't been able to get organized. Anyway, I just need to contact the previous owner to check on a couple of things."

"You can look that up very easily," Sandy explained. "You just go on the tax assessor's website."

"Awesome. Is there a log-in or password I need?"

"Property records are public information, so no. Hold on and I'll look it up for you."

"Wow. That would be great." Finley relaxed a fraction, but her heart continued its anxious pounding.

Derrick wouldn't lie to her. There had to be a mistake. Or an explanation.

"Let me get to my computer."

"Sure. Sure."

Finley resumed her pacing as she waited. Her nerves jangled, ratcheting up the tension again.

"Okay, here we go," Sandy said. "What's your street address?"

Finley provided the info, suddenly realizing she needed to write this down. She hurried to the sofa and dug her spiral from her bag. Poked around for a pen and then collapsed on the floor, pen in the ready position.

"The previous owner was Ted Walker." Sandy called off his address of record. "There's no telephone number."

"The address is perfect." Now for the big question. "What was the date of sale? From Walker to Reed? My husband bought the place before we married."

"All righty. Let me look back one second here."

Finley's heart thudded harder and harder as she waited for the news.

"Derrick Reed purchased the property on February twenty-second of last year."

The bottom dropped out of Finley's stomach. That couldn't be correct. She and Derrick had met in March. They'd married in April and then . . .

"Thank you." Finley cleared her throat. "This will really help."

"Anytime," Sandy assured her. "It's terrible what happened to your husband."

Finley managed a nod, then remembered Sandy couldn't see her. "Yes, it was. Thank you again."

Finley ended the call. Her body felt like ice. Her mind like a black hole. Why would Derrick have misled her about when he purchased the property? He'd told her at least a dozen stories about his ongoing reno over the months prior to their meeting.

She closed her eyes a moment and forced her mind to quiet. There would be a logical explanation. All she had to do was locate this Ted Walker.

A quick search of her favorite look-up service and she had a cell number for Walker. He was sixty-nine and had a wife named Suzy.

More pacing as she waited for an answer. The third ring and then a male voice. "Who's this?"

"Mr. Walker?"

"That's right. Who's calling?"

"My name is Finley, and my husband bought the house on Shelby Avenue from you. Derrick Reed."

"Yep, I remember him. Quite the persistent fella. He just showed up out of the blue one day and wanted to buy the place. He worried me to death, I'm here to tell you. I was in the middle of flipping it, and he just appeared and started throwing numbers at me. Wouldn't take no for an answer."

Her chest constricted. She forced a laugh. "That's Derrick."

"When the offer went high enough, I couldn't say no. I asked him why he was so determined to buy that rundown place, and he said his wife had fallen in love with it. I guess he wanted to make you happy."

Except she hadn't been his wife at the time.

"Thank you, Mr. Walker. I appreciate you sharing this with me."

"I sure was sorry to hear about his death. I hope you're doing all right."

"Thank you. I'm hanging in there."

"Well, if it's any comfort to you, I think he would have done anything to see that he got that house for you. Even when I told him I'd already planned out the place. Bought materials and all. He still wanted it."

Finley swallowed. Found her voice. "You picked out vintage white cabinets for the kitchen?" Every part of her stilled in anticipation of the answer.

"Me and my wife—yes, ma'am. We went to dozens of places, searching through old cabinets. People love that vintage stuff."

The urge to vomit rose in her throat. "You did a great job. They're perfect."

Walker rambled on for a bit, but very little of what he said sank in. Lies. Derrick had told her so many lies about the house. He'd gone on and on about his combing through junk and antique stores looking for just the right cottage-style cabinets.

When the call ended, she only stood there, looking around at the house she had believed was so much a part of their relationship—of him.

Her phone chimed with an incoming text message. She struggled to draw in a breath and forced herself to look at the screen. A text from Arlo, Jack's favorite jailhouse snitch. She opened it and read the words.

Preacher had a visitor today.

Another message popped up. This one an image.

Finley stared at the photo for a long time. All other thoughts disappeared.

Sophia Legard.

———

Drake Motel
Murfreesboro Pike
Nashville, 1:20 p.m.

Finley parked in the slot next to Jack's Land Rover right in front of the door to his rooms. The photo of Sophia Legard signing the visitor log to see the Preacher at Riverbend was startling to say the least. Particularly since Rudy Davis—the Preacher—was purportedly the best friend of Charles Holmes.

But even that eye-opener couldn't shake the haze of disbelief shrouding her.

Derrick had lied to her.

Her cell rang, shattering the silence. She swallowed, accepted the call without even looking at the screen.

"O'Sullivan."

"You coming in or what?"

Jack.

"Coming in." She ended the call and grabbed her bag and keys.

He opened the door, and she walked in, thankful for the dim lighting and the morgue-like temperature. He'd cleaned up the mess, but the wall still looked like a surgery patient who hadn't been sutured up after the operation.

"Arlo sent me a new photo."

Jack closed the door and strolled over to his desk. Papers and files were spread across the top in his general disorganized style. There were no motel furnishings in his place. The owner HAD allowed him to change everything about his space. Paint, carpet, the works. He basically did as he pleased, except when he made so much noise the manager got all out of sorts.

"Of the mystery woman? Is the quality of this one any better?" Jack picked up the bottle of water from his desk and settled into his chair.

"It's a different woman. This one paid a visit to the Preacher today—you know, Holmes's buddy who helped him find Jesus."

"Oh yeah?"

She showed him the image on her phone.

Jack's expression hardened. "Today? She was there today?"

Finley nodded, lowered herself into the nearest seat. She went on to give him the details of her conversation with Olivia and then her visit to Cecelia.

Jack stood, his face set in a grim expression. "What time do visiting hours end?"

"At Riverbend?"

"Where else?" He grabbed his keys.

"Three, I think."

"Good, that means we have time."

When Jack Finnegan made up his mind to do something, he didn't waste time. Asking questions was pointless.

———

Riverbend Maximum Security Prison
Cockrill Bend Boulevard
Nashville, 2:40 p.m.

Finley peeled her fingers loose from the armrests once the vehicle was in park. Jack had one speed: full throttle.

He'd called the warden on the way and arranged a visit with Rudy Davis. Once they were signed in, a guard escorted them to the visitation area. Davis had been set up in a private room. Inmates like Davis and Holmes weren't allowed any sort of freedom during visitation. Typically, visitors were separated by plexiglass with only a handset to speak through. If the meeting was face to face, the inmate had to be secured. Suited Finley just fine.

Davis was a lifer who'd murdered three people and managed a plea deal. Though she understood the methodology behind plea deals, she didn't particularly appreciate the system.

The guard paused at the door and reminded them of the rules. No personal contact with the inmate. And so forth.

Finally the door was opened, and Jack waited for her to enter first. They sat in the two chairs across the table from Davis, who was shackled wrists, belly, and ankles to the floor. His trademark Bible was clenched in his hands as if he might break into prayer. He was forty-five, not very tall, but fit as far as she could tell with him wearing prison garb. Dark hair and eyes. His face was nondescript. He was well educated. An undergrad degree in psychology, which made him all the more dangerous in Finley's opinion.

Davis glanced at Jack, but his gaze lingered on Finley. No surprise. He expected her to be the easiest to intimidate. She stared right back at him.

"Afternoon, Mr. Davis," Jack said, kicking off what would likely be a one-sided conversation.

Davis shifted his attention to Jack but said nothing.

"You had a visitor this morning," Finley said, taking a shot at him. "We"—she gestured to Jack and then herself—"are representing her and her daughters. We asked that she speak with you and see if you would help us understand why Charles Holmes is trying to hurt her family again."

This was mostly a fabrication, but he couldn't know for sure.

His eyes tapered into slits as he studied Finley, looking for some sign she was lying. He wouldn't find it. Finley was very, very good at lying. She was an attorney. She had to be good at it.

"I called her," he said, his voice not nearly as deep as she'd expected. Almost feminine.

"How did you get her number?" This from Jack.

Davis flashed him a look but gave his answer to Finley. "Information is easy to secure if you have the means."

Like drugs and basically anything else an inmate wanted.

"Why did you call her?" Jack asked.

Davis pressed the Bible against his chest as if what he had to say were coming straight from the heart. "I had a message for her."

Finley felt Jack stiffen. She placed a hand on his leg, then asked, "From Mr. Holmes?"

"No, no. From the Lord." He nodded somberly. "She badly needs to confess her sins before it's too late. The wrath is coming. Very soon."

"Did your friend Mr. Holmes ask you to convey that message?" Finley restated the question.

"The Lord asked me to convey the message, ma'am. She and her whorish daughters are doomed to the fires of hell if they don't confess their sins."

Jack pushed back his chair and stood. "We're done here."

Finley stood more slowly. Jack was already at the door by the time she pushed in her chair. "Thank you for your time, Mr. Davis."

"She's marked," Davis said quietly. "You'll see. They all are."

Then he launched into fervent prayer.

Jack didn't say a word until they were through security and out of the building. "Son of a bitch! Holmes is up to something. He's added a new level to this twisted game of his."

When they'd settled into his vehicle and had the air struggling against the heat, Finley reminded him, "You can't play a game without a willing participant. She came to see him. What does that tell you?"

Jack's mouth stayed shut in that thin line of fury while he drove through the gate.

"It tells me," Finley went on, "that Sophia Legard has reason to be worried. To jump through hoops. What do you think will happen when Siniard or the DA get wind of her little visit? She just wrote *guilty* across her forehead."

"I want to talk to her. Get her side of this story."

"Is that Jack the attorney talking or Jack the lover?"

He shot her a look. "Are you really asking me that, O'Sullivan?"

He barreled into traffic. Finley held on to the armrests.

He was pissed. He never called her O'Sullivan. She was his namesake.

"It's a reasonable question under the circumstances," she argued.

He drove. Said nothing.

"She's our client," Finley pressed. "Of course you need to find out why she felt compelled to visit the bastard. But the emotion I'm hearing in your voice is about more than the case. I'm not saying your heart is involved," she said when he continued the silent treatment. "I'm saying your ego is leading you. For whatever reason, she has dragged you into this case. And maybe you feel like you have to do a better job protecting her this time or some stupid macho thing like that."

"She trusts me."

"Does she? She had an affair with you. Is this about trust or about malleability? She called, and you came right back to her aid as if five years hadn't passed. As if," Finley emphasized, "the two of you hadn't drifted apart."

The next thirty seconds were filled with mumbled curse words. Mostly aimed at the possibility that Finley was right.

She was. No question. Sophia was counting on Jack to believe whatever story she gave him.

"She and I are going to have a serious discussion."

"Not without me," Finley warned.

"See if you can get a meeting. Now. Right now. The three of us."

Most of the trip back to Nashville was spent with Finley calling Sophia's cell and home number as well as Cecelia's and Olivia's cells. No one answered. Jack was so furious at their client he drove straight to the Legard mansion. There was no answer at the gate.

With him even more disgusted and still as mad as hell, he drove back to the Drake. Finley decided not to mention what she'd discovered about Derrick or the second warning from what was no doubt a Holmes follower. Jack had enough on his plate. He was teetering on the edge, and she wasn't about to be the reason he stumbled.

"You okay?" she asked when he made no move to get out of the vehicle.

"I fucked this one up, Fin. Didn't see what was coming. I feel like I've walked into a setup, but the endgame is unclear. I'd prefer you step away from the case and let me finish this one alone."

"What?" She laughed. "You think anything about this case could damage my reputation any worse than it already is?"

"Fin."

"Forget it. We're in this together, Jack." She reached for her door. "So don't go messing around with Jim Beam. I need you."

He nodded and reached for his door.

They were two of a kind all right. Broken and too damned hard-headed to admit defeat.

18

5:00 p.m.

The Murder House
Shelby Avenue
Nashville

Finley drove back to Shelby Avenue. She parked in the drive and stared at the murder house. For the first time since she'd moved in, she didn't feel at home. And she felt utterly alone.

She pressed her forehead against the steering wheel. Jack wasn't the only one who'd stepped in it. She'd missed something with Derrick. How was that possible? Her entire career had been based on her ability to read people and anticipate their actions to some degree.

Stop.

She lifted her head, stared at her reflection in the rearview mirror. Just because Derrick wasn't completely honest with her about the house didn't make their life together something bad or not real. The Judge had ensured he was intimidated by her family. Probably by Finley's career. Maybe he'd been trying to prove he had skills.

Even when you're in one of those big meetings with all those big shots, remember no one loves you the way I do.

She closed her eyes. He'd said that to her more than once.

Reaching for her door, she decided then and there that she would give Derrick the benefit of the doubt until it was no longer possible to do so. He wasn't here to defend himself. The least she could do was give him the benefit of the doubt.

Innocent until proven guilty.

She emerged, closed the car door, and was about to turn toward the house when she saw the lady next door. She stopped. Stared. How long had she lived in the neighborhood? She was the only person along this block well beyond childbearing age. The rest were young couples. Yuppies.

The woman stared right back at Finley. Apparently, some of her flowers required watering more than once a day. Maybe she'd gotten tired earlier and was finishing the job now. She wasn't exactly a spring chicken.

Before Finley could question her intent, she was walking across the street. The woman continued to stare at her as if she'd expected Finley would do exactly that.

"Hi." Finley stood on the sidewalk at the edge of her yard. "I just realized I've never introduced myself."

"I know who you are."

This close Finley could see that the woman was sixty plus. No makeup. Well-worn jeans and a tee proclaiming *I'd Rather Be Gardening*.

"Your name is . . . ?" Finley asked, not put off by her unfriendly attitude. Finley had never been particularly friendly to her. She hadn't even thanked her for calling 911 that night. Couldn't even remember her name.

"Helen Roberts."

"Have you lived in the neighborhood long?"

"Thirty-five years. My husband bought this place when we married. Been here ever since. He passed a couple years ago." Her fingers relaxed on the nozzle, and the spray of water stopped.

"My husband bought this house for us." She gestured to the murder house.

"Yeah. I watched him unload his stuff. I didn't realize he was married until you showed up a few weeks later."

Finley blinked. Still didn't want to believe any of that story. "Did you ever talk to him?"

Helen stared at her for a long while. "Nope. I talked to the man who owned it before. Ted. He worked on my kitchen sink once."

"Were you surprised when Mr. Walker sold the place?"

"He was always going to sell it. He just figured he would finish his work first. But your husband came along and wanted it just as it was. Ted said he worried him to death until he agreed to sell. I guess you wanted it pretty bad."

Finley managed a nod. Did everyone know this but her? "It was nice to meet you."

She turned to go home.

"I'm sorry about what happened," Helen said, stopping Finley's escape. "Never had nothing like that happen in this neighborhood."

Finley managed a tight nod. "Thank you. And thank you for calling for help that night."

When the older woman said nothing more, Finley started for home again.

"He must have done something big in the backyard."

The words followed Finley across the street. She paused on her side and turned back. "The backyard?"

Helen nodded. "He worked all hours of the night back there. I suffer with insomnia, so I sit on the porch a lot in the middle of the night. Until you moved in, he was out there every night doing something." She smiled, but it reflected no amusement, kindness, or even remote pleasantness. Just a twitch of her lips.

"Patio," Finley lied. "He wanted a nice patio."

Finley dug for her keys as she strode the rest of the way to her door, then unlocked it and disappeared inside. She leaned against the door and took a breath, then another.

"What the hell were you doing, Derrick?"

She tossed her bag on the sofa and walked to the kitchen to stare out the back door. The yard was nothing but an overgrown mass of green. Not necessarily grass. More weeds, she suspected.

What on earth would he have been doing back there? The water and sewer lines were in the front yard. No patio. No shed. No nothing.

But there had to be something.

The sound of her cell ringing echoed from the living room. She pulled her mind away from the troubling thoughts and went in search of the intrusion. The possibility that this could be another revelation related to their case or to her husband was not lost on Finley.

"O'Sullivan."

"Fin, it's Vern."

Nashville Driver's License Division. "Hey, Vern. Thanks for getting back to me." It was Saturday. She was lucky he was willing to go the extra mile.

"So I found three Alisha Arringtons. I have a seventy-year-old, an eighteen-year-old, and a thirty-year-old."

Based on the image Arlo had sent, it had to be the thirty-year-old. "I'll go with number three."

"You owe me big-time for this one," he warned. "I could lose my job."

"You know I'm good for it." Finley was well aware of the risk she'd asked him to take. She appreciated it more than he could imagine. "Rest assured, no one will ever know the information came from you."

He called off a Riverside Drive address. She thanked him again and ended the call. Nothing like a little drive to the East Side on a Saturday evening.

———

Arrington Residence
Riverside Drive
Nashville, 6:15 p.m.

The rock house was nice. The neighborhood a well-established one. Neat landscaping. Quiet block.

There was a vintage Volvo wagon in the drive, so hopefully someone was home. Finley pressed the doorbell and waited.

Ten, then fifteen seconds elapsed. She started to press the bell again, but the sound of footfalls had her waiting. The lock tripped, and the door opened.

The woman looked from Finley to her Subaru and back. "May I help you?"

"Alisha Arrington?" Finley asked.

"Yes."

Finley flashed her credentials—the ones she shouldn't carry anymore since she no longer worked for the DA's office. "I'm Finley O'Sullivan. I have a few questions for you."

Arrington's defenses fell into place. "Why would someone from the district attorney's office want to ask me questions?"

"It's regarding a court case, and I believe we can clear this up with just a few questions."

The woman wasn't happy about it, but she opened the door wider and allowed Finley inside. The door entered directly into her living room. "I'm sure you have me confused with someone else."

"Possibly," Finley agreed. "That's why I'm here. It's important that we sort this out."

Alisha made her way to a chair and sat down.

Finley did the same. The home furnishings and decor were modest and sparse. Beige walls. Beige carpet. Very clean and tidy. Finley understood this was not the woman she was looking for even before she took out her cell phone and showed the image Mickey had sent. "Is this you?"

Arrington stared at the image for a few seconds, then shook her head. "I don't have a hat like that or that sweater. She doesn't even look like me." She made a face and shifted her gaze to Finley. "What is this about?"

There was a slight resemblance. Mostly related to the blondish hair color and the line of her slim jaw.

"The woman in this photo was visiting an inmate in Riverbend—"

"The prison?" She shook her head. "I've never been to a prison in my life."

The shock and horror on her face backed up her words. "You don't know Charles Holmes?"

Alisha gasped. "The murderer?"

Well, that answered the important question. "You've never visited him or had any sort of contact with him?"

"No." She made an indignant face. "Why in the world would I do that? I don't even know him beyond what I've seen in the news."

"I wasn't able to find you anywhere on social media," Finley said, pulling the conversation back to her and away from Holmes.

"I don't do social media. Never have. Never will. In my opinion it's sinful. My cell phone doesn't even have internet."

Considering the woman who'd logged in at the prison would have had to show ID, generally a driver's license, there was only one explanation.

"Ms. Arrington, have you ever lost your driver's license, or perhaps had it stolen?"

Surprise flashed across her face. "I did lose it. I'd just moved to this house. It was just over four years ago. I went to have the electric changed to my name, but I couldn't find my license. I had to get another one straightaway."

"Have you noticed any irregularities with your credit report or perhaps anything else missing?"

She moved her head slowly side to side. "Not that I'm aware of."

Finley passed her business card. "You should check to ensure your identity is not being used by someone else in any other way."

"I will. Thank you."

Finley doubted she had anything to worry about. Alisha Arrington was likely a victim of circumstance. She'd been at the wrong place at the wrong time, and the woman who'd visited Holmes on all those occasions had stolen her license for that specific purpose. All the thief had needed was someone in the right age range and with the right color hair. Even the hair color wasn't a necessity. Hair color could be changed easily. The same for eye color. Buying colored contacts was as easy as buying mascara these days.

Whoever was pretending to be Holmes's sister had no intention of allowing her true identity to be known.

But why had she suddenly stopped the visits?

Was she the reason Holmes was so determined to revisit the case against him?

A deeper dig into his history was in order.

It was time to have a closer look at Charles Holmes's childhood and life before prison. The fake sister may have been close to him, maybe one of his trusted followers.

Finley couldn't think of a better distraction to keep her out of the backyard tonight. She longed to dig up the whole damned thing.

If there was anything back there, she wanted to know.

She was almost home when her cell shattered the silence in her car. *Seattle.*

Finley pulled over. She needed her hands free for this conversation, in case notes were necessary.

"O'Sullivan."

"This is Holly Thompson, returning your call."

"I appreciate you calling, Ms. Thompson." Anticipation gave Finley a kick of adrenaline. "As I told you in my voice mail, I'm investigating a case that involves your college roommate, Olivia Legard."

"I'm afraid you must have me confused with someone else," Holly said. "My roommate was Anna Patrick. I don't know anyone named Legard."

Was it possible Olivia had kept her identity secret from her roommate? Didn't seem like a reasonable scenario. Roommates—even when they weren't friends—shared intimate space. Big secrets were difficult to keep.

"Do you mind if I send you a pic to see if we're talking about the same woman who's using a different name?"

Thompson hesitated, then relented. "Sure."

Finley sent a pic of Olivia and waited. Her heart rate accelerated with each passing second.

"No, that's not Anna."

Okay, then. "Have you and Anna been in contact since leaving school?"

"We were close, so I'm sure we would have, but she died sophomore year. A car accident. I moved off campus after that, so she was my only roommate during college."

Finley was the one hesitating this time. "I'm sorry to hear that. Do you by chance have a picture of Anna?"

"I'm sure I do. It might take me a bit to find one."

"I really would appreciate it," Finley urged.

"Sure. Sure." Pause. "What exactly is this about?"

"Probably just a clerical error," Finley assured her. "You were listed as the roommate of Ms. Legard. Now that I've spoken to you, I only need to confirm the identity of your actual roommate."

"How strange. I'll send you the picture as soon as I can."

"Do you have an address for her family?" It was possible Finley wouldn't need any additional details, but better to have them than not.

"Oh, she didn't have any family. She was an only child and her parents had both passed. She didn't have a single relative. There were times when I envied her that freedom."

Another thought occurred to Finley. "One last question. Do you recall her major?"

"Of course. Advertising. It was all she talked about. She had big plans for an LA-based job."

Same major as Olivia. A new thread of tension tugged through Finley.

"Thank you, Holly, you've been very helpful."

Finley tossed her cell into the passenger seat and checked the street before jetting away from the curb.

She needed to talk to someone at the university. Unfortunately, that likely wouldn't be possible before Monday.

She damned sure intended to speak with both Sophia and Olivia before then.

Maybe this was as simple as a clerical error.

But it felt like a hell of a lot more.

19

Olivia

9:00 p.m.

Legard Residence
Lealand Lane
Nashville

I pound on the door again.

My heart is bursting in my chest. What's going on? Why is no one answering?

"Cecelia!" I shout my sister's name. "Mom!"

No answer.

The house is dark.

I no longer have a key, so I can't just unlock the door and walk in. I should have told Finley more. I should have told her the whole truth.

But I couldn't.

Not yet. Not yet.

"What do you want?"

The voice is so muffled I scarcely hear it.

"Cecelia?"

"Go away!"

"Please. Please, open the door and talk to me."

"You know I can't."

Renewed fear rushes through me. "Why can't you?" This agoraphobia stuff is bullshit. I should have told Finley that too.

"You've been talking to Finley. Now we're all in trouble."

I am so afraid. I knew this would happen. The finite control we've somehow managed these past five years is gone. Oh God. Oh God.

"I didn't tell her anything. I promise," I insist.

"Yes, you did. I know you did, because she came to see me today."

"I was worried," I argue. "You and Mom are avoiding my calls. I was afraid something had happened."

When my sister says nothing, I press my head against the door and wish it all away. But it will not go away unless I make it.

I was a victim last time, but I must not allow my emotions to make me a victim again.

"Open the door, Cecelia, and let me see what you've done."

"You're such a hypocrite," Cecelia snarls. "You're so certain I'm the evil one. We all knew who the bad twin was, and it wasn't me. You might fool other people, but you can't fool me or Mother. We know what you are."

My heart hurts, my stomach twists. We loved each other so much when we were small. Why did everything change?

"Cece, please. Just let me in so we can talk. I need to see you."

"No. I don't want to see you. Go away. Never come back."

I give up and walk back to my rental car. There is nothing more I can do. Whatever Cecelia has done is not my fault. I tried to stop her before and failed.

Why did I believe this time would be different?

I pull out of the driveway, thankful I remembered the code to the gate. They should have changed it long ago. Sheer arrogance kept them from it.

Driving back to my hotel, I change my mind and make a turn. I thread my way through the streets. I don't drive a direct route. I have no idea what sort of cameras the city has in place.

Eventually I reach my destination. I park at the curb on the opposite side of the street and watch.

Finley O'Sullivan is still up. The lights are on, and after I watch for a while I see her shadow move across a window.

She intrigues me. So smart and perceptive. Very perceptive. I'm certain she sees through Cecelia. Certainly she has my mother figured out. She was only ever out for herself. She had no time for my sister and me. It was Daddy who treated us like princesses.

I wish she had been the one to die.

I wouldn't have missed her much. I miss Daddy so, so much.

But the choice was not mine.

I smile. This time is different.

This time I'm going to have the final say.

I watch the house where Finley lives. She stays because she feels a duty to do so. He died and she didn't. I've read a great deal about her. She's so very interesting.

It's funny how life puts people in one's path. I would never have met Finley if my father hadn't been murdered and the monster sitting in prison hadn't decided to play his games.

I'm so glad we met. I like her very much. I like watching her. I wonder what she thinks of me. Maybe I'll ask her.

For now I'll be content knowing she's not far away. Only a few yards.

If I close my eyes, I can smell her skin.

I want to know her better.

I'll have to find a way.

20

Sunday, July 10

8:35 a.m.

The Murder House
Shelby Avenue
Nashville

Finley awoke that morning determined to hunt down Olivia and her mother or Cecelia—whomever she could find with the name Legard. After the chat with the supposed roommate late yesterday, she'd called all three women. No answer. No return calls came. Frustrated beyond reason, Finley had gone to the Legard home. No response at the gate. At seven a.m. this morning she had repeated that process, to no avail. Then she'd called Jack.

Jack had gotten the same when he'd called their clients.

Oh yeah, the ladies had apparently gone into hiding.

Finley had to kill some time or go crazy contemplating this afternoon's dreaded birthday party.

She should never have promised her dad she would go.

Walking the floors hadn't burned off the impulse to do something . . . anything. There had been only one option left for retaining her sanity—unearth whatever was in her backyard. From the moment the neighbor had mentioned Derrick doing something in the backyard, Finley had tried to quell the urge to check it out. But she had lost that battle.

She didn't actually own boots suitable for yard work or gardening, but Derrick had. She dug around on his side of the closet until she found the rubber boots he had kept by the back door *before*. She pulled them on over her socks, tucking the legs of her jeans inside. It was hot already, so she trudged to the back door and picked one of his hats. Gloves lay on the shelf above the coat-and-hat rack.

Phone was in her back pocket. Bottle of water and gloves in hand. She was ready to begin.

She walked out the back door and surveyed the small rear yard. Nothing much to see. Overgrown grass. A rusty firepit standing near the center. A couple of overturned plastic chairs. Sooner rather than later she really needed to get someone over here to mow the lawn. Her gaze narrowed as she kicked a clump of grass. Maybe she should cut the grass before poking around back here. Shouldn't take that long. Assuming there was gasoline and that she could start the mower.

Why not?

The garage smelled musty. Retrieving that screwdriver for Matt was the first time she'd been inside in ages. It had been Derrick's space. It wasn't like a new garage with an overhead door. It was old and small with barn-style doors that swung open. She flipped on the lights and picked her way to the mower. It was dusty. Even had a cobweb hanging between it and a nearby shelf.

"You never know until you try."

An hour and a half later she'd actually cut the grass in back as well as the postage-stamp-size plot out front. All that was left was the grass too close to the house, around the firepit, and along the fence. Her arms were tired and she was sweaty and dusty, but she felt good. Maybe it was time she started running again. She'd forgotten how a strenuous workout could help with stress.

At least now she could see the contours of the ground out back. There were a few ruts and a couple of former flower beds with that rubber landscape edging. She had never noticed any of it before. When she'd pushed the mower back into the garage, she'd grabbed a shovel. Derrick had all the usual yard implements. Something else she'd never noticed. There had been no yard work to do at her condo. Her parents had always had a gardener.

Pretty sad that she could get to thirty-two and not have ever cut grass until now.

She walked the backyard in a grid pattern. Like a crime scene, east to west, then north to south. Near the back, at the thick row of trees and hedges that separated her yard from the neighbor's behind her, there was a bit of a mound. It was grass covered, but after a year it would be.

With a covert glance around to ensure no one was watching, she started to dig. Her arms were burning and sweat was dripping by the time she hit something that wasn't dirt. Black. Plastic.

Her pulse skipped. Taking a deep breath, she scrubbed away more of the dirt with her gloved hands. Definitely a large plastic garbage bag. When she'd cleared enough dirt, she poked at the bag. Her breath caught. There was something inside. Since she hadn't found the opening of the bag, she opted to make one in the plastic. As soon as the black shroud was ruptured, the scent of decay hit her in the face.

She reared back. Coughed. Fought the urge to gag.

When she'd calmed her reaction, she dug around in the hole she'd made. Her gloved fingers wrapped around a slender, solid object.

Holding her breath, she pulled it from the bag.

Bone.

Adrenaline slammed into her heart.

Damn.

More clawing around in the bag and she discovered another bone. This one a jaw.

Dog.

Relief had her collapsing onto her butt in the freshly cut grass. Someone had buried the family pet.

Shaking her head, she scrambled up, tore off her gloves, and dusted herself off.

What was wrong with her?

There had to be a reasonable explanation for whatever Derrick had been doing back here. Shovel in hand, she spread the dirt back over the bag of bones. She swore at herself for being such an idiot.

She trudged around the yard again, kicking the slightest clump or lump she spotted. Surveying for sunken areas where trenching or digging might have been done previously. She found nothing.

Frustrated, hot, and exhausted, she grabbed the shovel and headed to the garage just in time for the rain. Was it supposed to rain? She stared up at the sky. She couldn't recall the last time she'd watched the weather news.

Ignoring the rain, she walked around the rear corner of the house, and her gaze collided with that of Helen Roberts. Her fuzzy white lapdog tugging at the leash, she gave Finley a nod from beneath her umbrella and walked on across the street.

Finley ducked into the garage feeling completely foolish. She tucked the shovel away. She'd forgotten the gloves. Didn't care. She was done. She kicked off the boots, closed off the garage, and plodded back to the house as the rain grew heavier.

She needed a shower. She had that damned party this afternoon.

Cranking up the heat on the tap, she climbed into the shower and stood there until her skin felt blistered. She washed her hair, forced herself to go through the motions of washing her skin and shaving the necessary areas. She should probably wear a dress to the party. She had one somewhere. She'd gone a little overboard after quitting the DA's office and burned half her wardrobe in the backyard firepit. She never wanted to dress that part again.

She rubbed the towel over her hair, then wrapped it around her body. When she'd first started at Jack's firm, she'd had a hard time getting into the groove. A few weeks later she had hit her stride, and life had purpose again.

She refused to allow whatever was going on with their damned clients or Metro and her husband's case to pull her back to that dark place. She'd worked too hard to escape. In whatever way this new detective tried to find some way to make Derrick look like the bad guy—or Finley, for that matter—she knew who the bad guy was. She knew why her husband was dead.

Before she could close that door, memories flooded her.

The murder weapon hadn't been found. The medical examiner had believed the weapon to be a baseball bat or other rounded club. Since they'd had nothing like that in the house, the perps had obviously brought it with them.

She and Derrick had made love that night. Showered together. Finley had grabbed a towel and rushed to the kitchen to turn off the oven. She'd almost forgotten about the meat loaf. As she turned to go back to the bedroom, someone attacked her from behind. The first blow to the back of her head had put her down. Rattled her for several seconds.

She'd seen the boots. Black. Like hunting boots. Whatever trousers the intruder had worn had been tucked into those boots or concealed in some other way. She'd heard the yelling. Objects shattering. The grunts. More shouts.

At first she'd had to drag herself across the floor. Eventually she'd risen up onto her hands and knees. She saw the boots again. Saw Derrick's naked legs. Blood on the floor. Struggling. Then she'd seen Derrick's face. Eyes unblinking. Blood trickling down his skin. Then the kick to her side.

He was there . . . over her. But he wasn't alone. There were three. She'd gotten glimpses, but those brief images were enough.

The one who'd raped her had whispered that message in her ear. *You take something from me. I take something from you.* Then there was nothing.

She'd awakened two days later in the hospital, her father on one side of her, Matt on the other. For weeks she hadn't been able to remember many details. Then, as the investigation played out and her frustration had grown, she'd started to remember bits and pieces. She'd tried explaining what she recalled, but no one had believed her. Over time more fragments had come to her, but by then her statements had been deemed irrelevant and unreliable, so she'd stopped talking and decided to find the evidence she needed on her own.

But what if she'd been wrong all this time?

The idea shook her to the very core of her being. Derrick hadn't been completely truthful with her. There could be a perfectly logical explanation . . . but what if he—

The shrill of her cell phone pierced the air, jerking her back to the present.

Finley headed in that direction, her legs shaking just a little. Reliving those memories still had that effect on her. She'd been raped, yes, but most of that horrific act had occurred while she was unconscious. The realization made her sick still, yet the other feelings she'd expected were oddly missing. She didn't want to feel any of it. Those emotions would make her weak. Would make her hesitate going forward.

Another ring, the sound seeming far too loud, as she fished around the sofa cushions for her phone. By the time she found it, a third ring had screamed at her.

Matt.

"Hey. Sorry, I couldn't find my phone."

He laughed. "This is why I carry mine in a holster on my belt."

"Ha ha. I hate anything confining around me." Including belts. She'd never been able to wear tight jeans. Somewhere in her childhood there was likely an explanation, but that was one place she and her therapist weren't going.

"So you're going to the birthday gala."

This was not a question—he knew she had no choice. "Gala?"

"That's what the invitation says."

"I wouldn't know. I didn't get one."

He sighed, the breathy sound familiar and comforting. "You're the daughter. You have a standing invitation to all family functions."

"Yes, I am going. Only so my father won't be miserable."

"That's very noble of you, Fin. I know he'll appreciate it, and your mother will also. Though her appreciation may go unspoken."

Finley did laugh then.

"You want me to pick you up?"

Have you ever seen him on a real date with anyone? Seriously. He only wants you.

Finley pushed Derrick's voice out of her head. "I would, but I need my own transportation in case I have to leave early."

"Ah, you're cutting out early. I got it. All right, then, I'll see you there."

"See ya."

She stared at the screen. Maybe she should have ridden with Matt. Then she could have gotten shitfaced. Wouldn't the Judge have loved that?

Finley forced herself to find something to eat. She hadn't bothered with breakfast, and at least two drinks would be necessary to stay at the party for a half hour or so. Food was essential. The fridge was mostly empty, but she found cheese that was only out of date by about forty-eight hours. Somewhere in this house there were crackers. Finding them took a whole five minutes. She sat on the back steps and ate the cheese and crackers, no matter that she didn't taste either one.

She stared at the lawn. The place where the dog was buried. She studied the contour of the grass. She closed her eyes and cursed herself for going down that path again. Who knew if Helen had seen what she thought she had? She was old and wore glasses with very thick lenses.

Finley shook her head. She recognized the strategy. Denial. Find a reason it couldn't be possible. Made ignoring the possibilities far easier.

She should get dressed and get moving so the Judge could pretend all was right in her world.

21

2:00 p.m.

O'Sullivan Residence
Jackson Boulevard
Belle Meade

Finley opted to park on the street outside her parents' compound. The gate was open with only a guard waving guests through without asking questions. He smiled at Finley and gave her a nod.

She rarely wore heels anymore, so the trek over the cobblestones was hazardous at best. Finley recognized most of the faces she saw. The hierarchy of the community. The city's elite. Exactly what she'd expected.

Entering the massive foyer with its sweeping staircase always impressed guests no matter how many times they had been to the house before. Belle Meade was that kind of community, and the Judge's home was a real estate star. Ruth bought the place two weeks before she and Finley's dad had married. Her parents had lived a couple of streets over. Their house hadn't been large enough to suit the future judge. After they passed, she'd sold the homeplace and paid off the mortgage on this one. She always said they would have approved. They were gone before Finley was born, so she had no idea.

The flowers and decorations were impeccable. Lots of whites and blushes and soft greens. Several beverage bars were set up throughout the downstairs area and outside. Waiters with freshly loaded food trays roamed the crowd offering all manner of tasty delights. There were champagne fountains, chocolate fountains, and a veritable array of who's who strolling the red carpet that made a path through the center of the house to the rear gardens.

Finley snagged a flute of champagne from a passing tray. She didn't really like champagne, but her mother always bought the best. Might as well enjoy some aspect of the next half hour or so.

Matt appeared at her side. "My, my, Ms. O'Sullivan, you certainly clean up well."

"It's the only dress I had that wasn't wrinkled." She'd once owned a steamer, but she had no clue where it was now.

"You look great."

She laughed softly. "This shade of green reminds me of a car you owned in college."

He laughed then. "That must be why I like it so much."

She turned to him, looked him up and down. Matt was the only person she knew who could pull off a white linen suit. He had that perpetual tan and just the right color hair and eyes to make it work.

"Maybe you didn't notice . . ." She leaned closer to him. "But every female—and some males—in the room are openly eying you."

"Actually, I think they're eying you."

She muffled a laugh to prevent the champagne she'd just chugged from spewing forth.

"Fair warning," he said. "The trinity is gathered out by the gazebo. They're talking business. You might want to avoid the area."

"Thanks for the heads-up." She would steer clear for sure.

"Did you by chance have an unauthorized chat with DA Briggs's daughter?"

Finley sipped her champagne this time. "I did. She was full of information." She grinned up at Matt. "Did you know she and Cecelia were quite notorious in high school?"

"I can only imagine." Matt leaned closer. "So you know, Briggs is not happy. I'm supposed to mention that you'd better not approach her again without her attorney present."

"He didn't have the balls to tell me this himself?"

"Apparently not."

Matt put his arm around her shoulders. "Come on. Let's go find the lady of honor and wish her a happy birthday."

"Whatever." Finley downed the last of the champagne, left the glass on a tray table, and grabbed another from a passing waiter. This one went down the hatch too.

"Easy, tiger," her friend whispered close to her ear.

"All better now."

The Judge was in the great room. Dressed in a well-fitted rose-colored sheath, she stood with her back to the fireplace since a massive painting of her in her robes hung above it. Finley's father, sporting a taupe suit and a tie that perfectly matched the Judge's dress, stood at her side, smiling like always.

The receiving line was endless.

"I'll just wave from here," Finley suggested.

"Of course you won't." Matt ushered her around the crowd and right up to the Judge. "Happy birthday, Judge," he said with a broad smile.

Ruth O'Sullivan looked from Matt to Finley, only the slightest glimmer of surprise flashing in her eyes. "Thank you for coming."

Matt leaned in and kissed her on the cheek. "I wouldn't have missed it for the world."

Matt was too nice.

Ruth turned to her. "Finley." She looked her up and down as she reached for her shoulders. "So marvelous to see you, sweetheart." She leaned in and left a kiss on Finley's cheek.

Then she did what she always did. Introduced her daughter to the gathered crowd as if she were a doting mother and Finley an adoring child.

"Happy birthday, Judge," Finley announced.

Those closest laughed at Finley's joke. Her mother would know that it wasn't really a joke. She hadn't called her *Mother* in a long while now.

Her father skirted around the Judge and gave Finley a big hug, allowing the guest of honor to move back to her receiving line duties.

Being a good friend, Matt shook hands with her father and then ushered Finley into the dining room. "We should find a place to talk."

"That sounds ominous."

The concern in his eyes warned it was indeed ominous.

"Let's go up to your old room." He glanced around. "We need some privacy."

"Sure."

They used the staff staircase in the kitchen to avoid adding to the rumor mill. Finley had no idea if her old room was still *her* room. For all she knew the Judge could have cleared it out and turned it into a fifth guest room.

She opened the door and switched on the light. To her surprise the room remained exactly as it had been her senior year of high school.

"Looks the same," Matt noted.

White walls. White carpet. White bedding. The only color was in the photos of places Finley had visited up to that point in her life. Paris. Madrid. Sydney. Dozens of other places. Her father had made sure Finley was well traveled. The Judge was generally too busy to accompany them, which was always a relief.

"She was so annoyed when you refused to have pink walls," Matt reminded her. "You remember, she had that designer fly in from New York and create this magnificent"—he spread his arms wide apart—"fairy-princess fantasyland. And you came undone. You hated it."

"I was ten years old," she grumbled. "She took my room from clouds and butterflies to her vision of a fairy tale."

"You were so upset, your dad and Jack painted it white the next day while Ruth was in court. She was furious when she found out."

"The story of our relationship. We never saw eye to eye on anything."

"She loves you anyway."

Finley turned to him, studied his face. "Whose friend are you, hers or mine?"

He held his hands up, palms out, and moved them side to side as if erasing the words. "My bad. I guess being in this room had me sentimental for a moment."

"What's going on, Matt?"

"Briggs has openly voiced that he wants you off the Legard case. He's claiming you're unreliable. Lawrence has that new detective, Houser, digging up all the dirt he can on your and Derrick's relationship and his . . . murder."

"Briggs wants the Legard case to go away again without any new bones being unearthed," Finley said, anger and frustration fighting for equal billing. "His one and only daughter was connected to the sister Holmes named as the one who supposedly wanted Lance Legard dead. I've already gotten too close for his liking." Besides, he was looking for a way to ensure anything she did or had done didn't make him or his office look bad. Protecting his office—or, more specifically, himself—was his top priority.

Matt sat down on the bed. "Fin, there is no doubt in my mind that there's something bigger than we know here. The question is, are you willing to pay the price for finding the answer. You've just regained your balance after what happened last year. I don't want to see you taking the wrong risks too soon."

"Houser came to see me." She couldn't keep this from Matt any longer, and it was the perfect segue for moving on.

He nodded. "You mentioned he had."

"What I didn't mention was his claim that Derrick bought the house only a couple weeks before we met."

"How's that possible? Derrick had been working on the place for months before you met."

"That's what he told me. But when I called the previous owner, he said the same thing Houser did. In fact, the house wasn't even for sale, but Derrick just kept upping the offer until the guy sold it to him. Derrick insisted his wife had seen the house and fallen in love with it. Derrick and I hadn't even met at that point."

"Damn."

Finley sat down beside him. "Exactly."

"I can do some digging if you want. See if Houser has found something more he hasn't shared yet."

"I would appreciate it very much. Obviously my contacts at the DA's office and Metro are a little thin right now." She'd never had that problem before.

"I really hate to broach this subject, but how well did you research Derrick before you married?"

She shrugged. "The usual. No criminal record. Not even a speeding ticket. Good credit. Solid work record. He didn't have any close family, so I don't really know anything about his relatives."

Matt leaned forward, braced his forearms on his knees. "I'm guessing the Judge conducted a similar background review. If there was anything to be found, she would have found it."

"Unless," Finley braced herself for saying out loud the possibility that had been nagging at her, "he was using an alias."

"Unless that, yeah." Matt looked her in the eyes. "Any reason to suspect he did?"

"Not yet."

At this point she was just waiting for the other shoe to drop.

"We'll figure this out," he promised. He touched her elbow. "Come on, let's get back to the celebration before the Judge sends the cavalry looking for us."

They were halfway down the stairs when something in a photograph caught Finley's eye. She paused, stared at the framed eight-by-ten. It was one of the Judge's pet-project committees. There were photos like this all around the house. The Judge never met a bragging opportunity she didn't like. Finley couldn't recall the name of this particular committee. Something related to preserving the history of the city. But it was the face next to her mother's that had caught her eye.

Sophia Legard.

Finley leaned forward and looked more closely. Sophia's left arm was coiled around the Judge's right. What the . . . ? How old was this photo? She stared at her mother to try to gauge when it was taken.

"Something wrong?" Matt moved in beside her.

"Is that . . . ?" She pointed to the face she was certain belonged to her client.

He looked from the photograph to Finley. "Sophia Legard. I didn't know she and the Judge were friends."

"Neither did I." Finley's cell vibrated. She fished it out, her attention still glued to the images in that photograph. She glanced at her cell. Jack's name scrolled across the screen. "It's Jack. I'll catch up with you," she said to Matt.

He gave her a nod and headed back down to the party.

"Hey, boss, you are not going to believe what I just found."

"I need you to come to the Legard house now."

The hollowness of his voice told her something was very, very wrong. A frown tugged at her face. "What's going on?"

"Come now, Fin. Right now."

"On my way."

Rather than track Matt down, she sent him a text. She walked out of the house and had reached the cobblestones when someone stepped into her path.

Briggs.

She drew up short. He said nothing, only glared at her.

"Is there something you need, Mr. Briggs?"

"Stay away from my daughter," he said softly, but the look on his face, in his eyes, was anything but soft. "I don't know what you think you're doing, but you'd better watch your step, O'Sullivan."

"I'm doing my job, sir. I haven't broken any laws." That anyone knew about, anyway.

"You ambushed her. Allowed her to think you still worked for me."

"If that's what she thought, she reached that conclusion on her own. I never said I still worked for you."

"I gave you a shot," he said, fury humming in his words, "and you threw it away. We're all keeping eyes on you now."

"Good. Maybe you'll learn something."

Finley walked around him. She had no more time for his blustering. Jack needed her.

22

3:20 p.m.

Legard Residence
Lealand Lane
Nashville

The gate was open in anticipation of her arrival.

Finley rolled through. Parked. Jack's Land Rover was there. No other vehicles in front of the house. No cops. That could be a good sign. Maybe whatever had gone down wasn't the worst-case scenario.

She climbed out of her Subaru and headed to the front door, all the while wishing these shoes were in hell. Her feet were killing her. When she was halfway across the veranda, the front door opened.

Olivia stood on the threshold looking like a wrongly convicted prisoner who'd just been released.

Suddenly Finley wanted to grab her and shake the hell out of her. Why hadn't she been answering her phone? Why wasn't she at her hotel last night?

"Hurry." Olivia, oblivious to Finley's fury, motioned for her to come inside.

The door slammed shut behind her. Finley turned to the younger woman. "I called you like ten times last night and this morning. What the hell, Olivia?"

She stared at Finley as if she had no idea what she was upset about.

Before she could stop herself, Finley let her have it. "I spoke to the woman who was listed as your roommate at USC. She never heard of you. You want to explain that?"

"What?" Olivia shook her head as if Finley had spoken some foreign language she didn't understand.

"Holly Thompson."

Olivia made a confused face. "Who's Holly Thompson?"

Before Finley could calm enough to answer, Olivia shrugged. "My roommate was Tanya Smallwood. I don't know any Holly Thompson."

Finley's fury fizzled. "Why does your file at USC say your roommate was Holly Thompson?" Nita had gotten the information directly from a source at the university.

Olivia's head moved side to side. "I have no idea. A mistake of some sort."

Shit. Finley took a breath. "We'll figure that out later. What's going on? Where's Jack?" And what the hell was he doing here without her? Finley kept the last to herself.

"Come with me." Olivia grabbed her by the arm and ushered her through the house until they reached the kitchen. Jack was there. Seated at the island with his head in his hands.

Finley's gut wrenched. "What's going on, Jack?"

He lifted his head, met Finley's gaze.

"Mother's dead," Olivia blurted before Jack could respond.

Had there been an accident? "What happened? Where's Cecelia?"

"Cecelia is MIA," Jack said. He stood. "We've searched the house. She's not here."

Somehow, they weren't giving her the answers she needed. "What happened to Sophia?"

"I found her," Olivia volunteered.

Oh hell. Finley swung her attention back to the younger woman. It was difficult to discern whether the woman was excited or maybe in shock. "What does that mean, Olivia?"

"I couldn't get an answer from Mother or from Cecelia. Maybe that's why I didn't get your calls," Olivia offered. "I called them over and over. Finally, even though I didn't want to ever come here again, I couldn't shake this bad feeling. I drove over and came inside. Mother was . . ."

Her explanation trailed off, and Finley turned back to her boss. "What the hell happened?" She clenched down on her whirling emotions and muttered, "Why did you come here without me?"

"I didn't have a choice." He shook his head as though she should understand and he couldn't comprehend why she didn't. "She's upstairs in her bedroom."

Finley didn't wait to hear more. She hurried to the entry hall and up the stairs. There was likely another route to the second floor, but she wasn't interested in tracking it down. She rushed from door to door until she found the luxurious double set that led to the owner's suite.

Sophia was still in bed. One arm hung down the side along with a silk comforter. She looked as if she were sleeping except for the enormous knife protruding from her chest. Finley winced. There wasn't as much blood visible as she would have expected, but she wasn't a medical examiner. For all she knew, the majority of the blood loss was under the victim for some reason. Exit wound? Could a knife have an exit wound? Maybe it went all the way through.

Whatever the case, the woman was dead. Son of a . . .

"I think my sister killed her."

Finley turned to the door, where Olivia had stalled in her tracks.

What the hell was Jack thinking calling Finley instead of the police?

"You found her?" Finley confirmed, grappling for her mental footing.

Olivia nodded.

"Did you come into the room?"

Olivia shook her head. "I could see from here." She gestured vaguely. "The blood and the knife. I assumed it would be pointless to check for a pulse."

All spoken so logically . . . so damned emotionless.

"Did you call 911?" The answer was no, but Finley felt compelled to ask. Besides, she was pissed all over again.

How the hell had this happened?

"First I searched the house for Cecelia. I was worried she might be . . ." She gestured to the bed. "Hurt or something. But I couldn't find her. That's when I realized she may have done this. The alarm was still active. If anyone else had opened the door and come inside, it would have gone off." She shook her head, squeezed her eyes together. "I just don't know. Then I called Jack. Mother would have wanted me to call him first."

The comment had Finley's head ready to explode. "Exactly how did you get in?"

"The door was unlocked. I opened it and entered the code for the security system. Fortunately, it was still the same. Like the gate code, they never changed it."

Finley clamped her mouth shut, walked out of the room, and stormed back down the stairs and into the kitchen.

"Did you go in the room?" she demanded of her boss. Soon-to-be ex-boss if he had fucked this up any worse than it already was.

He stared at Finley, his expression somber.

Damn it! "Just tell me you didn't touch anything."

"I didn't touch anything. I just looked at her. It was clear she'd been dead for a while."

Thank God. "We have to call this in."

Olivia rushed to Finley. "What about Cecelia? What if she didn't kill Mother? What if someone took her? The killer may have forced her to reset the alarm."

Fair point. Except . . . "I thought you were convinced Cecelia killed her?"

Olivia's face blanked. "I can't be sure. I wasn't here. I don't know what happened."

Finley stepped closer to her, pinned her with a cautioning look. "What are you not telling me, Olivia? You and Cecelia—even your mother—have been skipping all around some unsaid thing. I'm telling you right now, if you don't come clean, I'm out of here. Jack might be willing to represent you, but I won't have any part of it."

If there was one thing Finley hated, it was a liar. Unless she was the one telling the lie for a damned good reason.

Had Derrick lied to her?

She blinked away the thought.

"Fin," Jack begun.

She held up a hand. He'd done and said enough already. She imagined the fact that Sophia had visited the Preacher yesterday wasn't lost on him any more than it was on her. What was it he'd said? *She was marked?* Holy hell.

Olivia took a step back as if fearing there was about to be an explosion. She shook her head. "I told you I was worried, but you blew it off. Now my mother is dead and my sister is missing. My sister who never leaves the house. Someone must have taken her."

There she went, shifting blame again.

"We'll search the house once more, and then we're calling this in." Finley hesitated. "What about the cameras? Doesn't your security system have cameras?"

Olivia nodded. "I checked the system. Hoping to learn what happened. But the cameras were turned off."

Of course they were. Finley turned to Jack. "You stay put. I don't want you dropping so much as a hair anywhere else in this house."

He didn't argue with her. Just sat down and pressed his palms together as if he might pray. Too damned late for that too.

Finley kept Olivia with her as they moved through the massive home. Olivia's former room was like Finley's at the Belle Meade house—just a room with no personality other than a random photo here and there of the twins. Cecelia's room, on the other hand, would have made a great episode of *Hoarders*. Stuff—clothes, soiled dishes, towels—was everywhere. The bed was piled high with photo albums and more stuff save for a narrow place on the right side where she presumably slept. There was no television. No radio. No phone.

"Did you find Cecelia's cell phone?"

"It's not here."

Finley faced her. "Have you ever known your sister to leave the house?"

Olivia hesitated.

"I'm asking if she's truly agoraphobic or if the illness is a cover."

Olivia looked away. "I'm not entirely sure."

Lie.

"Don't lie to me again," Finley warned.

"I believe she has left when it suited her. In my opinion the agoraphobia thing is the way she kept Mother under control."

Maybe not the whole truth, but part of it. "All right, let's keep going."

Half an hour later it was clear Cecelia was not in the house or the attached garages. Another twenty minutes were necessary to check the pool house and detached garage as well as the gardening shed.

Back in the kitchen, Finley explained to the younger woman what would be happening next. "The police will want to question you. Jack will be with you throughout the questioning. He'll let you know when to talk and when not to. If he speaks, you be quiet. Do not give any additional information. Answer the question asked as concisely as possible. If you don't know the answer, say so."

Olivia nodded. "I remember from last time."

Jesus Christ. This was going to be a shit show.

Finley ushered Olivia to the small table in the kitchen and had her sit. Then she grabbed Jack by the arm and prodded him into the massive entry hall.

"Are you up for this?"

He worked up a glare and directed it at her. "I'm fine. It's just—"

"This whole thing is a bad idea, Jack. You are personally involved and—"

"Sometimes you can't help being personally involved. Shit happens."

Okay, so she couldn't argue the point. She heaved a breath. "All right."

He shook his head. "I'm sorry. This is just . . ."

"Yeah, well, time to call it in. Am I doing it, or are you?"

He reached for his cell. She put a hand on his to stop him. "I'll do it." She started to suggest he keep Olivia calm, but frankly, she seemed calmer than anyone in the house other than the dead woman upstairs.

Finley stepped out onto the veranda and made the call. Her next call was to Matt. She didn't want him blindsided by this. He wanted to rush over, but they both recognized that would be a mistake.

The ambulance arrived first. Someone had to do the official call on the victim's status. Two police cruisers arrived next and began the protocol of securing the scene. When the detectives arrived, Olivia and Finley were separated and interviewed individually. Then Jack had his turn. Luckily, neither of the detectives was one Finley had pissed off recently.

By the time the questioning was over, a flock of reporters had gathered outside the gate. Leaving would be a bitch.

When the time to exit came, uniformed officers backed the reporters away from the gate so Finley could leave. Olivia was in the back seat with a blanket over her so they wouldn't be followed. Jack left right behind her and took a different route. Since he was the representing attorney, hopefully any ambitious reporters would follow him.

When they were far enough away and no one had followed, Finley gave Olivia a task. "You can sit up for now. I want you to call the security company. If possible, find out the times the house was entered and exited today using the security code. And find out when the cameras were shut down."

One of those detectives would be doing that very thing, if he hadn't already. The fewer steps she and Jack were behind, the better.

As Olivia sat up, the blanket shifted off her face. "If she hasn't changed the pin number, I can."

"Give it a shot," Finley urged as she focused on driving. "And don't lie to me, Olivia. I will be confirming whatever you tell me."

Olivia made the call. Finley mentally crossed her fingers. They needed that information.

By the time she reached Olivia's hotel, she was fairly confident they had no tails. Olivia had recalled the property pin—her parents' wedding anniversary—and passed along the information obtained to Finley. Meanwhile Finley had called the hotel manager, and he'd given her instructions on the best way to get Olivia to her room. Rather than pull up in front of the hotel entrance, she drove into the garage and parked in the staff parking area. She escorted Olivia inside through a service entry. Security had blocked the corridor and monitored the service elevator to ensure no one had boarded ahead of them.

Good thing Jack had a lot of friends in this city. Other than the Judge and the trinity, most people liked him, which was immensely useful in situations like this one.

Olivia unlocked the door, and they entered together. Finley checked the room. All clear. "You need to stay in your room. Get room service when you need something. Call me or Jack if you have any trouble or feel you need someone to talk to. It would be best if you didn't talk to anyone else."

"I won't. I don't have any friends left here, so there's no one to talk to. Unless Cecelia calls."

"If Cecelia calls, talk to her," Finley amended. "Don't scare her off—just try to get her location. We need to find her."

Olivia nodded.

"If the police come, don't say a word until Jack or I get here."

Another nod.

"Call me if you need me."

Finley hurried back to her car and got away without being followed by anyone who showed an interest in her vehicle. She put through a call to Jack. "You back home?"

"Yeah."

"You okay?"

"Yeah." He knew what she was asking.

"If that status changes, I want to hear from you."

"Don't worry, I'm okay."

"I had Olivia call the security company. The alarm was deactivated at nine this morning, then reactivated at nine forty-five. It wasn't deactivated again until two this afternoon, which would seem to confirm Olivia's story."

"Sophia never struck me as one to sleep in," he countered. "Why would she be in bed until nine?"

"It's Sunday. She's older now, and she's been under a lot of stress," Finley offered.

"Maybe."

Finley inhaled a long, deep breath. "Look, I asked Olivia about the roommate, and she assured me there was a mistake. She spouted off another name without the slightest hesitation. Maybe . . ." It was possible, Finley had to admit.

"I'm listening," Jack prodded.

"Maybe Holly Thompson was a clerical error." There, she'd said it.

"Your gut is telling you," he countered, "that you should still check it out."

"Yeah."

"Do it, Fin. At this point, I'm not banking on anything being what it appears to be on this one."

"You're right. I'll call you later." Finley ended the call without telling him she would be making an in-person contact tonight to be sure he was okay.

Turning onto her street, she spotted a vehicle parked at the curb in front of her house. What now? She'd had more unexpected visitors in the past two days than she'd had all year.

As she rolled closer, she recognized the car.

The Judge.

"What the hell?"

Finley parked in her drive and took a long, deep breath. Her mother had never been to this house before, at least not to Finley's knowledge. Being in the neighborhood at all would likely have the Judge in hives. For a minute or so Finley sat right where she was. Getting out would set off a chain reaction that couldn't possibly end well.

Her mother broke before she did. The driver's side door opened, and the Judge herself popped out and headed up the walk. She still wore the rose dress from her party. Finley exhaled a long breath and then did what she had to do. She got out of her car and faced the woman who gave birth to her.

This was as good a time as any to ask her about the photograph.

"Did you get bored with your party?" Finley hadn't meant to sound like a smart-ass, but there it was.

"We need to talk."

Finley walked to the porch, unlocked the door, and went inside. The Judge followed. The next fifteen or twenty seconds elapsed with the Judge surveying the shabby living room with its stained and cracked ceiling and worn-out furniture.

"Why are you here?" Finley asked at last. And where was Dad? The only way he wouldn't have come with her was if she hadn't told him her destination.

The Judge's attention settled on Finley. "Why on earth are you still living in this place?"

"Well, *Mother*, this is my home."

She made a face. "Your condo is your home. This is . . ." She glanced around again. "Some sort of penance."

Finley wasn't wasting another second with whatever this was. "Why didn't you disclose that you and Sophia Legard are friends?" The Judge obviously had not heard about the murder. Finley would hold on to that news for a minute.

The Judge looked taken aback. "I have no idea what you mean."

"The photo on the stairs," Finley clarified. "One of your precious preservation committees. You and Sophia are standing arm in arm and all smiles for the camera."

The Judge considered her accusation for a moment, then frowned. "I know who she is, and we have served on various committees together over the years, but I wouldn't call her a friend. More like an acquaintance."

Whatever. It wasn't like Finley could ask Sophia. "She's dead," she said bluntly. "Murdered. I just left the scene."

If she'd expected her mother to show some sort of emotion, Finley had been kidding herself.

"When we're finished here," the Judge announced, "I'll call Chief Lawrence in regard to your somber news."

"What do you want?" As far as Finley was concerned, they were finished now.

"You and Jack are in over your heads." The Judge's dark eyes, a perfect match to Finley's, probed for a reaction.

"Jack is one of the best attorneys in the state," Finley countered. "He is far from in over his head."

"He's an alcoholic who has already seen his best days. You—by association—are ruining any hope of turning your career around."

"*This* is my career. I'm an investigator for Jack's firm." Finley worked hard at keeping her emotions at bay, but it wasn't easy. Anger hummed beneath her skin. Hurt, disappointment, and other emotions she refused to label tugged at her.

"You are just like your father. Fall once, and you're down for the count. Grappling and taking whatever comes your way."

Ah, the old "Dad could have done so much better for himself" lecture. How many times had Finley heard that one?

"I think Dad did exactly what he wanted to, and so am I. If you don't agree with my choices, then that's an issue you'll have to work out for yourself."

The Judge stared at her for another five count. She was a beautiful woman. Far more so than Finley would ever hope to be. High cheekbones. Wide eyes and a perfect nose. Hardly any lines on her perfect skin. Her hair was thicker and richer than Finley's. Even at sixty she remained trim and fit. But it was the ice-cold heart that beat beneath all that beauty that pushed Finley away.

"Finley," she said as if the analysis had been spoken aloud, "this case is only going to grow more complex and more stressful. Look at the events that have occurred just today. I really wish you would consider what's best for you just once."

Enough. "Since I'm certain this visit would be considered inappropriate, I'm going to have to ask you to leave, Judge."

Rather than argue, the Judge executed an about-face and walked out. Finley watched from the window until she was gone. She rushed to her bedroom and changed into jeans, sneakers, and her fav old Vandy tee.

She grabbed a bottle of water, her bag, and her keys. She had some follow-up work to do. If her estimation was correct, the timing would be perfect.

23

8:45 p.m.

Legard Residence
Lealand Lane
Nashville

Finley had had to remind herself to slow down as she'd blown out of her driveway. It never ceased to amaze her how very angry the Judge could make her. Even after all this time and the many, many occasions they had squared off, Finley still could not prevent the gush of outrage. Never mind that trickle of disappointment or hurt or some stupid emotion or the other that never failed to make a thready appearance.

"You will never learn," she muttered as she entered the code to the gate Olivia had given her and waited for it to open. She rolled through and parked in front of the Legard mansion. The lack of blood around the vic kept nagging at her, so she'd decided to come back and prod whatever info she could from whomever remained at the scene.

The crime scene investigators were still at it. She had known they would be. The van sat next to a police cruiser. A house this large would take some time. They wouldn't want to risk missing anything useful in the way of evidence. One or more uniformed officers would be around here somewhere. She was surprised one hadn't hustled out already to send her packing. But then she supposed they hadn't expected anyone to get beyond the gate.

On the way over she'd come up with several scenarios to explain why she had to return to the house.

She made it all the way into the entry hall before she was caught.

"Excuse me, ma'am—you can't be in here."

She turned toward the dining room to face the man who'd spoken.

A smile tugged at her lips. Lady Luck was on her side.

Tommy Hanes.

Finley said, "Hey, I didn't know you were working CSI now." Tommy was a former beat cop. He had been the first on the scene when Derrick was murdered. She didn't remember him there since she'd been unconscious, but he'd visited her in the hospital a few days later.

A big grin flashed across his face. "Hey yourself." His arms swung ever so slightly as if he had to resist the urge to walk over and hug her.

She'd received a lot of unexpected hugs after what had happened. Southerners were huggers.

"I'm the investigator for the firm representing the family. I just stopped by to make sure the place gets locked up after your team is done. With all that's happened, someone needed to."

"Sure thing. I'll personally see to it." He glanced around, pretended to ignore the fact that she wasn't wearing gloves or shoe covers. "We'll probably be here for a while."

"Now that I know you're here, I'm not worried at all." She looked around the vast hall. "The place is huge. Every time I'm here I'm stunned all over again at just how big it is."

"You've been here before, then?" He visibly relaxed at the news.

"Oh yes. I was here today when the victim was discovered."

"It's pretty bizarre. What happened, I mean," he clarified.

"It really is. I found it particularly strange there was so little blood. I suppose it may have been beneath the victim." She held up a hand. "Despite my curiosity, I knew better than to touch anything."

He looked around again. Listened for the sound of his colleagues moving around in other rooms. "Between you and me, I don't think there was enough blood for the stabbing to have been the cause of death." He shrugged. "The ME will be the final word on that, of course."

"I totally agree. Something doesn't fit here." She shrugged. "I'm sure the ME will run all the usual tox screens."

He scoffed. "Oh, count on it. Janzen is the best. And he's fast. The chief put a priority on this one."

"That's good to know." She had a contact in Janzen's office.

"This is an odd family," he said. "No offense, but I don't envy you figuring this one out."

"No kidding." She backed toward the door. "I should get out of your way. Thank you for taking care of the place. We should catch up sometime."

A blush swept across his face. "Sure thing."

It was good and dark when Finley walked out the door and to her car. That had been a lot easier than she'd anticipated. Now, the big questions were these: If the knife didn't kill Sophia Legard, what did? And, if that was the case, what was the point of the big knife?

Two very good questions for the twins.

Assuming they found Cecelia. And she was still alive.

Finley called Jack as she climbed in and pointed her Subaru in the direction of home. She brought him up to speed on what the CSI team had found—or, more accurately, what they hadn't found. While she had him on the phone, she told him about the Judge's unexpected visit. Jack immediately launched into a monologue about how this was just further proof that the Judge actually cared about Finley. Rather than listen, she pondered how it was that she and the Judge could have nothing in common. Couldn't see a single thing through the same lens. Most daughters had issues with their mothers during puberty and the emotional roller-coaster ride of the teenage years. But Finley and her mother's issues had magnified only after all that. While Finley was away at school, it wasn't so bad. They rarely saw each other or had time for calls. Her mother had been anointed with her robes, and Finley had been buried in exams. When Finley returned to Nashville to begin her career, things had gone downhill.

If not for her dad and the occasional case that landed on the Judge's docket, she and her mother would likely never see each other at all anymore.

Finley ended the call as she turned into her own driveway, and she was damned tired. It had been a long day. She put the car in park and shut off the engine, then reached for the door.

"I need your help."

Finley froze. Her gaze shot to the rearview mirror.

Cecelia Legard sat up in her back seat, the same blanket her sister had used for hiding pulled around her.

What the hell?

Finley tightened her hold on the door handle to prevent lunging over the seat and shaking the woman. There were many answers she wanted, but first things first. "Are you injured?"

"No . . . just scared."

"Do you know something about what happened to your mother?"

"No," she wailed. "It wasn't me. I've been hiding all day. I didn't know what to do after I found her. I panicked and went into my place."

"Your place?" Finley had searched the house and the grounds.

"In the attic there's a maintenance room. It's climate controlled like the rest of the house. I discovered it when I was a kid. I used to hide there to smoke."

"Did Olivia ever go there with you?" Finley would be pretty pissed if she learned Olivia had known about the hiding place and ignored it during their search.

"No. Just me. That's how I knew I'd be safe there. No one knew about it."

"I searched for you," Finley said. "Why didn't you come out then? I called your name over and over."

"You can't hear anything in there. It's like soundproof or something."

Made a sort of sense. If the home's heating and cooling systems were part of the maintenance area, then there would certainly be soundproofing.

"When I dared to sneak out and have a look, the police were everywhere. The last time I came out to look around, I saw your car. I figured it was my one chance to escape. I . . . I wrapped my arms around my head and made a mad dash to your car and hid under the blanket."

"You should have come out and spoken to the police. They're looking for you," Finley warned. "They're running your photo on the news and social media asking that anyone who sees you call it in."

Cecelia leaned forward, her lips trembling. "I'm telling you," she cried softly, "I didn't do this. I'm running for my life."

"Let's go inside," Finley said. "We can talk, and you'll be safe."

"Thank you."

Finley got out of the car and walked to the door. The idea that she should call the police flitted through her mind, but her need to hear the rest of what Cecelia had to say overwhelmed any concern for the rules or her own safety.

Cecelia was slower getting out. She was cloaked in the blanket like a swaddled baby; only her head was covered too. She made her way to the porch, bumping into anything in her path. When she was inside, Finley closed and locked the door.

"Have you eaten? You need water?"

Cecelia burrowed into the sofa, still swaddled in her blanket. "I'm not hungry."

"You need water whether you eat or not."

Finley grabbed two bottles of water from the fridge and joined her on the sofa. She placed the water on the table and turned to Cecelia. "Tell me what happened."

"I got up this morning, and Mother wasn't in the kitchen. I made coffee and sat at the island and waited for her. But she never came down. I called up to her, but she didn't answer. So I went to her room . . ."

Her hands closed over her face, and she sobbed for a moment. Finley draped an arm around her shoulders in a gesture of comfort. "I know this is difficult, but I need your help right now."

Cecelia swiped at her eyes and nose and nodded her understanding.

"When was the last time you saw your mother alive?"

"At dinner last night. She was all upset. She had a call from someone that morning. She had to leave. She said it was urgent. But she acted strange after she came back. Even at dinner she just sat there at the table. Didn't eat or drink or talk."

The Preacher had claimed he'd called her. Evidently that part of his statement had been true. "Do you know who called her?"

Cecelia's head swung side to side, more tears slipping down her cheeks. "She wouldn't say, but I know she was going to that prison."

"How do you know this, Cecelia?"

"Because she took money from the wall safe. She said she was going to pay someone to end all this so we wouldn't have to worry anymore. Did she go visit *him*?"

"Who?" Finley asked, pretending not to know who she meant.

"Him," she pressed. "Holmes?" Hope glinted in her eyes.

"Your old friend?" Finley pointed out.

"I didn't know him." Her gaze lowered to the sofa.

Definitely a lie. Finley opted not to go into what Bethany Briggs had told her at this point. "What time did you find your mother . . . still in bed?"

"I dreamed about bad things last night." Cecelia reached for a bottle of water. The blanket fell away from her upper body. No sign of blood or injuries. "It woke me up over and over. And I kept hearing voices." She opened the water and chugged several swallows.

"Are you sure the voices weren't part of your dreams?"

She shrugged. "I don't know. Maybe."

"But you eventually went to sleep and woke up this morning?"

She nodded. "I went downstairs, and later I went back up looking for her. I found her in the bed." She stared at the water bottle in her hands, picked at the label.

"Can you tell me what you saw?"

"She was just lying there." Her hand went to her chest. "There was that big knife from the kitchen in her chest."

"You recognized the knife?"

She nodded. "I knew this would happen."

"What do you mean?"

"Olivia. I knew she would kill us. You'll see—I'll be next. That's why I hid. I knew she'd be back to finish the job."

"How can you be sure it was Olivia?"

"She said she was going to do it. She said it was the only way she would ever be free."

"Do you have any evidence she came into the house and did this?"

"Her fingerprints are probably on the knife, right?"

"Not if she wore gloves."

"She knows the code to get into the house. It's the only way someone could have come in without waking me up."

"I'm afraid that won't be enough to prove Olivia came into the house and hurt your mother. You could have hurt her and be trying to blame your sister." Not to mention that the code hadn't been changed in ages.

Cecelia's eyes widened in panic. "She's all I had. She took care of me. What am I supposed to do now? I don't even know. Why would I hurt her?"

"Did you hurt your father?"

"No! I didn't do anything. I told you this! The letter wasn't mine. It's him and her. How easy would it have been for her to copy my handwriting? They did this, and now they're trying to frame me."

"Who do you mean?"

"Holmes and Olivia. It was always them. They are the ones who started all this. Now they just want me out of the way so they can have everything."

People had killed for a hell of a lot less. Not that Finley found Cecelia even remotely convincing.

"Your best friend from high school, Bethany," Finley countered—it was time to go there now—"claims it was you who had a relationship with Holmes." Bethany hadn't claimed any such thing, but she'd been lying or—at the very least—evading. Either way, Finley wasn't above stretching the truth to prompt an honest response.

"Bethany is lying." Cecelia held Finley's gaze as if she might actually be telling the truth now. "She's the one who was obsessed with him."

And just like that, a hint at the real story popped out.

"You were with Bethany all the time," Finley pressed, hoping for more. "You were best friends. You had to know him too."

Cecelia rolled her eyes. "No one—not even Bethany—could ever tell us apart. Can she prove it was me?"

Finley had to give her that one. "Tomorrow Jack and I will sit down with you and Olivia and get some answers. If she did this, we will see that she can't harm you."

"No you won't."

Finley watched her carefully. "Why do you say that? Have Jack or I promised you something we didn't deliver? Your mother asked us to represent you and Olivia, and we've done all we could and will continue to do so."

"You don't know her," Cecelia cried. She dragged in a big breath and went on. "This is what you have to do. You have to find her. Because if she finds me first, she'll kill me. I'm sure she has been looking for me all day. She's probably watching this place right now."

"Let's stay calm," Finley suggested. "The door is locked, and I'm right here with you. I can protect you."

"The way you protected your husband?"

The jab hit its mark. Finley struggled to breathe. "I should call Jack and let him know you're here and safe."

Cecelia grabbed Finley's hand when she stood. "I'm sorry. I didn't mean to say that awful thing. I'm just scared. That's all. You don't know her the way I do."

Finley patted her hand, then tugged hers free of her iron grip. "You're going to be fine. I'll call Jack, and we'll figure this out, okay?"

She nodded.

"Drink your water. After I talk to Jack, let's try to eat something. You'll feel better when you've eaten and had some rest." This was likely a lie, but if it worked, Finley didn't care.

Cecelia grabbed her bottle and twisted off the top.

"I'll be in the kitchen talking to Jack."

Finley had to admit she was a little reluctant to turn her back when she walked away. Cecelia was on some kind of ledge, and she was inching closer and closer to the edge. Olivia's warning that her sister was dangerous echoed in Finley's brain. But then, Cecelia insisted that it was Olivia who was dangerous.

Thankfully Jack picked up on the first ring. "I found Cecelia," she told him instead of bothering with a hello.

"For the love of God, please tell me she's alive."

"She is." Finley glanced beyond the open doorway. Cecelia sat on the sofa clutching her water bottle, her gaze fixed on something only she could see. "She says Olivia killed Sophia."

"What do you think?"

"I think it's a toss-up. Either one or both could be working with one of Holmes's followers. After what the Preacher said about her visit, who the hell knows?"

"Yeah, that's what worries me. I should call Olivia at the hotel and make sure she's where she's supposed to be."

"That's probably a good idea. This is getting a little hairy, Jack. We're missing something here."

"The something we're missing could be whatever went down at Riverbend."

"Cecelia said her mother took money with her and claimed she was going to end this thing."

Jack blew out a loud breath. "I sure as hell wish she would've spoken to me first."

"Yeah, well, she didn't."

"I think it's time we got these two sisters together and had a come-to-Jesus talk. This whole sister-against-sister thing has gone on too long."

It was difficult to believe that their first meeting with Sophia and the twins had been only three days ago. It felt like weeks. But Jack was correct—it was past time the twins came clean.

"You're right. We can have a meeting first thing in the morning. Give the two of them time to calm down and reflect on the idea that all they have left is each other."

"I'll set it up with Olivia. We can meet at the office or her hotel."

"See you then."

Finley braced herself and walked back into the living room.

The blanket lay on the floor by the door, but Cecelia was gone.

Finley checked her bedroom and bath. No Cecelia. She grabbed her keys and rushed outside. She couldn't have gotten far.

24

Cecelia

10:30 P.M.

I am going to die.

No one can save me now. My sister will kill me.

She sent me a text saying she knew where I was and would be there soon. I panicked and ran.

But she was already there. Waiting.

She had a gun.

I'm going to die.

"What did you tell Finley?"

I stare up at Olivia. Other than the blonde hair, looking at her is like looking in the mirror. She is as much me as I am. A spontaneous split during development. Two people created from one. We share everything.

Except she is evil.

They've always thought it was me. But it's not. It's her.

Too late now. She's already won.

Mother is dead.

"I told her the truth," Cecelia said. "That you killed Mother."

Olivia laughed. "Are you kidding me? You know you're the one who killed her."

I am huddled on the floor. She is pacing back and forth in front of me. I know what's happening. I've seen it before. She is losing touch with reality.

I shake my head. "I would never hurt her. She was all I had." I blink back the burn of tears. She hates it when I cry.

"You just don't remember," Olivia challenged. "You killed her, and I came looking for you and you were gone."

"I was hiding from you."

"Liar."

I do lie. Sometimes. Maybe more than sometimes. But she lies all the time.

She *is* a lie.

My stomach sinks a bit. I don't want to think about that . . .

"You know what I have to do now, don't you?" She crouched down in front of me and stared into my eyes with her matching ones.

"I know what you want to do," I say. There's a difference. She doesn't have to do it, but she will because she wants to.

Then it will be as it was in the beginning, and there will only be one.

"You know it's the right thing to do. We can't go on like this."

Maybe she's right. The past five years have been so miserable. Our father is gone. Now Mother is as well.

What's the point?

"Why does it have to be me?" I don't want to die. Really, I don't.

"You'd rather it be me?" Olivia demanded.

I thought for a time, but there was only one answer.

"Yes."

It was supposed to be that way.

25

Monday, July 11

10:00 a.m.

Davidson County District Attorney's Office
Second Avenue North
Nashville

Parking in downtown Nashville was the absolute worst.

Finley was grateful Jack had picked her up for this command performance. District Attorney Briggs and Chief of Police Lawrence wanted a meeting with all involved in the Holmes case. Generally this was something Jack would handle alone, but Finley's presence had been requested. She'd had to cancel her meeting with Detective Houser. When he didn't complain, she figured he'd already heard about the chief's request.

She resisted a yawn as she climbed out of the Land Rover. Her search for Cecelia had gone on until two a.m. Jack had rushed to Olivia's hotel, but he'd gotten no answer. A hundred bucks to a maintenance guy on duty had gotten Jack a look inside her room. Olivia was MIA as well. At two, Jack had insisted they both needed some sleep. They could continue the search the next day.

Morning had arrived and the call from Briggs had come, prompting the rush to his office. Maybe he'd heard she and Jack had lost complete control of the situation.

One client was dead and the other two were MIA.

Surely the situation couldn't get any worse.

Jack opened the door to the lobby of her former workplace. How many times had she walked through those doors believing she was on top of her world? Life had been good.

Until it wasn't.

Forcing the thoughts aside, she headed with Jack to the bank of elevators. If she weren't dead on her feet, she might work up enough enthusiasm to attempt some level of conversation with her boss. They stepped into the elevator car together. Jack punched the necessary button for the floor they needed and leaned against the back wall. Finley did the same.

When the elevator bumped to a stop, Jack turned to her. "Don't sweat this, kid. We're not taking any shit from these guys."

Finley smiled as she followed him into the corridor. She really did love the guy. They were two of a kind for sure.

The others were already assembled around the table when she and Jack were ushered into the conference room. The meeting was already in full swing.

"Obviously, Finnegan," Siniard accused as Jack pulled out a chair for Finley and then one for himself, "your clients are involved in this tragic turn of events in ways we can't even begin to fathom."

Jack smiled. "One of my clients is dead and another is missing. Considering *your* client has a cult following capable of God only knows what, I'd say there's a lot going on *we* can't even fathom."

Finley for one was grateful Jack didn't mention the other missing client. It was bad enough that they knew it. No need to tell the world just yet. She reached for the carafe in the middle of the table and poured herself a coffee while relishing the start of a battle between the best and a runner-up.

"What we have here," Briggs spoke up, "is a hell of a mess. This ridiculous proceeding is a travesty, and nothing good will come of it. Your client, Mr. Siniard, should never have been granted a new trial."

Siniard laughed. "I refuse to justify that statement with a response. Everyone at this table knows the law."

Finley glanced around the conference table. She'd sat at this table many times during discussions exactly like this one. Deals were hashed out. Pleas were bargained. But there would be no deals today.

This was not going away quietly.

"I'm still reeling from the idea that one of your clients," Chief Lawrence said to Jack, "called you to the scene of a murder without calling the police first. And that you and your investigator"—he pointed a finger at Finley—"wasted valuable time before making the call yourselves. You contaminated a crime scene. Potentially rendered whatever evidence is found worthless."

"There was the matter of calming down our client, Chief," Jack said. "Our first obligation was to her."

"Bullshit," Lawrence raved.

"I'm sorry, gentlemen," Jack offered. "If we're not here to discuss Mr. Holmes admitting this entire fiasco is a fantasy, then we're done."

Go, Jack!

"We're here," Briggs said, "because lines are being crossed." He looked at Finley as he said this. "I want to make it clear that I will be bringing these issues to Judge O'Sullivan for review."

"You do what you think you have to, Briggs," Jack assured him. "If the Judge can find fault with any of our known steps, I'll be the first to suggest sanctions."

The key word, Finley mused, being *known*.

"I'm watching you," Siniard said, his gaze burning through Finley.

Yeah. Yeah. He should tell her something she didn't already know.

Jack turned to Finley. "Let's go."

They stood together and walked out of the conference room to the sound of dead silence.

They were out of the building and on the sidewalk before uttering a word to each other. Too many ears.

"Can you believe that shit?" Jack snapped as he stalked toward his Land Rover.

"I can." Finley lengthened her stride to keep up with him. "Their case is flimsy, and they know it." The single piece of evidence Siniard had was that handwritten note supposedly from Cecelia.

They climbed into Jack's vehicle.

"The problem is," he said as he started the engine and prepared to merge into traffic, "they opened a can of worms with this case, and now they can't close it back up. All kinds of shit is spilling out."

"Like Bethany Briggs and her relationship with Cecelia."

"Bingo. The last thing Briggs wants is to have to admit that he pushed the Holmes case through to protect his little girl's reputation." Jack made the turn that would take them back to Finley's house for her car.

"I'm guessing Lawrence threw his support behind Briggs and now he's worried it'll come back to bite him in the ass." Finley hated when the powers that be played God.

"If we don't find our clients," Jack warned, "this will not end well."

"I'll keep trying to track them down." She'd already called a friend who had a friend who could illegally track cell phones. Hopefully he could help. Her cell vibrated. She checked the screen. She'd forgotten to take it off silent after they'd left the conference room. The kitchen manager from Riverbend. Maybe news from the prison would turn this crappy day around. "It's Mickey."

Jack pulled to the curb in front of her house while she answered the call.

"What's up? I have you on speaker—Jack is here with me."

"I may have an opportunity for you."

"We could use one," Jack said.

"Our man Holmes is having a visit with the doctor today, and there's a nurse who called in sick, so a sub is supposed to be coming. I've made the necessary arrangements for you, Finley, to be that sub for the appointment with Holmes at one. Can you handle that?"

"I can. Where should I hook up with you?"

"The usual place. I'll have a uniform and badge for you."

"Thanks, Mickey," Finley said. "See you in a couple of hours."

"This might not be the best idea," Jack warned as she put her phone away. "Siniard is watching you."

"Trust me." Finley gave him a wink. "He'll never know I was there."

For a moment Jack hesitated. It wasn't like him to ignore an opportunity. "I don't want to be the reason you fall again, kid."

Ah, the Judge had gotten word to him that Finley working with Jack was a bad thing. Anger and frustration and other emotions too raw to name whirled inside her. She took a moment. Steadied her composure.

"This is all I have, Jack." She looked directly at him then. "I want to do this. If I were anyone else, we wouldn't be having this conversation." When he would have argued, she held up a hand. "Just let me do what needs to be done."

He nodded. "All right. Just don't get caught."

She laughed. "That is definitely not part of the plan."

"All right. I have to get back to the office," Jack said. "I'll give you a call if I hear anything from either of the twins."

"You know . . ." Finley reflected a moment before going on. "I'm not so sure we're anywhere near figuring those two out."

"Sophia once said they were like daylight and dark. Meant to be, but never at the same time."

Finley thought about that for a moment. "She was right." Finley climbed out. "See you later."

He gave her a nod and drove away.

She watched Jack go, then checked her cell. She had time to go by the Legard home. Maybe she'd drive by Bethany's home too. Cecelia may have gone to an old friend.

Finley considered another item on her mental checklist. She should try reaching someone at the university in California too. She leaned against her car, pulled out her spiral, and turned to her notes on Olivia as she put through the call. Six minutes later she finally reached the proper office. She ID'd herself as Olivia and asked about the glitch in her file. The clerk assured her that she would check into the situation and get back to her. Finley wasn't holding her breath. The request was a little low on the priority scale for the clerk to rush.

At this point she fully expected any and all things that came out of the twins' mouths to be lies.

Finley tucked her spiral along with her cell into her bag. For what came next she needed different transportation. She pushed away from her car and started toward the garage. Across the street, Helen Roberts stood in the yard watering her plants the way she did every day, sometimes twice. Finley waved. Roberts threw up a hand in a sort of nonwave.

As strange as she thought the woman was, she imagined that Roberts thought she was a little on the strange side too. Maybe a lot.

Riverbend Maximum Security Prison
Cockrill Bend Boulevard
Nashville, 12:30 p.m.

Finley didn't get another deep breath until she parked behind the prison commissary. She shut off the truck's engine and thanked her lucky stars she'd made it with no issues. Derrick's truck hadn't been taken out of the garage in a year. It was a straight-up miracle the tires weren't flat and the battery wasn't dead.

She'd had no tail when she left her neighborhood and didn't pick one up on the route to the prison. If Siniard sent his minion to check up on her, he would find her car parked in her driveway.

Jack didn't need to worry—she had this.

Mickey was waiting for her at the docks. He gave her a nod and passed her a badge. The name on it was Jenny Schultz.

"You ever done any nursing?" he asked as he guided her inside and to a place where she could change clothes.

"No, but I've spent enough time in hospitals and rehabs to have an idea what they do." This was sadly very true.

He grinned. "You'll do fine. Besides, Doc West is a big flirt. Just smile, and he'll overlook any mistake you make. If he's not in there when you arrive, then he's probably off for a smoke."

Finley wasn't worried. Unless there was an emergency surgery, she could handle most anything thrown her way.

The staff restroom was clean and utilitarian, and there was a locker where Finley found a pair of scrubs. She changed and stowed her bag. She tidied her ponytail, added a little lip gloss for the doctor's benefit, and she was ready.

Mickey left her at the infirmary door. She took a breath and went inside. As an investigator, there were times when she had to adopt a different persona. This should be particularly interesting. Inside, the large space was empty. As Mickey had said, the doctor was likely visiting a designated area for a few puffs.

While she was alone, she walked around the room and familiarized herself with where the various items were stored. By the time the doctor showed up, it was time for the inmate's appointment, and she had a reasonably good handle on the layout of the room.

"Good afternoon, Ms. Schulz." West looked her up and down as if he could see beyond the boxy scrubs.

"Doctor." She smiled. "I'm thrilled to be working with you."

A big grin claimed his face. Before he could say more, the door opened and two guards escorted Holmes into the room. Finley busied herself inventorying the items arranged neatly on the counter while Holmes was settled into a chair, his shackles attached to the floor. Once he was secure, the guards stepped back outside the door to wait.

The prisoner gave Finley a once-over before cutting his eyes away. He didn't look that different from the five-year-old media images she had seen. Long, unruly dark hair, sort of curly but mostly just tangled looking. He had those really light blue eyes. Good cheekbones, strong jaw. He had all the right features to draw in the young and the naive.

Dr. West went about his examination, and Finley acted attentive, though her services really weren't needed. Holmes was complaining of lower-back pain and requesting pain medication. She imagined there was a significant number of calls for pain meds among inmates.

The doctor assured Holmes he would check his file and see what he could do. He stepped into his office and closed the door. Through the window in the door, Finley watched him open a file and sit down at his desk to review.

"I haven't seen you before."

This was the first time Holmes had spoken directly to her.

"I haven't seen you before either." She busied herself with reorganizing the instruments on the tray next to the exam table.

"But I know who you are," he said, his voice low, for her ears only.

"I know who you are too," she said with a nod.

"You're that lawyer whose husband was murdered last year. You work for Jack Finnegan."

The man watched the news. Give him a gold star. She looked him dead in the eye. "Are you going to rat me out, Charlie?"

He sniggered. "No way. I'm having too much fun."

"Well, that's good. Maybe you'd like to tell me about this game you're playing."

He produced a properly put-off expression. "I don't know what you're talking about." His face shifted into one of regret or sadness. "I sure hated to hear about Sophia Legard. Life has been hard on her. Bless her heart. I told y'all Cecelia was a bad one. She's the whole reason I'm in here. Anybody who would wish their own parent dead is pure evil."

Finley barely restrained the urge to roll her eyes. She felt confident he was well aware what evil looked like. He saw it in the mirror each time he looked. "Why did you target the Legard family?"

"You've got it all wrong, ma'am. Cecelia sought me out," he insisted. "She knew what she wanted, and she thought I was the one who could help her. May God have mercy on my soul for being so weak."

Okay, now she might just vomit. "I don't believe you, Charlie. This whole thing is just a lie to get attention. *You* are a liar." She met his gaze. "No one is going to believe anything you say."

He grinned. "All I've ever wanted was to take care of the people close to me. My family."

"Or maybe it was just the thrill of driving that Jag a few hundred miles that made taking a man's life worth the risk? Not really your MO based on all we learned after you were arrested. You primarily saved your violence for those who seemed to deserve it—in your opinion."

He laughed, a dry sound. "Don't waste your time trying to figure me out. Just tell Jack he can't win this one because he doesn't see what's right in front of him."

"This is your chance, Charlie, to say something that might make me believe you," Finley offered.

"My good friend Preacher tells me everyone has a time to die. I guess it was just Sophia's time. Like it was her husband's when he died. What will you do when it's your turn to die, Finley O'Sullivan?"

"I don't know, Charlie. What about you?"

Dr. West rose from his desk. There wasn't much time.

"I think I'd go to Paradise. I was always my best in Paradise."

"Paradise?"

He grinned. "See, I told you there was a lot you didn't know, and now you have a chance to see that I'm telling the truth. I didn't kill Lance Legard."

"You said Cecelia hired you to kill him," Finley countered.

"You keep at it, and you just might find out the most important truth of all."

"And what is that?"

He made a soft chuckling sound. "I lied."

Oddly enough, for that one instant . . . she believed him.

The doctor strolled back to the patient, and the rest of Finley's time in the same room with Charles Holmes was spent watching him play the part. His back was killing him. He wasn't sure how he could continue handling the pain. He needed some relief. The man certainly knew how to work the people around him. He was smart. Much smarter than he presented himself to be. A manipulator.

Finley had his number.

When he wasn't working the doctor, he was eyeing her. He understood that she recognized exactly what he was doing, and he liked it. Her presence emboldened him. His followers, all those people who hung around him before he'd ended up here, had incited him. Gave him extraordinary courage. And made him dangerous.

Charles Holmes was a very dangerous man.

Particularly when things didn't go his way. Like the man who'd allegedly attempted to rob him and the one who'd dared to go after his girlfriend. Maybe Legard was dead because Holmes never made it in the music business.

After the appointment, Finley excused herself for a break. She hurried to the usual meeting place. She left her borrowed scrubs and badge with Mickey and climbed into the vintage Ford truck. She checked her cell for messages. Nothing from Cecelia or Olivia. Nothing from Jack. She had missed a call from Matt.

Once she was on the highway headed home, she returned his call.

"Sorry, I was in a meeting," she explained. Technically it was true. She wondered what Matt would think if she told him about the things she did these days to get what she wanted.

She decided then and there that she should keep those things to herself.

"Your ears must have been burning today, Fin. Seems like Jack's source was right. Briggs is leaning on Lawrence to have his guy Houser amp up his game. I'm guessing he believes if he makes your personal life a living hell, you'll fall down on the job on the Legard case."

Outrage belted her, but she pushed it back. Didn't matter that she had known this would be the case. "I guess he doesn't know me as well as I would have thought after four years of working together."

"Apparently not. Anyway, don't be surprised if Houser starts giving you a hard time. Watch your back, Fin."

"Count on it."

"What the hell happened with Sophia Legard?" he asked. "You think Cecelia killed her?"

"The jury is still out, but I'm not convinced. Cecelia says it was Olivia." Finley wouldn't put it past them to be working as a team.

Charles Holmes's voice echoed in her brain. *I lied.*

What else was new? Every damned person involved in this case was lying.

"Well," Matt said, "you didn't hear this from me, but the ME says Sophia was dead before she was stabbed. Looks like she emptied a bottle of prescription sedatives. The empty bottle was found under the bed. Whether she had help doing so is yet to be determined."

Finley wasn't surprised. "Makes sense. There was very little blood at the scene." Could Sophia have killed herself? And left her daughters to fend for themselves in this mess? Didn't seem likely. Unless she'd reached her limit.

Finley knew better than most that everyone had a limit.

"Did she seem suicidal to you?" Matt asked.

"No. I have to say she did not. I was just thinking that she didn't strike me as the sort who would bail on her daughters in a time of crisis, even if it was exactly what they deserved."

She heard voices in the background, and Matt piped in, "Gotta go. I'll talk to you later."

"Later."

Her cell chimed again, and this time it was Jack. As soon as she accepted the call, he launched into the news that Sophia had died of an overdose.

"I just heard the same news from Matt. You think there's any chance she was ready to check out?"

"No way. She wanted to make sure Cecelia and Olivia were cleared of any wrongdoing. She wouldn't take the easy way out. Not until this was done anyway."

"That was my thinking." Finley gave him a quick overview of her meeting with Holmes.

"Does this Paradise he mentioned mean anything to you?" Jack said, sounding weary.

"Doesn't ring a bell for me. I'll touch base with Detective Montrose and see if he can offer any insights into what Holmes may have meant."

"Check in when you can."

"Will do." She tossed her phone aside.

If Cecelia and Olivia had nothing to hide, they should come forward and help work this all out.

Both were lying. Keeping secrets.

She thought of Cherry Prescott Inglewood. She had her own secrets.

Honestly, most people did. The only real trouble was if the part they kept to themselves really mattered in this grand scheme.

Seth Henderson's widow firmly believed that Cherry had an affair with her husband. But Cherry insisted it was Legard with whom she was having an affair. What about Sophia and her affair with Jack?

There was Alex Collins. He'd been close to Legard. Close enough to know things, and yet he'd never said a word about the P-trap or Henderson five years ago during the investigation into Legard's murder. He was Legard's assistant, and yet he hadn't seemed to know about the man's alleged obsession with Cherry.

They'd all lied.

Did that make any of them murderers?

Who knew? Finley damn well intended to find out.

26

3:00 p.m.

Montrose Residence
Delmas Avenue
Nashville

Retired Detective Montrose lived in a nice neighborhood in a neat little craftsman bungalow. Finley was surprised at the array of blooms bursting in the landscape. Evidently the man had a green thumb. Finley would kill a plastic plant.

She'd called, and he'd agreed to meet. He'd asked that she come to his house since his recent round of chemotherapy had given him hell.

She knocked on the door, and he called out for her to come in. It was cool inside, a much-needed respite from the muggy heat outside.

"In the living room," he said a little less loudly and a whole lot shakier.

The narrow entry hall led directly into the kitchen, passing the living room on the left and the dining room on the right. Montrose sat in a recliner, various prescription bottles and a large drinking cup with a straw on the table next to him.

He chuckled, the sound weak. "Spending my life as a cop, I always figured I'd go down in a shootout or a high-speed chase. I never expected dying to look like this."

Finley made herself at home on his sofa. "I guess there's something to be said for a measure of advance notice."

"Maybe." He glanced around the room. "I'd offer you tea or something, but you'd have to go the self-service route."

"No need. I'm good. Really."

"You said on the phone you had an opportunity to speak with Holmes. I won't ask how that came about. I do hope it was worth the effort. He likes to play games."

"He knew who I was, which I'd expected." A frown needled its way across her forehead. "I'm sure you heard about Sophia Legard's death."

"I did." His chest rattled with a deep, shaky breath. "Makes you wonder if we'll ever really know what happened in that family." He shook his head. "I wonder if in the end she still thought all she'd done to protect her daughters was worth it."

As Cherry Inglewood had pointed out, Finley didn't have children, so she couldn't answer the question. She could, however, say with complete certainty that she would marry Derrick again even if it meant living through the night he was murdered all over again. Was loving him worth the pain?

Yes.

Even if he lied to you?

Finley dismissed the thought. "Do you believe one or both of the Legard twins might be capable of murder?"

"No question," he insisted. "Is either one capable of planning and executing a murder? Maybe not. An impulse kill is a whole different animal. I believe anyone could be capable of murder if the circumstances were just right. But to deliberately set out to take a life—to plan it just so—is something else altogether."

Finley basically agreed with his assessment. "Holmes said a couple of things to me that I'm trying to fit into this puzzle."

"Let's hear them. Maybe I can help. I suppose I know as much as anyone about the evil bastard."

She hoped the mysterious remarks might just ring a bell for the detective. "Holmes said that he'd only ever wanted to take care of the people he cared about. Those close to him. His family. I'm assuming he was referring to his Manson-like followers. There's no mention of family in his case file or on the net that I could find."

"As far as we know, he had no siblings. He was born in a small community—more a curve in the road—called Francisco, Alabama, near Huntland on the Tennessee-Alabama line. His parents died when he was very young. Murdered. He moved from foster home to foster home until he was seventeen, and then he took off. He's spent most of his life as a drifter. A thief. And, as we learned after his arrest, a murderer. The strangest thing about him, to me, was the fact that he was never caught in any of the bigger crimes he later confessed to after his DNA came up a match in those scenes. There were never any complaints from foster parents. At least none we found. I found it quite strange there was nothing in his past that even hinted at violence."

"You discovered nothing that suggested he may have seen his parents' killer or participated somehow in their murders?"

Montrose shook his head. "Since he was only seven, I guess no one really considered the possibility. Looking back, maybe they should have."

"The reason I'm asking is that Sophia had been stabbed, although there's reason to believe the stabbing was not the cause of death. If he ordered someone to do it, he may have had the knife left behind to show us it was him." Lance Legard had been stabbed multiple times with a switchblade-style knife.

Montrose contemplated the idea, then nodded. "It's possible. She was killed at home, you say?"

Finley added, "With the security system active."

"Who else knows the code besides Olivia and Cecelia?"

"We could be looking at a large number of people. Olivia said the code hadn't been changed in years. It was still the same as it was before her father's murder."

"Definitely a complication, but I might be able to help you there. What about the cameras?"

"All the cameras were inactive."

"Then you need a list of everyone who had the code back then."

"If you have that list," she said, hopeful, "I might just have to hug you."

"I do."

He directed Finley on how to find the list in his office. He was far too weak to be puttering around the house. The home health nurse had stepped out for a break during Finley's visit. She would return shortly, he assured Finley.

The list was in the file on the desk just where Montrose said it would be. She had never been so grateful for an organized man. She wandered back to the living room, already skimming the list.

"This is fantastic," she said, shooting him a grateful smile.

"I can't guarantee you it's complete. Any of those people could have told anyone else."

Unfortunately true.

"Was there anything else . . ." He paused for a breath. "That you wanted to ask about?"

Finley realized he was losing his battle with exhaustion. "Yes, thank you for reminding me. Holmes said when he died he wanted to go to Paradise. That he'd always done his best there. I assumed it was a line he learned from his pal the Preacher."

"Paradise?" The detective's eyes perked up. "There was a place—maybe it's still in business—in one of those back alleys around Broadway. It was called Paradise. It was one of those places you had to know about. Not listed on the net or anywhere else. As I recall, it was a favorite hangout of his."

Finley's anticipation spiked. "I will definitely check it out."

"Be careful," Montrose warned. "It's not the sort of place nice girls hang out."

She smiled. "Thanks. I really appreciate everything."

She considered telling him that all the nice had been beaten out of her the night her husband was murdered, but she changed her mind.

The nurse appeared just as Finley was leaving. She started the engine to get the air-conditioning going, then sat in her car long enough to send Jack a text telling him where she was headed. Even as an ADA she'd never gone out into the field without letting someone know where she would be.

A rap on her window made her jump. She stared at the man standing outside her driver's side door. Older, fifty or more. Shaggy gray hair. Needed a shave. Wore a plaid shirt. All these things she noted as he pointed to a piece of folded paper he held, then started to unfold it. Once the page was open, a single handwritten word filled the larger portion of the white space.

HOT.

The man pointed at her and then walked away, the paper fluttering to the ground.

She was close to the truth, it seemed.

When the Holmes follower had disappeared from view, she shifted into drive, but her phone chimed with an incoming text, stalling her. She read the message. Jack confirmed that he'd heard of the place and echoed Montrose's warning urging her to be careful.

Finley drove away. She might not be as nice as she used to be, but careful was her middle name.

Paradise
South Broadway
Nashville, 5:00 p.m.

According to the posted hours on the door, the club didn't open until six, but there were people inside prepping for the night. Finley had checked in with Sandy, and the owner of the property was Maurice Cosgrove. He had been the owner/operator of the place for twenty years.

No reason he shouldn't remember Charles Holmes since, according to Montrose, he had been a regular here. No live bands, but there was always a DJ in the house. Lots of wild lights and even elevated cages those who wished to show off their dancing skills could utilize. Alcohol was served. A good many drug arrests had gone down outside the building over the years. But never inside. Word was Cosgrove was obsessive about keeping the place clean. This venue catered to the rich and famous. Even the infamous, apparently.

Finley walked up to the first person she spotted inside. "Is Mr. Cosgrove here?"

"Checking in a beer delivery in the back."

"Thanks." Finley didn't wait for an invitation. She walked beyond the bar and through the staff-only doors. The driver of the beer truck had just rolled in the last of the order. Cosgrove signed the invoice, and the driver was on his way.

Cosgrove turned and noticed he had company. "Can I help you with something?"

She extended her hand. "Finley O'Sullivan. I'd like to speak to you about the Charles Holmes case, especially as to what your relationship was with him and any details you can provide related to the time he spent frequenting your establishment. I understand he was a regular."

Cosgrove nodded. "Now there's a blast from the past. Just so we're clear, he and I didn't have a relationship other than him regularly patronizing the place. Twice a week usually. Sometimes three."

Finley nodded. "Did you ever see any trouble out of him? Any violence?"

"He gave all indications that he was a lover, not a fighter. Believe it or not, considering what we know now, there was never any trouble here with him."

"Was he into dancing?" This was more like a dance club than just a hangout place.

"Not really. Not that I recall anyway. He usually hung out until he hooked up with someone, and then he was out of here."

"Was he working the crowd for more than a pickup?"

Cosgrove shrugged. "I can't say for sure, but judging by the one-offs he left with, I suppose anything is possible. He was a popular guy. Had his own little group of fans who hung around him."

She showed him photos of Cecelia and Olivia. "Did you ever see either of these women here with him?"

"The twins." He laughed. "They were here on a fairly regular basis." He shrugged. "One of them was, anyway. She hung on his every word. I never got it. The guy was not what you'd call handsome and had no real personality. He was nothing more than another wannabe country music star. But they flocked to him like he was the last loaf of bread on the shelf with snow in the forecast."

When Finley would have asked her next question, he held up a hand. "Before you ask, we do not and never have served alcohol to minors. We do, however, allow entrance to seventeen- to twenty-one-year-olds."

Finley hadn't planned to ask about his door policy, but she nodded her understanding to appease any worries he might have had. "Was there ever anyone in particular you noticed him with? Maybe one woman who kept up with him more than anyone else."

"You know, I told the detectives on the case all this last time around. And they never investigated it as far as I know. I guess they figured they had their killer. No need to waste time. At any rate, there was this one girl who spent a lot of time with him. I don't know if she's relevant."

"Can you tell me anything more about her? Describe her?"

"I can't remember her name. She had dark hair and eyes. Kind of petite. Always well dressed. You might look on the bulletin boards up front. People used to leave photographs of their visits here. We had photo booths back then. The crowd loved them. The woman you're looking for may be in one of the posted photos. I can't be sure, but it's worth a look. If you have more questions, just ask."

"I'll do that. Thanks." She retrieved a card and passed it to him. "Please call me if you think of anything else that might be relevant to our case."

"Sure thing." He accepted her card, started reading the info there as she walked away.

At the front of the building Finley found the four large bulletin boards on each side of the corridor that stretched from the double entrance doors to where the club opened up, zooming three stories high and extending the width and remaining depth of the building. The boards were crowded with the narrow strips spit out by a photo booth. It took a little time, but Finley found one of Holmes all hugged up with a young woman she recognized immediately.

Cherry Prescott Inglewood.

27

6:28 p.m.

Inglewood Residence
Morning Glory Court
Brentwood

At the gate Finley pressed the call button.

A full ten seconds elapsed before the lady of the house said, "Yes."

"Finley O'Sullivan. I apologize for showing up unannounced, but it's urgent that I speak with you now."

Another extended pause before the gates began their slow swing inward. Finley drove through and parked. By the time she was out of the car and up the steps, Cherry was waiting on the porch just outside the door. A yellow swimsuit adorned with a wrap in pastel colors showed off her fit body and her nice tan.

"We should talk out here. My husband is in the pool with our son, and I'd like to get back to them."

"Tell me about this." She held up her cell and showed the shot she'd made of Cherry all smiles while hugged up with Charles Holmes, the bland photo wall in the background.

Cherry looked away. "I was young and foolish. Everyone hung out at the Paradise." She shrugged. "People would grab you and drag you into one of those old booths for a memento. It was free, and everybody did it."

Really? Did she think she was getting off that easily? "This is Charles Holmes. You claimed you'd never had contact with him. Never even met him . . . and yet here you are." Finley put her phone away. "I'm guessing you forgot about that incriminating photo."

"I didn't want to get dragged into this." Cherry bit her lips together and considered what she wanted to say next. "My husband doesn't know I spent some time in places like that one. I'm just trying to protect my son and my marriage."

"I can understand that. Really I can. But you have to understand, one of my clients is dead, another, maybe two, are missing. No matter that Holmes is in prison, I one hundred percent believe he has something to do with this. If you know anything about him—anything at all—you need to help me find the truth."

"I can't help you." Cherry reached for the door.

"If you refuse to help me," Finley warned, "I'll have no choice but to turn this information and the photo over to the detectives investigating his claims."

Fury snapped in the other woman's eyes. "Are you threatening me?"

"No," Finley said. "I'm only informing you of the choices we are both faced with. You can help me, or you can help the police."

"He's crazy," she said with a covert glance around. "Completely and totally nuts. He's another of the reasons I had to go into hiding. I changed my hair." She shuddered. "It was terrifying."

Something on her right cheek, near her hairline, captured Finley's attention. A slightly darker area shaped in a triangle or maybe a diamond. Birthmark? Finley hadn't noticed it the last time they spoke or in any of Cherry's many, many images on the net. Maybe she'd forgone makeup since they were in the pool.

Finley refocused on the conversation. "So the two of you had some sort of relationship?" Sure as hell sounded that way to Finley.

"I guess you could say we were friends. I had a lot of girlfriends who loved clubbing. Charlie—" She closed her eyes and took a breath. "He liked meeting new women. I introduced him to a lot of my friends. Everyone, myself included, was in awe of him back then. He was charming and confident. Talented. He could make you believe anything."

"Did you ever see Cecelia or Olivia Legard with him? Maybe you introduced him to the twins. You worked for their father."

"I didn't introduce him to either of them. Cecelia and her friends came to Paradise all the time, using fake IDs. In fact, I told her father they were playing with fire. Cecelia hated me after that."

"You're certain it was Cecelia."

"As certain as I can be. She said she was Cecelia. Her friends called her Cecelia."

"Was Bethany Briggs one of the friends who hung out at Paradise with her?"

"Yes. I'd seen her photo in the paper. She was like Miss Nashville once. I couldn't understand how they were friends. They were so jealous of each other."

"Did Holmes ever talk to you about Cecelia or Bethany? Make any comments at all about either of them or their families?"

"He said he was intrigued by Cecelia. She was like him somehow, and that turned him on."

The more she said, the angrier Finley became. Cherry could have told Finley this days ago. "Maybe Sophia Legard would still be alive if you'd told me this the first time we talked."

"You don't understand," she argued. "I would do anything to protect my son."

"Did you consider Cecelia one of his followers?" Finley was beyond pissed off, but she couldn't risk pushing the woman too hard or she'd shut down. Or maybe worse—her husband would appear and shut Finley down. Right now Finley had some leverage, as the husband didn't know. She did not want to lose her upper hand.

"She was infatuated with him. Bethany too. They followed around after him like he was a god. A lot of women did. He had that kind of draw." She hugged her arms around herself. "He could talk people into things."

"Then why would he kill Lance Legard and confess?" The more Finley learned about his so-called charisma and his following, the less sense what he'd done made. "How did a kid like Cecelia get him to do her bidding?"

"I don't know. The only thing I can tell you for a certainty is that he is very, very dangerous. If he finds some way out of that prison, there won't be anyplace anyone who talked to the police will be able to hide."

"Is there anyone in particular who knew him especially well? Someone who might be able to help me put all the pieces together?"

"Cecelia. She was closer to him than anyone else."

"She claims she didn't know him and had no contact with him."

"She's lying. Even Lance said he couldn't believe anything his daughters told him."

Finley looked her straight in the eye and asked the question that really counted. "Did you or your husband hire or otherwise encourage Holmes to kill Lance Legard?"

"No! Elton was prepared to drag Lance into court and damage his reputation. But murder?" She shook her head adamantly. "He would never even consider such a thing."

"Would you?"

"No. Of course not."

"What about Sophia? Did you have anything to do with her murder?"

Shock claimed Cherry's face. "No! I haven't been in that house since . . . *before*."

"But you have the security code to the property."

"What? I had it when I worked for Lance, but they've surely changed it by now."

Finley didn't correct her. She'd only wanted her reaction since her name had been on Montrose's list.

"If you think of anything else," Finley urged, "I need to hear from you. I don't want to have to show up at your door unannounced again, asking questions you should have already answered."

"I will call. You have my word."

Finley wasn't convinced her word was worth much, but it appeared to be all she was prepared to offer at the moment.

As she drove away from the McMansion, she put through a call to Jack. "Can we meet at Olivia's hotel? I need to bring you up to speed on my meeting with Montrose and my discoveries about Paradise. And it's time we pushed Olivia a little harder."

His answer was immediate and resolute. "On my way."

———

Margaritaville Hotel
John Lewis Way South
Nashville, 8:00 p.m.

Finley and Jack arrived at the hotel about the same time. She climbed into the passenger seat of his vehicle and gave him an update on what she'd learned about the club called Paradise and the photo of Cherry with Holmes.

"Can't be a coincidence that Holmes confessed to killing Legard," Jack suggested, "and Prescott had an affair with Legard—one in which he was reportedly obsessed with her."

"I'm with you," Finley agreed. "There's a big chunk missing, and Cherry is somehow involved in it." She told him about the Holmes follower who'd let her know she was hot now.

"The part I'm having trouble with," her boss said, "is why was Henderson's widow so convinced the woman was having an affair with her husband if it was really Legard?"

"Cherry may have lied about that as well. It's entirely possible she was involved with both."

"We may have no choice but to see what Mr. Inglewood believes happened."

"Maybe."

For now, Finley wanted some answers from Olivia Legard.

The hotel lobby was surprisingly deserted as they walked through to the bank of elevators. During the ride up, Jack said, "Wallace turned in his resignation today."

"Why?" The guy was barely out of law school when Jack gave him a job. Paid him way too much in Finley's opinion.

"Said he's moving to Alabama with his new fiancée. Apparently, her folks live in the Birmingham area and the two of them have decided to relocate."

"Do you have anyone else on your radar?"

"Why would I need anyone else? I have you."

The elevator stopped, the doors slid open, and Finley still hadn't decided exactly how to respond.

They exited the car and headed toward Olivia's room. A housekeeping cart was parked in the corridor, and Olivia's door was open.

Jack made a face. "If she's not answering her phone and she's not here, we've got a real problem, Fin."

"Tell me about it."

They walked past the room. The door was ajar, and housekeeping was inside. Seemed late in the day for housekeeping rounds, but this may have been a busier-than-usual checkout day.

Finley paused. "Go back to the lobby and wait for me. I'm going in there."

"I'll be at the bar. I need a Pepsi."

"Order one for me too."

As Finley walked back to Olivia's door, she took out her cell and focused on the screen, then walked inside.

"I'm almost finished," a female voice said.

"No problem." Finley kept her face turned downward. The room was a suite, so she left the housekeeper to her work in the sitting room and disappeared into the bedroom. She'd learned a long time ago if you did a good job of acting like you were supposed to be somewhere, people generally believed it. Most people assumed most other people were doing what they were supposed to be doing.

The bedroom was empty. No big surprise.

Bed was made. Finley checked the nightstands. Both were empty. On the right side of the bed, a phone charger lay on the bedside table. She moved to the dresser and picked through the items in the drawers. Underwear. Feminine products. Every item was arranged carefully. Undergarments folded precisely and stacked in neat rows. The closet was the same. Each dress, blouse, and pair of slacks hung on its hanger the exact same distance from the garment hanging next to it.

"Can you say too much time on her hands?" Finley mumbled.

Two pairs of flats, three sets of heels, and one pair of sneakers lined the closet floor. Most were sandals. She crouched down and checked inside the sneakers. Mud smeared on her palm. She turned the pair over. Muddy.

She hummed a curious note. "Where have you been in the mud, Olivia?"

Finley thought of Cecelia showing up at her house and then disappearing. Had she gotten mud on these sneakers at Finley's house and then put them here to frame Olivia? Finley couldn't remember what kind of shoes she had been wearing. Or maybe Olivia had taken a walk in Finley's muddy backyard to make it look as if Cecelia was trying to frame her.

She closed the closet doors and checked the bathroom. Cosmetics and the usual bath products. Toothbrush was dry. Inside the shower and tub were dry. No dirty clothes strewed about. Didn't seem as though Olivia had been back last night. At least not for long.

The door in the other room slammed, and Finley stilled. Hopefully the housekeeper had finished and left. If Olivia had returned, Finley would have some explaining to do.

To err on the safe side, she flushed the toilet and walked through the bedroom and into the sitting room. She'd dropped by to check on Olivia and realized she desperately needed to use the bathroom. Housekeeper was here, so Finley figured Olivia wouldn't mind.

She needn't have worried. She was alone.

"Where are you, Olivia?"

28

9:25 p.m.

The Murder House
Shelby Avenue
Nashville

When Finley pulled into her driveway, her headlights flashed over a figure standing on her front porch.

Olivia.

Finley wanted to storm up to the porch and rant at her, but since she'd had the opportunity to snoop in her room, she decided not to bother. She emerged from the car and rounded the hood.

"Jack and I have been worried."

Olivia stepped away from the door so Finley could jab the key into the lock.

"I'm sorry. I had to think all this through. My mother is dead. My sister is missing, possibly dead too. I wanted to disappear again. I was just plain scared."

A perfectly reasonable explanation—to a point. Finley pushed open the door and flipped on some lights. "You're supposed to trust me. You're supposed to trust Jack. We're not going to get through this if we don't have trust."

Olivia followed her inside, her expression crestfallen. "I'm really, really sorry. I do trust you and Jack. I think I just panicked."

Where had she heard this before?

"Have you talked to Cecelia?" Finley tossed her bag on the sofa and sat. She was too tired to worry about food.

Olivia shook her head. "I haven't, and this is the first time she's been out of touch for this long. Mother took care of her. Always. This is why I'm so worried that someone took her."

"No one took her," Finley announced. "She was here last night."

"So you know now the agoraphobia is a lie?"

"I stopped by the house to check on how the forensics part of the investigation was going, and while I was inside, she claimed she covered her head and hid in my car. The answer to whether the phobia is real remains up in the air."

Olivia's face turned to one of confusion. "Why didn't she call me and let me know she was okay? Why didn't you call?"

Her confusion visibly shifted to frustration.

"You haven't been answering your phone," Finley pointed out, restraining her own frustration. "At least not for me or Jack."

Olivia pulled out her phone and checked the screen. "I have no missed calls from either of you." She faced her screen outward for Finley to see.

She waved her off. Didn't matter. They were beyond a few missed calls at this point. Besides, call logs could be erased. "Cecelia believes you killed Sophia."

"What? That's insane. Where is she? We need to talk about this. She can't possibly believe I would hurt Mother."

"She disappeared on me last night. I looked for hours. Never found her. For all I know she could be hiding in a neighbor's garage. She's pretty shaken up."

"So am I!" Olivia stood and started pacing. "I can't believe this. Cecelia is the one who always lies. She has always been the trouble-maker. How can she blame me for this?"

"Whoever came into the house and killed your mother had the security code." Finley had gone over the list provided by Montrose and circled the names of folks she wanted to interview.

Olivia stared at Finley for a few beats. "Like I told you, the code hasn't been changed in years."

"Assuming we can find Cecelia again," Finley said, "the four of us need to sit down and figure this all out. One or both of you is lying. Jack and I can't help you if you're not telling us the whole story."

"I've told you all I know. The first time we met, I explained to you that my sister can't be trusted. She lies." Tears rolled down Olivia's cheeks. "She terrifies me, but she is still my sister, and now I'm all she has left."

"Tell me about her relationship with Holmes—and don't leave anything out. I've already been to Paradise, the place they hung out together. I've spoken with the man who runs the place. He remembers Cecelia." Finley shrugged. "Of course, it could have been you, pretending to be Cecelia. You told me you did that sometimes for tests at school."

Fear sparked in Olivia's eyes. Good. She should be afraid. Finley had run out of patience for their games.

"Cecelia was a little obsessed with him. She and Bethany would go to that place just to be around him. To watch him. It was really stupid."

"You never went," Finley pressed.

"I did once." She dropped her head for a moment before meeting Finley's eyes again. "Cecelia was sick with some kind of bug. I'd heard her talking to Bethany about him so much that I was curious. So that night I went. I pretended to be her. But I never spoke to him. I stayed in a dark corner and just watched. I was too afraid to talk to him. I left at the first opportunity I had."

"Why would you keep any of that from me? If Holmes has his way, Cecelia will be going to prison."

She looked up at Finley then. "The truth? She needs to be in prison where she can't hurt anyone else."

Finley felt weary of her waffling and decided to move on. "Were you aware your father was having an affair with Cherry Prescott?"

"Did Cherry tell you that?" Olivia scoffed. "Cherry has no room to talk about anyone. She was in tight with Holmes. You can ask Cecelia. Cherry was very close to him. Almost like an old married couple who liked playing around with other people."

"Cherry says she didn't really know him."

"She's lying." Olivia's hand went to her throat. "Oh my God. She worked with my father for nearly a year. She was like his personal assistant. She would have known the security code."

Finley opted not to confirm.

"She worked with Dad in his home office on several occasions. She was always coming in and out."

"How did your mother feel about that?"

"She was busy with her own interests." Olivia looked away.

"I need to know what that means, Olivia." Finley already understood, but she wanted the daughter's side of things.

"She had other men. They both cheated on each other. It was like a game they played. Always trying to one-up each other."

Sounded like the couple had enjoyed the pain of hurting each other. Not unheard of.

"I'm going to follow you back to your hotel," Finley said. She was fed up with the sisters going back and forth with their stories. She had someone else she needed to see. "I want you to stay there until you hear from me or Jack. Don't let anyone in, and if you hear from Cecelia, call me immediately. If she shows up at your hotel, demand to meet her in the lobby or restaurant where there are other people."

Olivia nodded. "I'm sorry I've caused so much confusion, but I did try to warn you the first time we met."

Finley wasn't so sure if it was Olivia who had warned her about Cecelia or the other way around on their first meeting. Didn't matter. Right now, the only thing she wanted was to get to Bethany Briggs.

———

Rainbow Room
Printer's Alley
Nashville, 10:30 p.m.

Bethany and her fiancé were seated at the bar having drinks. No doubt after already having had a lovely dinner and catching a snazzy show. The Rainbow Room was famous for both. Finley sat at the opposite end of the bar and sipped a glass of overpriced white wine while she waited for Bethany to spot her. Bethany really needed to speak with her live-in housekeeper. She had been only too happy to give Finley her employer's location. Not that Finley was going to tell.

The bride-to-be laughed and snuggled up to her future husband. Happy. Carefree. The world at her fingertips.

Then the happy lady spotted Finley. Her bright, carefree expression fell. Finley hitched her head and slid off the bar. She walked to the ladies' room without glancing back. Bethany would follow.

She wouldn't dare blow off Finley's unspoken request.

The elegant ladies' room was unoccupied, which made what Finley had to do considerably easier. Bethany walked in, fury darkening her carefully made-up cheeks.

"You're not supposed to bother me again."

Finley walked over to the door and locked it, then leaned against it. "I'm sorry, am I bothering you?"

Bethany's hands settled on her designer-clad hips. "What do you want?"

The patent fact that she didn't threaten to call her daddy spoke volumes about what she had to hide. Finley was counting on the weight of guilt and fear.

"You lied to me, Bethany. You said you and Cecelia never had anything to do with Holmes, but I have proof you did. In fact, Cecelia was crazy about him. The two of you hung out with him on numerous occasions at a place called Paradise."

Bethany's lips tightened together in a flat line. Red rose up her throat and spread across her cheeks.

"There are photos of you and Cecelia hanging all over him. How do you think the DA is going to feel when he sees those?" This part was fiction, but Bethany couldn't be certain. Like the owner said, everybody used those photo booths. It was the thing to do.

"That's a lie," she snarled. "I was—" She caught herself. Clamped her mouth shut.

"You were too careful? Made sure no photos were left on the bulletin boards?"

No answer. Oh yeah. Finley had her now.

"I'm not interested in outing your past to your fiancé or to your father," Finley assured her. "All I need is the truth about Cecelia and whatever relationship she had with Holmes. Anything you know about either of them could make all the difference."

"She didn't care about him," Bethany said, her voice hollow. "Cecelia didn't care about anyone except herself. She was jealous of her sister's relationship with their father. It drove her crazy that he thought Olivia was the good daughter and Cecelia was always making mistakes."

"What kind of mistakes?"

"Missing curfew. Getting caught trying to sneak back in the house. Stealing her mom's jewelry. Skipping school. Passing out at some party and having to be picked up. She just wouldn't keep her shit together. We were kids, we all screwed up, but she just didn't care or was too arrogant to put forth the effort to stay out of trouble."

"She was a screwup," Finley said. "I've got that. But that's not telling me what her fascination was with Holmes."

Bethany stared at the floor a moment. When she looked at Finley once more, she asked, "Is she still missing?"

"She is."

"Then you don't know where she is, and you can't protect me from her."

Now, this was new. "Are you concerned that what you know could make you a target?"

"If she's out there and still alive, you're damn straight. She will kill me if she finds out I told."

A one-eighty from her last version of her and Cecelia's relationship. Not that Finley was surprised. Every damned one of the women involved in this case was lying about something.

"If what you know is so dangerous for you, why haven't you gone to your father? He would see that you were protected."

"Because I can't tell him about her without telling him about *me*."

Well, there was a motive and a half. One Finley knew well. "She has something on you too."

"I was the one in love with Charlie."

Finley hadn't seen that one coming. "Okay."

"I was afraid to talk to him at first, so Cecelia helped me out. I became deeply involved with him for a few weeks. But then he grew tired of my neediness, so he blew me off for another of the fools hanging on to his every word. I mean, we still hung out, but the physical relationship was over. The problem was, I ended up pregnant. Cecelia went with me to the clinic and had me over at her house that night. She really helped me out."

Whoa. Briggs would have a cow if he heard about this.

"Did Holmes ever know?"

"No. I was afraid he would try and make me keep the baby or kill me for killing it." She drew in a big breath. "This was another reason I needed to hang around. To make sure he wasn't suspicious or anything."

"This is the reason you don't want to spill whatever it is you know about Cecelia?"

"Isn't that enough? I did awful things. And she knows. She could ruin my life." She glanced at the door, knowing her fiancé was out there wondering where she was. "If she doesn't kill me first."

They were at a standoff. Finley had to think fast, or Bethany was going to rush out of there without telling her anything.

"Look, there are ways to find out things if you know those things in advance," Finley explained.

At Bethany's confused expression, she went on. "Say if you stole something from someone's house and the homeowner didn't know—but your best friend was with you. If your best friend told someone, that someone could go to the homeowner and ask to see their security footage, which would show you entering the house. They could use seeing that footage to explain how they knew about the theft without ever mentioning your friend."

Bethany nodded slowly.

"What I'm trying to say is that if you tell me what Cecelia did or whatever it is you know that could change the course of my case, I can guarantee you that I will not use your name or the information unless I have no other choice. Keep in mind that I'm very good at coming up with ways to get information and to explain in a roundabout way how I got it."

Hopefully she'd proven that skill.

"Cecelia wanted to hire Holmes for a job." Her hands flew to her face, fingers rubbed at her temples. "She will kill me if she finds out I said this out loud."

Jesus Christ, could she not get on with it?

"Anyway, I guess something went wrong, because the next day her father was murdered and Charlie was arrested for killing him."

"Are you saying that Cecelia hired Holmes to kill her father?"

Shit. Jack wasn't going to like this.

"No." Bethany shook her head adamantly. "She wanted to hire him to kill the bane of her existence. Her sister."

Olivia.

29

Olivia

11:30 p.m.

I park well down the street from my childhood home. It will be best if no one sees me going in, which is why I have to do this well after dark. Last night was extremely difficult because Cecelia refused to cooperate. I finally managed to force her into the gardening shed. Restraining her was yet another struggle. I have never felt such relief in my life as when she sat helpless before me, her hands and feet fully secured.

Well, that isn't true. I felt incredibly relieved when I left nearly five years ago. Mother was going to see that Cecelia never had the opportunity to hurt anyone ever again. She would keep her in the house and tell everyone that she'd developed agoraphobia after Father's murder.

Mother had set up a perfect life for me in San Diego. I wondered at the time if it was the life she wished she'd had. She hadn't been happy in a very long time.

The plan seemed perfect. What could go wrong?

But then Charles Holmes started his crazy shit all over again. He is the reason our lives have fallen apart a second time.

The reason everything has turned upside down.

The reason I had no choice but to return.

My destination is the side gate Cecelia used back in high school for sneaking in and out at night. The key was hidden under one of the stones in the column. A little tug, and a stone comes free of its place—and there's the key.

With a single twist I unlock the gate and slip through. Heart pounding, I hurry to the shed, the bottles of water and the snack crackers in my bag bouncing against my leg. I slow my breathing and remind myself I have everything under control now. This is for the best.

I creep inside without turning on the overhead light. The flashlight app on my cell helps me thread my way to the back, behind all the tables and shelves the gardeners and landscapers used over the years.

"I brought you—"

My breath catches.

She is gone.

My heart threatens to leap out of my chest. Cecelia is gone.

She might be anywhere. Doing anything. How in the world did she escape?

A crunch beneath my right shoe draws my attention to the floor. Cecelia has torn open a bag of wood-mulch nuggets and used the pieces to spell out a message.

YOU ARE DEAD.

30

Tuesday, July 12

9:00 a.m.

The Murder House
Shelby Avenue
Nashville

Finley used her towel to swipe the fog from the mirror over the bathroom sink. She finger combed her wet hair and trapped it into a ponytail. She still hadn't found her hairbrush. She studied her reflection. Sighed. The circles under her eyes were darker than usual. Last night had been a long one.

After her meeting with Bethany, she'd called Jack, and they'd gone to talk to Olivia—who was, of course, nowhere to be found. She wasn't at her hotel as Finley had instructed. Not that she'd actually expected her to be. Calling her cell got them nowhere.

Cecelia was still MIA. Her phone now went straight to voice mail on the first ring. The battery was dead.

Ultimately, they'd decided on a stakeout. Jack had taken the hotel where Olivia was supposed to be. He knew the manager, who'd insisted he use a comfy corner reading nook with a free tab for soft drinks and coffee.

Finley, on the other hand, had spent the better part of the night strolling the perimeter of the Legard property or sitting in her car eyeing the main entrance. If Cecelia had wanted her sister dead five years ago, maybe she still did. Finding both of them as quickly as possible was crucial.

A thermos of coffee and a couple of energy drinks had kept Finley's eyes open all night. There were moments when she wasn't sure she was actually awake. Reminded her of cramming before exams in college. During law school, since Matt had been a year ahead of her, he had always grilled her before exams. Only it was more like he was cross-examining her in a murder case than quizzing her for the coming test.

She smiled. She should call him and let him know what was going on. They hadn't talked since—God, she couldn't remember when. Her mind was a blur this morning.

Five days since she and Jack first interviewed the three Legard women, and every damned thing had gone to hell.

A firm series of knocks on the front door shook her from the sorts of thoughts one drifted into when sleep deprived. She checked her reflection one last time and headed for the front door. Another firm trio of knocks sounded before she reached her destination. A peek out the window told her the two suits on her porch were cops.

She hoped like hell they didn't have another dead client. This was not looking good for Jack's firm. She opened the door. "Did I win the lottery?"

"Ms. O'Sullivan, I'm Detective Gordon Barry, and this is Detective Bob Tanner."

Though she didn't recognize the faces, she knew the names. The detectives on the Holmes/Legard case. Definitely not good.

"How can I help you, Detectives?"

"We need you to come downtown, ma'am. We have some questions."

"You can ask me anything you'd like right here." The home field advantage was always preferable.

The two shared a glance. So that wasn't happening.

Ah, it gets worse.

"Ma'am." Tanner spoke this time. "This will go a whole lot faster and a lot smoother if we just get on with it."

Translation: Come with us quietly. Now. Or there will be unpleasant moments.

"I have the right to know what this is about," she pointed out. Even a suspect being arrested had the right to know the reason.

"Cherry Inglewood went missing yesterday," Detective Barry explained.

There it was—the not-good part she'd expected.

"What about her son? Is he okay?" Finley hoped this mess hadn't spilled over to the child. Brantley was what? Four years old?

"Yes. He's with his father," Barry confirmed. "According to the home-security surveillance system, you were the last person besides her husband to see Mrs. Inglewood before she disappeared."

Finley nodded her understanding. "I'll get my shoes."

She slid her feet into a pair of sneakers and grabbed her bag. Her cell was in the back pocket of her jeans. Since she hadn't dressed for a trip downtown, she glanced at her chest to see what was plastered across her white tee. She'd grabbed the first one her fingers landed on this morning.

Allegedly, it proclaimed.

Fitting, she decided.

She locked her front door and followed the detectives to their car, where Tanner opened the rear passenger door for her.

"Thanks." As she was getting in, she noticed Helen Roberts watering her plants and watching her. She didn't bother looking away when

Finley noticed her. She never did. Finley gave her a little wave, but the woman didn't wave back. Just watched.

Finley didn't really care what her neighbors thought of her. Once a murder happened in your house, everyone around you expected the worst.

If Cherry Inglewood was lucky, her disappearance would not be the worst-case scenario.

———

Nashville Metropolitan Police Department
Murfreesboro Pike
Nashville, 9:50 a.m.

The protocols for questioning were conducted the moment the three settled around a generic metal table in the blindingly white interview room. Finley was infinitely familiar with the proceedings.

"What was the purpose of your meeting with Mrs. Inglewood?" Detective Barry asked.

"She worked for Lance Legard at the time of his murder. Mrs. Inglewood was close to the family and interacted on a regular basis with Legard's daughters, Olivia and Cecelia. Attorney Jackson Finnegan directed me to reconstruct the events surrounding the murder of Lance Legard—to the degree possible. In order to do so, it was important that I understand the relationships between the parties involved."

"Did Mrs. Inglewood mention any concerns she had related to the case, or with any party involved with the case?"

"No."

This was not the answer Barry had been hoping for, but Finley felt confident it was exactly what he'd expected considering she was an attorney—she wasn't going to say more than necessary. Certainly not something that would cast her clients in a bad light.

"Did you feel she was in any way distressed or concerned for her safety?" Tanner asked, choosing a different strategy.

"I did not." Unless her husband finding out what she and Cherry had talked about counted. "Have you questioned her husband? Statistics show that in most situations like this, the husband is involved."

"The husband," Barry said, annoyed now, "came home to find his four-year-old son alone because his wife was missing. He is not involved. He gave us free rein in the house and with the security system."

Which, of course, made him innocent of any wrongdoing. "I wish I could help, gentlemen. Really I do. But I have only met Mrs. Inglewood on two occasions. Both times at her home, where the video surveillance surely shows my departure—alone."

"What about your firm's clients," Tanner asked, "Cecelia and Olivia Legard? Cecelia has been named in the pending Holmes case. Can you vouch for the whereabouts of your clients?"

"You're aware, of course, that Sophia Legard was murdered and Cecelia is missing. To the firm's knowledge, she remains missing. As of this morning, Olivia is officially missing as well."

Tanner and Barry shared a look, then Barry said, "We've had no report of Olivia Legard as a missing person."

"I just reported it," Finley said. "We searched for her all through the night, and I was just getting ready to come in and file the report when you showed up at my door."

"So of your three clients," Tanner suggested, "one is dead and two are missing."

"Sadly, yes."

"What did you and Mrs. Inglewood talk about?" Barry asked. "Specifically."

"We talked about her relationship with Mr. Legard and her interactions with the family." She'd already said that.

"Can you be more specific?" Barry pressed.

"No. My answer is sufficient."

Another shared look between the partners.

"Can you talk to us about her answers?" Tanner asked.

"She worked for Mr. Legard. She occasionally saw his wife and his daughters either at the office or at his home."

"Did she talk about any issues with Cecelia Legard?"

"No."

"Was Sophia Legard aware of Inglewood's affair with her husband?"

"I was referring to Mrs. Inglewood's professional relationship with Mr. Legard."

Tanner rolled his eyes. "Did Inglewood know if Sophia Legard was aware of the affair?"

"Any answer I provide to that question would have to be supposition."

"Why were you and Inglewood talking on the front porch?" Barry wanted to know.

"She didn't want to disturb her husband and son. The reopening of the case has been an unpleasant experience."

"You're stating for the record," Barry said, "that no part of your conversation with Mrs. Inglewood was or could possibly be related to her disappearance?"

"No," Finley said. "I'm stating that I have no idea if our conversation was related."

"She could be a hostage of one or both of your clients," Tanner suggested.

"She could have run away with the circus," Finley offered.

The detectives weren't happy with her answers. But it wasn't her job to make them happy. After she'd signed her statement, she was free to go. Except her car was at home.

"Your ride is waiting in the visitor parking area," Barry said when she asked. He opened the interview-room door and waited for her to exit.

"Thanks."

She wound her way through the building toward the front entrance. Where the hell was Cherry? She wouldn't have gone anywhere willingly without her son. It was possible she thought dropping out of sight would be best for her son and husband, but Finley doubted that was the case. More than anything else she wanted to protect her son and marriage.

Was she with Cecelia and/or Olivia?

Not if she was lucky.

Jack's clients were looking less and less like victims of Charles Holmes's delusions and more and more like clever perpetrators of something Finley feared was bad for all involved.

Finley thought of the mud on Olivia's shoes and how it had rained the night after her mother's body was discovered. That was the night Cecelia had disappeared from Finley's house.

Images of digging around in her backyard whizzed one after the other through Finley's mind.

What had Cecelia been wearing that night? Sneakers? Maybe the same ones Finley had spotted in Olivia's closet at the hotel? Were the sneakers an attempt to frame her sister?

Who the hell knew?

Finley burst out the main entrance. Before she had time to consider what the hell else the twins were up to, Detective Eric Houser was walking toward her.

"I'm supposed to give you a ride home."

A setup. Finley wasn't surprised. Cops were the same as lawyers when it came to getting what they wanted. They weren't above a little out-of-the-box ingenuity.

"I appreciate it." She did. Mostly.

He led the way to his car. "I started the engine to cool the interior."

She was grateful, because even at eleven in the morning it was hot as hell. She settled into the passenger seat. He slid into the driver's seat and fastened his seat belt. She should do a background search on the guy. He was new to Metro. Where had he transferred in from? Married? Her gaze flitted to his hands on the steering wheel. No ring. Couldn't be older than midthirties.

He exited the parking lot and merged into traffic. "I'm hearing all sorts of stories about how people are disappearing in the Legard case."

Finley made a noncommittal sound in response.

"I'm glad I'm not working that one."

To this she said nothing. His nonchalant tone and happy-go-lucky "I'm just driving you home" attitude had already warned her where this was going.

Silence stretched for a few blocks. He was hoping she would ask him something about Derrick's case. When she didn't, he had to figure out how to kick off the conversation himself.

"Did you look into when your husband bought the house?"

She hated being right all the time. At least he hadn't leaped ahead of where she was with his allegations. "I did, and you were correct. I must have misunderstood the timeline."

"You talked to the previous owner?"

He knew she had, or he wouldn't have asked. "I did."

"He told you how Reed said he was buying the place for his wife, and the two of you hadn't married yet."

"He did."

More silence. One block. Two. Then three.

"Had you seen the house at that point?"

She hadn't met Derrick at that point, which was where he planned to take the conversation. He was as easy to read as a flashing neon sign.

"No."

"Had you ever been in the neighborhood?"

"I've lived in Nashville my whole life. It's possible."

"You hadn't even met Reed at that point, had you?"

"No."

Another turn, and the murder house came into view. Home sweet home.

"Do you believe this is some indication that Reed had targeted you for some reason we don't know as of yet?"

He was the first to test those waters . . . except for her, of course. In the past twenty-four or so hours, the idea had crept into the back of her mind. Not going there yet.

He glanced at her, expecting an answer.

What did she believe about Derrick?

She believed Derrick had loved her. Who could fake it that well?

She believed the short time they'd had together was the most amazing time of her life.

She believed her husband was murdered by someone related to Carson Dempsey in payback for her putting away his son, which had prompted his untimely death.

She believed she didn't know the whole story of Derrick's past.

That was as far as she had allowed herself to go.

"No," she said in response to his question.

Houser pulled to the curb in front of her house. He turned to her. "Come on, Ms. O'Sullivan. You have to see that what I'm suggesting is the most likely scenario."

"Derrick got a great deal on the house." She met Houser's intent gaze. "He may have been attempting to get a better deal by weaving a story about his wife being in love with the house. Since at the time I had no knowledge of the house, why would his story have had anything to do with me?" She shrugged. "Think about it, Detective. There's no connection between me and the property. Why would purchasing that particular property have anything at all to do with me?"

While he floundered for a comeback, Finley took the opportunity to make her exit. "Thanks for the ride."

She rounded the hood and walked to her house. Houser drove away. She'd just unlocked her door when her cell vibrated.

Jack.

"Hey," she said, pushing the door inward and tossing her bag on the sofa.

"I'm at the office. Detectives Barry and Tanner are here to question me about Inglewood and the twins."

"At least you weren't hauled in for your questioning." She gave him a quick rundown of the questions they'd asked and her responses before moving on to her plan for the day. "I'm heading to Francisco, Alabama, to see if I can track down anyone who knew Holmes and his bio parents. We're missing something, Jack. I'm starting back at the beginning to try and find whatever the hell it is."

"I was thinking the same thing. Just be careful. I want regular check-ins."

"Will do."

She didn't tell him about Houser. Jack had enough to worry about without her adding an unknown problem to the pile.

And there was a problem. As much as she would prefer to pretend there wasn't, she wasn't that naive. Until she had a grasp on what the problem was, she couldn't begin to understand the magnitude of it.

For the first time since Derrick was murdered, she wondered if she really wanted to.

Would it matter now?

It certainly wouldn't bring him back.

31

1:15 p.m.

State Route 65
Francisco, Alabama

Montrose had been right. Francisco was basically a curve in the road outside the small town of Huntland and just across the Tennessee state line. The area was thickly wooded, the road narrow, and the houses few and far between. No cell service—at least from her carrier.

She'd stopped in Huntland at the Town and Country Café to grab a bite of lunch, though she wasn't that hungry. Based on the few offerings in the little town and the lack of patrons at the others, this was the place more of the locals patronized.

A gentleman at a neighboring table had been only too happy to talk about the thirty-year-old murder of the Holmes couple. Their small farm was owned by the Granger family now. Their closest neighbors had been the Wrights, Chester and Gladys. Though advanced in age, the Wrights still lived in the old Victorian just down the road from the house where Charles Holmes spent his early childhood.

This was Finley's next stop. If the Wrights were able and willing to talk to her, their insights could be invaluable.

Finley was grateful for her Subaru when she turned into the drive-way leading to the Wright home. Rocky, rutted, and long. Trees crowded in on either side. The shade was nice, but it made it difficult to see what lay beyond each curve, and there were plenty of tight little curves.

When the gravel drive ended amid a green expanse of lawn in a wide clearing, Finley felt as if she'd slipped into a time warp. The farm implements lined up beneath a metal-roofed shed were old and rusty. The house stood tall and was mostly white. Lots of peeling paint. Chippy style, the fixer-uppers would say. An old truck, a relic from the middle of the last century she would guess, sat closest to the house.

She got out, swatted at a fly, and surveyed the area. No sign of dogs that might not appreciate her appearance. She adjusted her blouse. Since she was interviewing strangers, she had exchanged the tee for a nicer top. Looking the part was generally helpful.

Finley headed up the stone path that led across the green lawn. The porch steps looked solid enough, so she made her way up and stalled at the top.

The reason she hadn't seen a dog was that it was sprawled on the porch enjoying the shade. The big black-and-white animal lifted its head, looked her up and down, then promptly lowered his head once more without so much as a growl.

"Good doggie," she murmured.

The double set of doors was narrow and fronted by screen doors. She opened the one on the right and knocked on the wooden door beneath. The lack of sound beyond the doors gave her little hope that the Wrights were home.

A fly or gnat flew around her head again, and she swatted at it.

A couple more knocks were required before someone stirred inside. The flip of a dead bolt, and then the door opened.

An elderly woman with white hair tucked into a bun eyed her. "You lost, hon?"

"Possibly," Finley offered. "I'm looking for Mr. and Mrs. Wright."

"Who is it?" a male voice called from somewhere deeper in the room. A gray head poked its way between the petite woman and the door.

"You've found us," the woman said. "You selling insurance or religion, girlie?"

Finley smiled. "No, ma'am. I'm from Nashville. I work for the Finnegan Law Firm, and I'm here to ask you about the Holmes family who used to live next door."

The man, presumably Chester, scowled. "If she's a lawyer, send her on her way." He grumbled a few swear words as he ambled away from the door.

"You a lawyer?" the woman asked.

"I'm an investigator," Finley said without answering the question.

"What're you investigating? Doug and Wanda Holmes were murdered a long time ago."

"I have questions about their son."

Chester's head was suddenly next to his wife's again. "Why?"

Finley reminded herself that these folks probably rarely had company and needed to be sure who they were letting into their home.

Before she could answer, the lady glowered at her husband. "Go fix some iced tea and quit giving her the third degree."

He disappeared again, mumbling more of those colorful expletives. Gladys opened the door fully. "Come on in. You look a little flushed. Let's have some iced tea, and we'll talk about your questions."

The house was filled with antiques and smelled of fresh-cut flowers. Wood floors looked in pristine condition, with vintage rugs here and there. Tall windows were up, allowing air to circulate, and a huge metal ceiling fan turned slowly overhead in the parlor, stirring the air.

It wasn't particularly hot in the house, but it wasn't actually cool either. Finley supposed if you sat nice and still you'd be quite comfortable.

"Sit anywhere you'd like," Gladys directed. "Chester will be along with the tea."

"Thank you." Finley settled on a well-loved sofa adorned with a crocheted throw hanging across the back.

The lady of the house sat in one of the upholstered rockers that flanked a marble-topped table.

"They were young when they died." Gladys set her rocker in motion. "Doug had just turned forty-two. Wanda had us over for cake. She was only forty. It was a terrible tragedy."

"Both parents were murdered?" The details of the case were a bit sketchy. Home invasion. Parents shot and killed. Boy found hidden in the barn. There hadn't been any real forensic work as far as Finley could determine. Few reports at all, in fact.

"Well," Chester announced as he entered the room carrying a tray of glasses filled with iced tea, "that depends upon who you ask." He placed the tray on the table between the rockers. Handed a glass to his wife and then another to Finley. He settled into his rocker and claimed the final glass.

"If you had asked Joe Keaton," Gladys said, "the police officer who investigated the case—he passed away a while back—anyway, he would've told you it was a home invasion. Doug and Wanda had a little money and some nice things. There was no money found in the house. A few things were missing. A gold-coin collection and a pistol, along with the rifle used to kill them."

"The murder weapon belonged to the victims?" Finley asked.

"Yep," Chester said. "That part right there don't add up to me."

"Not one bit," Gladys put in.

"Why was Detective Keaton convinced otherwise?" Surely there was some sort of evidence, though she'd found nothing in the meager contents of the case file. The missing items may have been sold prior to the incident. Or perhaps they were simply hidden, and no one had found them.

"Officer," Chester corrected. "He wasn't no detective. The closest detective then, and now, is in Winchester on the Tennessee side or Scottsboro on this side."

"Officer Keaton was from Huntland," Gladys explained. "Everyone always called him 'cause he was so close by."

"Who called him?" Something else Finley hadn't found in the file.

"I did," Chester said.

"So you discovered the bodies?"

"Heard the gunshots. I didn't think too much of the first one. Folks run off unwanted critters with a gunshot. Bobcats, coyotes, and such. Doug wasn't one for hunting, so I figured he'd had to run off a critter. But when I heard the second shot, I knew something wasn't right. I told Gladys to stay in the house, and I drove over there."

"You didn't see a fleeing intruder when you approached the house?"

He shook his head. "Wanda was on the sofa." He grimaced. "Just sitting there with her eyes wide open and a big-ass hole in the center of her chest."

"Language," Gladys scolded.

"Anyway, her dress was soaked in blood. The sofa too," he went on, ignoring his wife. "Doug was in his chair, blood all down the front of him. The bullet had torn through the underpart of his chin and throat and ripped through his brain. Don't sound like no home invasion to me."

"You believe he committed suicide after shooting his wife?" Though the trajectory of the bullet sounded feasible, the fact that the weapon used was missing basically ruled out that scenario.

"I sure do."

"What about the weapon?" she countered. "If he shot himself, who took the weapon?"

Chester shrugged. "I don't know, maybe the boy. All I know for sure was Doug hadn't been happy for a while. He and Wanda were having some trouble."

"I hate to speak ill of the dead," Gladys interjected, "but the last time I talked to Wanda just a few days before, she said Doug was very upset with her. Things were pretty rocky."

"Not happy about what?" Finley looked from one to the other. Chester seemed the most forthcoming.

"They always had trouble with that boy," Chester tossed in. "There was something wrong with him."

Something else the file on Charles Holmes hadn't shown.

"Now, you don't know that for sure," Gladys chided. "He was a little odd, that's true. But Wanda never told me anything about him being trouble."

"Tell that to the people he killed," Chester contested.

"Just because he lost his way and started doing bad things when he grew up," Gladys argued, "doesn't mean he came into this world a bad seed."

Chester grunted. "Doug told me he was too quiet. Just sat around watching them."

"Well, Doug couldn't deny him," Gladys interjected. "The boy looked just like him with those piercing blue eyes."

"I'm just telling you what the man said," Chester griped. "In fact, he said it was even worse after the new baby was born."

"Wait." Finley held up both hands stop-sign fashion. "There was no mention of a new baby."

"Poor thing was only a couple weeks old," Gladys explained. "I guess they figured it was better just to keep the baby out of the mess and let someone adopt her."

"Her?" Holmes had a sister? The possibilities flashed like a movie on fast-forward in Finley's head.

"I don't think Doug wanted another one," Chester said. "He was afraid it would be like the boy. He told Wanda they weren't having no more kids. Period."

"I guess Doug thought they were in the clear since she'd had so many problems. You know, down there." Gladys sighed. "But next thing you know, she was pregnant at forty years old."

Still reeling at the news, Finley asked. "The boy was seven?" She'd figured it was better to confirm, since little else in the file had been correct.

"He was," Chester said. "He'd finished first grade that year, and then his birthday was right before school started back."

"If you're convinced this was a murder-suicide," Finley said, "why was it officially listed as a home invasion?"

"Doug and Joe were friends," Chester explained. "Close friends. I guess he didn't want to believe his friend would kill his wife and then himself. I figure he's the one that got rid of the rifle and maybe the other stuff to make it look like something it wasn't."

"Did Officer Keaton have a wife or anyone with whom he might have confided his thoughts on the case?"

"He had a wife. Don't know if she got the real story, though," Gladys offered. "No one save us ever thought any different than the official report as far as we know."

"Did you talk to anyone about your feelings?"

"We decided it was best if we stayed quiet," Chester said. "It wasn't going to change anything. They were dead. They had no other family. No need to make it any worse than it was. Dead's dead."

Finley could see how they'd come to that conclusion, but the lawyer in her couldn't get right with it. "Charles was put in foster care?"

"Over in Alabama," Gladys said. "We never did know where he ended up until that big trial in Nashville a few years back."

"What about the little girl?" This was the part that had Finley's pulse racing.

"Officer Keaton seen to it that she was adopted." Chester nodded, sipped his tea.

"How did he do that?" There were laws about those sorts of things. Procedures to be followed. There was absolutely no record of Holmes having had a sibling.

"Well, there really wasn't any record of the new baby," Chester said. He placed the sweating glass on the marble-topped table between himself and his wife.

"There had to be medical records," Finley countered.

"Wanda preferred doing things all natural," Gladys said. "She never went to the doctor or hospital with either one of her kids. Doug delivered the boy. But he was so mad he refused to deliver the girl."

"Surely Mrs. Holmes had some sort of help." This was over the top.

"I helped." Gladys nodded. "She sent Charlie over here to get me. I almost missed the whole thing, but I helped her finish up. Doug stayed out in the barn the whole time."

"You got to understand," Chester said, "these people mostly kept to themselves. Wanda rarely did any of the shopping, or even left the house for that matter. Especially once she looked pregnant. She didn't get out at all."

"Nothing wrong with staying home," Gladys grumbled. "Wanda was a good person."

"Didn't say she wasn't," Chester pointed out.

"Who could I ask about what happened to the baby?" Finley couldn't go back to Nashville without something on this baby.

"I guess you could ask Keaton's wife, Penelope," Gladys said. "She probably knows who took care of the adoption."

"Does she still live in Huntland?"

"She's in Winchester now," Chester said. "Lives over on North High in one of those fancy historic homes. She was never the friendly type. I doubt she'll want to talk to you."

"Unless," Gladys said with a scowl, "there's something in it for her." She sniffed. "That's just her way," she added as if attempting to temper her unkind words.

"Is there anything else you can tell me about the boy or his parents?"

"Just odd," Chester said. "Not necessarily bad, mind you—just plain old odd. Like I said, for the most part they kept to themselves."

"Thank you so much for your time and the tea." Finley stood, anticipation roaring in her ears. She had to find that cop's wife.

Gladys walked her to the door. "Good luck, hon. I hope you find whatever it is you need."

Finley thanked her. Far more than luck would be required, she imagined, to find the answers she needed. But she had to try.

———

Keaton Residence
North High Street
Winchester, 2:30 p.m.

Google hadn't given her much about Joe Keaton or his wife, Penelope, but she had learned when they'd purchased the historic home and how much it had cost. Only a few months after the murders, and it cost far more than a cop could afford on a small-town salary.

She had a feeling about what had happened to the baby girl, and it was more like a sale than an adoption. She also suspected the money and other items missing from the Holmes house had gone toward the purchase price of this property.

Penelope had never remarried or held a job. She lived well on her husband's retirement and the large insurance payout she'd received when he was killed on the job.

That was the other interesting aspect. Keaton had transferred from Huntland to Winchester a couple of years after the murders. Then, ten years later he was shot in his cruiser while eating his lunch. No one witnessed the shooting. There hadn't been any body cams in the

Winchester Police Department nearly two decades ago. His murder remained unsolved.

Finley rang the doorbell. The yapping that followed was from a tiny white dog that stood in a window staring out at her.

The door opened, and Penelope Keaton considered Finley. "Can I help you?"

"My name is Finley O'Sullivan, and I'm trying to locate the daughter of Wanda and Douglas Holmes."

Penelope flinched at the name. Panic widened her eyes. "I'm sorry. I don't know anything about that family. I'm afraid I can't help—"

Before she could say more, Finley rushed on, "This is concerning an estate that has been left to her, and there's a substantial reward for whomever helps me find her."

The panic faded. "An estate? I was under the impression there was no extended family."

So much for her not knowing anything about the family.

"I suppose that's what everyone thought," Finley said, running with her cover story. "Apparently Wanda had fallen out with her family when she married Douglas, and they lost touch. Her mother recently passed away, and my firm has the task of finding the heirs. Since Wanda died, that leaves no one but her children. We've located the son, but he knows nothing of what happened to his sister."

Worry surfaced in Penelope's eyes, and her posture stiffened. "I'm not sure I can help you. It's been a long time."

"Any help you can provide would be greatly appreciated, and as I said, there is a substantial reward."

Penelope blinked. "I can certainly try, but I can't make any promises." Her words were tentative.

Ah, money. There was never enough.

"I'd really hate for her to be left out of her inheritance."

"Leave me your name and number," Penelope said, "and I'll let you know if I can find out what became of her. I remember my husband said she was adopted privately, but I don't know the details. My husband passed away, so . . ." She shrugged.

There she went, laying whatever happened at her dead husband's feet. Finley withdrew a business card from her bag and passed it to the lady.

"Thank you so much. I look forward to hearing from you."

Finley walked to her Subaru, climbed in, and drove around the block. Then she parked a short distance from the Keaton home to watch. Penelope Keaton wouldn't wait long before making some sort of move to earn that substantial reward. Being a cop's wife, she likely knew better than to use the phone or email to make that move.

Finley was counting on her making an in-person attempt. Hopefully right away.

Less than half an hour later, Keaton left her house and hit Interstate 24 all the way to Nashville. Finley followed, keeping a safe distance. Keaton drove to Sylvan Park Lane, parked in front of a neat little bungalow, and went to the door. After a couple of knocks the door opened, and she went inside.

Finley had called Jack during the drive and given him an update. Unless the status had changed in the last half hour, there was still no news on the search for the twins or for Cherry. Finley was more convinced than ever that Cherry was in this up to her eyeballs.

The sister connection could be nothing. A waste of time. But Finley couldn't ignore it. She thought of all the female followers that had flocked after Holmes. Several had criminal records. Others didn't. Most were attractive.

But the only one on Finley's radar was Cherry Prescott Inglewood. She was the right age. She didn't have the same startling blue eyes as Holmes, but her eyes were definitely blue. Really dark, but blue nonetheless. The rub was that her background search showed her parents were still alive, and there was nothing that suggested she had been adopted. With a private adoption and basically a newborn, it was possible she might not be aware she'd been adopted. Either way, Finley intended to confirm the identity of the sister.

Her cell vibrated on the console. She glanced at the screen.

Matt.

"Hey." Was she supposed to have called him back on something? Sleep deprivation was scrambling her brain. "Did I forget to call you back?"

"No. No. I just wanted to make sure you're okay. With Cherry Inglewood missing and the twins MIA, I was worried about you. I heard you were questioned downtown."

Finley leaned fully against the seat. Too damned tired. "Apparently I was the last person besides her husband to talk to Cherry before she disappeared."

"You believe she's more a part of this case than you first thought?"

"I do. I tracked down the neighbors of Holmes's biological parents. Looks like their deaths weren't as cut and dried as the case file showed." She shared the details the Wrights had claimed and the news about the little sister as well as her own thoughts regarding her identity.

"Could Inglewood really be the sister?" Matt asked.

"I can't be sure, but it makes sense. She may have been the mystery woman who visited him. The Alisha Arrington."

"Keep me posted. I have a dinner meeting tonight, but I want to hear from you when you get home."

"You got it."

The call ended, and her full attention shifted to the house across the street. She had googled the address but didn't find much. The place was a new build. She'd searched Cherry's parents. Both were still alive and listed as living in the Hermitage area. Maybe this had nothing to do with Cherry. Then again, if Finley was right and Lance Legard had been bothering Cherry, she certainly could have asked her brother to take care of the situation.

Finally Keaton exited the house and hurried back to her car. Her face looked red as if she was angry. She got into her car and zoomed away. Yeah, probably angry. Finley considered following her, but she needed to know who lived in this house . . . who Penelope Keaton had just quarreled with.

Finley was out of the car and walking toward the house before she could overanalyze the situation. She knocked on the door. It flew inward, and a woman glowered at her, then blinked in surprise.

"Can . . ." She shook her head. "Can I help you?"

Her cheeks were flushed, her eyes red from crying. So there had been an exchange of some sort.

"My name is Finley O'Sullivan. I'm an investigator." She stared directly at the woman. "I need to know who you are and why Penelope Keaton came to see you."

"I can't talk about this!" The woman's face crumpled, and she burst into tears, her body slowly sliding down the doorframe to the floor. "My daughter is missing. Oh my God, she's missing."

There was her answer. Had to be Cherry's mother, no matter that this wasn't listed as her address. Finley crouched down next to her. "I don't know what's happening, but I might be able to help."

The story flowed out of the woman in great gasping chunks. Her name was Elly Prescott. She and her husband hadn't been able to have children. They'd lived in Winchester decades ago; her husband had been an ER doctor. Officer Keaton was aware of their situation. One night he had come to them with a newborn little girl. He told them the mother had died of a drug overdose and the father was unknown. He hated to see the baby go into foster care. Elly's husband and Keaton had made a deal. Cherry was that little girl. Now Keaton's wife was back to say she needed to reveal what had happened to the baby unless Elly was willing to pay her for her silence. The Keatons had come to them for money time and again over the years. It was never enough. But the

Prescotts were so afraid of losing their daughter that they did whatever necessary. Even after they moved from Winchester to Hermitage and then to Nashville, the blackmail continued. It seemed they couldn't escape or hide from Penelope Keaton. And now Cherry was missing. Elly had been instructed to stay home in case Cherry contacted her. Elly's husband was with Elton and their son, Brantley.

"Mrs. Prescott, I can assure you," Finley said, "this blackmail is about to stop."

Penelope Keaton would not get away with torturing these people any longer.

The older woman wiped her eyes with her fingertips. "I don't understand why this happened. There's been no ransom demand."

This woman had no idea about Cherry's bio parents. "Ma'am, were you told the names of the parents?"

She shook her head adamantly. "We agreed not to ask any questions, and the Keatons promised to never share our names. No one would ever know she wasn't ours. We accepted her as our own and never looked back."

Finley braced herself for a storm. "Do you recognize the name Charles Holmes?"

If possible, Elly Prescott paled to an even lighter shade. "What're you saying?"

Half an hour later Finley was convinced the Prescotts had had no idea Cherry might be the sister of Charles Holmes. As an adult, their daughter had certainly never mentioned knowing him. Finley gave Prescott her card and told her she would be hearing from her. Until then she was to stay calm and to avoid Keaton. The police were doing everything possible to find Cherry.

Finley left, needing to get to the office ASAP. She wanted to talk to Jack, and then, together, they would go to Detectives Barry and Tanner with this.

Her cell rang, and she answered without taking her eyes off the traffic keeping time with her.

"O'Sullivan."

"I need your help."

Finley almost slammed on the brakes. "Cherry?" It was Cherry's voice, but her contact list told Finley it was Cecelia.

"I don't know how much time I have," she whispered.

Finley did slow down then. A horn blared behind her. She ignored it and pulled to the side of the highway. "Where are you?" Her fingers gripped the phone tighter. "I need to know where you are."

"She's going to kill me," she cried softly.

"Cherry, who's going to kill you? Where are you?" Finley repeated, her pulse pounding in her ears. What the hell was Cecelia doing? Had to be Cecelia. Cherry was calling from her damned phone.

"It's Cecelia." Cherry whimpered. "Wait! I think she's coming back."

Finley held her breath, and still her heart thundered. She wanted to scream.

"Okay." A gasp echoed across the line. "She's still arguing. She forgot about her phone when Olivia arrived. But she could come back any second. Please, please help me. They're crazy."

"Olivia is there?" Damn it! Finley fought the urge to get out of the car and pace along the side of the road. "Tell me where you are!"

"They're screaming at each other." Cherry made a fretting sound. "Please tell my son I love him."

"Cherry," Finley said firmly, "where are you?"

"I . . . I think we're at the castle. You know, off Centennial Boulevard. I've been here before. A lot of us who hung out at Paradise used to come here . . . to smoke dope and stupid shit like that. Oh God . . ." A keening sound echoed from her.

Finley checked the traffic and eased back onto the highway. "The old prison? Are you sure? Didn't they shut that place down a while back? It's restricted. Maybe guarded twenty-four seven. People may have gotten in there five years ago but—"

"I don't know," Cherry cried softly. "When they dragged me out of the trunk, I saw . . . a *No Trespassing* sign. And . . . and what looked like a chapel in the distance."

She stopped talking. Finley heard a voice or voices in the background. Her heart thudded harder. The voices faded.

"Did you call the police?" Finley asked, pressing harder on her accelerator.

"The police? No! Then Elton will know and . . ." She started to sob. "Please. You can help me. I know you can. He can't know any of this."

It was far too late for the woman's husband to be kept out of the loop, but Finley opted not to point out the obvious.

"I'm on my way," Finley assured her. "Tell me more about what you saw when you got there."

"She . . . she forced me through a door," Cherry said, whispering again. "There . . . there was a sign on the door. *Maintenance*. We went down some stairs. It's like a basement with long corridors. Please help me! She has a gun!"

Finley's heart sank into her gut. "I'm coming," she promised. "Just stay on the line with me as long as you can."

The call dropped.

Finley stared at the now black screen.

A horn blared.

She swerved back into her lane.

"Damn it!" Finley couldn't risk calling her back and alerting Cecelia or Olivia if the phone was not silenced.

She called Jack. Got his voice mail. Hung up and called Matt. Voice mail.

"Shit!" She waited for the beep and left him a message about the call from Cherry.

Her thumb went instinctively to the nine, but she hesitated. If she called 911 and alerted the police, all three women could end up dead. Cecelia had a gun.

That would not end well.

She thought of Cherry's little boy, and she flung her phone onto the passenger seat.

Finley wanted these women alive.

32

5:30 p.m.

The Castle
Centennial Boulevard
Nashville

Finley drove around the decaying castle that fronted the old state prison until she could see the chapel. She parked at the nearest entrance and scrambled out of her car. She had tried Matt again and left a second voice mail.

She glanced around. Didn't see anyone. Didn't hear anything except the rumbling of the traffic on the nearby interstate. She silenced her cell, tucked it into one of her back pockets and her keys into the other, then started walking. Graffiti marred the walls. Discarded trash littered the ground. Vandals. Teenagers looking for a cool place to do stuff they couldn't do at home. Apparently, that hadn't stopped. A safer place for the homeless than the street. Anyone could be hanging out here if there were no longer any guards. The last Finley recalled reading about the place, parts of it were used for storage.

MAINTENANCE.

She spotted a door like the one Cherry had mentioned and headed toward it.

The door opened with ease. She went through it, allowing it to close behind her. Scenes with the lead character entering an unlocked door in every bad horror flick she'd ever watched scrolled through Finley's head.

As Cherry had said, there were stairs that disappeared downward. Peeling paint and evidence rodents called the place home kept Finley watching her step.

She imagined there were tunnels and underground storage or mechanical rooms all over the property. Hopefully this was the right one. Back in high school some of her friends had slipped in and explored the prison. She'd never had any desire to do so. Really didn't now, but if she could find Cherry and the twins, it would be worth the effort.

Effort . . . or risk?

She would know soon enough.

The stairs ended at the entrance to a long, relatively wide corridor. Since it was underground and there were no windows, she was grateful for the lighting, dim as it was. At least the emergency lighting was still operating. She started forward, listening carefully for any sound.

Still nothing. Her arms and legs tingled with the rush of adrenaline pulsing through her veins. Why hadn't either of the twins called her?

Was this some sort of final retribution? Some showdown?

Or just a plan to force a confession?

But from whom?

Olivia swore Cecelia was the one. Cecelia said the same about her sister.

Was Cherry caught in the middle, or had she played some more pivotal part in the murder than she'd shared so far?

Finley cleared her head. What difference did it make? More importantly, why now?

Somehow Charles Holmes had prompted all this with his decision to request a new trial.

Had this been his ultimate goal? A showdown of some sort between the three women closest to Lance Legard?

Drawing all the players back into this sick game of who did it?

Finley started moving again. When she reached another corridor that went left and right, she paused once more. She didn't see anything resembling a door in either direction. Didn't hear a damned sound.

She hadn't seen any other vehicle. But Cherry had said she'd been in a trunk. Cecelia must have driven her mother's car since she didn't have one of her own. If Olivia was here, where was her rental car? Finley supposed one or both could have parked anywhere and walked to their destination.

She moved on. The silence had a sort of swell about it, as if she were underwater. A creepy feeling tapped its way up her spine. Up ahead, she saw a door on the right. About time. She was beginning to think there was nothing down here but empty corridors to nowhere.

"I knew you'd find us."

Finley whirled around. Cecelia stood a few yards behind her. She appeared uninjured. Her jeans were muddy. Her pink tee was stretched and wrinkled as if someone had tried tugging it off her. Her short shaggy brown hair stood in tufts here and there as if she'd been wearing a hat. A large canvas bag or purse hung on her shoulder, rested against her hip.

Where was the gun?

Finley ordered her heart rate to slow. For the good it would do.

"Are you all right, Cecelia?"

She nodded. "I'm glad you came. We're all here. To finish this."

Finley ignored the pulse pounding louder in her ears. "What can I do to help?"

Cecelia walked directly up to Finley, grabbed her hand, and pulled her forward. "You can be the jury."

Finley didn't argue. Just allowed herself to be tugged forward. They rushed along the dimly lit corridor until they reached a door on the right. Cecelia opened the door and entered more slowly, almost warily.

Finley stayed close behind her. An overturned table and several chairs sat in a disorganized pile. Boxes, taped and labeled, stood in precarious stacks. That dusty, closed-up smell crowded into Finley's lungs.

A gasp echoed from somewhere deeper inside. "Help me . . ."

The soft cry drew Finley's attention to the corner on the other side of the room. Cherry sat huddled into herself, her knees pressed against her chest, her arms locked around her legs. There was blood on her forehead.

"You okay?" Finley asked.

Cherry lifted her head to meet Finley's gaze. "I think so."

"She's only here because I was afraid you wouldn't come otherwise." Cecelia pointed to the other woman.

Finley gave her a nod. "I understand. How do we begin?" She dismissed thoughts of whether the gun was in Cecelia's bag and focused on the moment.

"She'll kill us all," Cherry warned. "She has a gun!"

Now that Cherry had brought it up, Finley turned back to Cecelia to ask about the gun. She was tugging at her hair.

But it wasn't Cecelia. *Blonde.* It was Olivia.

Wait. Wait. Wait. Finley studied the woman. Her blonde hair was tousled and lopsided.

Not her hair. *A wig.*

The muddy jeans and wrinkled pink tee were what Cecelia had been wearing.

A fresh wave of adrenaline fired through Finley. The wig—expensive, realistic. She glanced at Cecelia's—or whoever's—hands. No flashy red nails like Olivia's. Stick-on nails? Was it the residual glue that Cecelia had always been picking at? An almost calming rush of knowing rolled through Finley. There was only one twin.

The question was, Which one?

Olivia or Cecelia reached into the bag and drew out a handgun.

Finley steadied herself and addressed the woman based on who she appeared to be for the moment. "Olivia, you don't want to hurt anyone."

"She's guilty too." Olivia gestured to Cherry. "But that's not why we're here." Her attention shifted to Finley then. "It's about what Cecelia thinks I did." The hand holding the weapon wobbled. "I need to clear my name."

"What does Cecelia think you did, Olivia?"

"She thought it was me," she said, her chin lifting in defiance. "But it wasn't me."

"I don't understand. Can you be more specific?" Finley felt the phone in her back pocket vibrate. If she was lucky, it was Matt. When she didn't answer, he would come.

She knew he would.

He never let her down.

"She thought I killed him, but I didn't." Olivia's eyes flashed with emotion. "I loved him. I would never hurt our father." She shook her head, the wig flopping precariously. "She said she saw me, but it was a lie. She just said it to make Mother hate me. It's the only possible explanation."

"It was him," Cherry screamed. "Charles Holmes killed your daddy. You know that, you crazy bitch."

Olivia turned to Cherry, the gun shaking in her hand. "Shut up, you whore!"

"Olivia," Finley urged, "it was Holmes. It wasn't you. We know it wasn't you." She had to bring the tension down a notch or two.

"Cecelia said she saw me." Olivia pounded on her chest with her free hand. "She said I stabbed him over and over. And Mother believed her. Mother always loved Cecelia more than me. She shouldn't have believed her."

Oh shit. "Did you have a fight with your mother?"

"No. We didn't fight. She kept saying Cecelia was upset because of what I did to him and that's why all this happened. I kept telling her Cecelia was wrong, but she wouldn't listen. She swore she would never have been able to live with what happened if what Cecelia said was a lie. She took all those pills right in front of me, and then she told me to just let her die if I didn't believe her." Olivia fell silent for a long moment. "I didn't believe her. I knew it was a lie. But she wasn't supposed to die. I thought she was just saying those things to make me calm down. She would never be so foolish as to swallow real pills like that. It was another game. It had to be."

But it wasn't.

"She's going to kill us," Cherry ranted. "Do something!" she railed at Finley.

Finley held up a hand for Cherry to stop. "It's okay, Olivia. I understand what happened. You didn't hurt your father, and you didn't believe your mother was serious about the pills. It was a misunderstanding."

"I didn't want her to die." The barrel of the gun lowered slightly. "I only wanted her to finally believe me. Holmes told the world it was Cecelia, and Mother still didn't believe I was innocent. Cecelia was always her favorite. Always. Always. Always."

"Olivia." Finley dared to take a step in her direction. "I need to talk to Cecelia now. See what she has to say for herself."

"She ran away. She always hides from the truth." Olivia brushed at a wisp of hair stuck to her cheek. "Mother was always fixing everything for her. I warned her, but she always, always believed Cecelia. She should have listened to me." She shook her head, almost dislodging the wig. "No one ever listens to me."

"I'm listening to you, Olivia. Let me talk to Cecelia and see if we can get this sorted out." Finley produced a kind smile. "You can trust me."

"Don't you see?" Cherry shouted. "She has—I don't know—like split personalities. There's no telling what she might do next. We need help."

Finley ignored her. Hoped to hell the woman with the gun—whichever twin she really was—would as well. "Please, Olivia, let me help."

Olivia reached up, removed the wig, and tossed it away. She ran the fingers of her free hand through her short brown hair. Her gaze collided with Finley's. "I saw my sister stabbing our father. I already hated her." She shrugged. "Father thought Olivia was perfect." Her face twisted in anger. "But he was wrong. I wonder what he thought when she killed him." She blinked, the move in a sort of slow motion. "I tried to get Charlie to help me be rid of her, but he only laughed at me."

"How can you be sure it was Olivia?" Finley asked carefully, needing something concrete.

"It was Charlie," Cherry cried, her voice wobbling after so much shouting. "He killed him!"

Finley kept her attention fixed on the twin—Cecelia apparently—and the gun. "Please tell me why you thought it was Olivia."

"I saw her stab him. Over and over and over. I was frozen. In shock. I wanted to stop her, but I couldn't. I couldn't move. Then she started feeling around on the floor for her phone. I guess she'd dropped it. When she found it and started calling someone, I ran away. I couldn't . . ."

"Why didn't you tell your mother or the police?"

She stared at Finley for a long time before she spoke. "Mother wasn't home that day. Didn't matter. I couldn't. I think I was a little afraid it . . . it was me." She shrugged. "We pretended to be each other sometimes. I couldn't decide if I saw it or if I *did* it." She shuddered. "But later, after I'd calmed down, I remembered clearly. It was Olivia."

"I told you." Cherry was on her feet now, hunkered down in the corner but poised to cut and run. "She has totally lost it. She's *evil*."

"Did you tell your mother then?" Finley moved another step closer to Cecelia.

Cecelia shook her head. "I told you she wasn't home. Her car wasn't in the driveway, so I just hid in my room and pretended I saw nothing." She shrugged. "By the time she came home, I thought maybe I had imagined it. The garage was clean. Father wasn't there. His car wasn't there." She stared at Finley as if beseeching her to believe. "It wasn't until the police came the next day that I knew he was really dead. When Charlie confessed, I was confused, and then I was glad. His confession was easier to believe. I didn't have to wonder if I was the one anymore."

"Did you ask Olivia about what you thought you saw?" Another step disappeared between them. Finley struggled to keep her respiration level. Being calm was essential if she hoped to keep Cecelia calm.

"Not until after the trial. I guess I blocked the whole thing. Then one day I saw her in the garage looking for something, and it all came back to me."

Finley didn't need a map to see where this was going.

"I don't know what happened. I . . . I was so angry . . . so hurt. And then I just stared at her . . . lying there. Not moving. Blood." She touched her head. "I thought I was looking at myself. I wanted it to be me." She frowned. "Mother understood. I told her, I suppose. Or maybe she saw us." Her face twisted in pain and confusion. "She took care of everything. She took care of us. Olivia went away to school. Started a whole life for herself out in California." Anger suddenly twisted her features again. "Olivia should have stayed there, but no. Mother said she had to come back because of *him*! She said if Olivia didn't come back, everyone would know what I had done. So I let her come back."

Finley was next to her now. "You didn't mean to do it," she assured the younger woman as she reached for her arm. "It was a mistake."

Cecelia nodded. The hand with the gun fell to her side. "If Olivia hadn't come back, she would still be living happily in California and no one would know." She smiled sadly. "But she wouldn't go away until she showed everyone what I had done."

"Olivia doesn't have to come back anymore," Finley promised her. She reached for the gun. "We don't need this anymore."

When Cecelia didn't resist and Finley had the gun in her hand, relief gushed through her, weakening her knees.

Cherry collapsed against the wall. "Jesus Christ, I thought I was dead."

Cecelia reached down and picked up the blonde wig from the floor, then tugged it on. "Can I go home now? I'm very tired."

Finley tucked the gun into her waistband. "Sure." She pulled Olivia close to her. "Let's get out of here."

The corridors seemed twice as long as they had been when Finley passed through them coming in. Her lungs felt as if she couldn't get enough air. Claustrophobia, she decided. This place would make anyone uncomfortable.

Cherry trailed after them, sobbing softly.

Olivia leaned close, pressing her forehead against Finley's temple. "Don't trust her," she murmured.

Finley glanced back. Cherry trudged along, head hung low, arms hugged around herself.

"Okay," she whispered back to Olivia.

"I told Cecelia over and over that it wasn't me. It was someone else she saw."

The words were spoken so quietly Finley barely comprehended what she was saying. She nodded, the other woman's head still nudged against hers.

"That was the night Mother went to one of her charity auctions and I sneaked out to Paradise because Cecelia was home sick. I wasn't even home when my father disappeared. Cecelia was the only one there."

Finley's heart started that rapid staccato again. She reminded herself she couldn't trust anything this woman was saying. Hell, she couldn't even be sure who she was. But she could listen, and she could prompt her to keep talking.

"You think Cecelia killed him?"

Olivia paused, turned her gaze to Finley's, their faces almost touching. "How could she kill him and be watching at the same time?"

Valid point. Finley ushered her forward, hoped she would keep talking. "But if it wasn't you . . . ," Finley murmured, leaving the suggestion hanging.

Olivia paused again, stared directly into Finley's eyes. "It was someone who looked like me."

"Why are you just standing there?" Cherry snapped. "We have to get out of here. I want to get home to my son."

Cold seeped into Finley's skin. She turned to the other woman. "Sorry. Olivia needed a break."

Cherry stared at her, shook her head. "How the fuck do you know which one she is?" She shuddered, more tears spilling down her cheeks. "Please just get us out of here."

A new possibility building inside Finley, she urged Olivia forward once more. They reached the final corridor that would lead to the stairs, and Olivia suddenly removed the wig and tossed it on the floor. She pulled free of Finley and turned to Cherry.

"It was you." The accusation echoed in the long corridor.

Finley readied to make a move to stop whatever was about to happen.

Cherry drew up short. Looked from Olivia to Finley. "What the hell is she talking about?"

Finley thought of how badly Cherry had needed to escape Lance's obsession. How she'd disappeared . . .

Was she the woman who had visited Holmes every month? Her long-lost brother. The realization swept through Finley's veins like a fire tearing through dry woods.

"I thought it was my sister," Cecelia said, taking another step toward Cherry. "But it was you. I only saw you from behind. I was several yards away . . . I just assumed since it was our garage . . . our home . . ." Cecelia moved her head side to side. "I was wrong. It was you."

"She really is insane." Cherry threw up her hands and backed away. "I'm not having this conversation."

Finley thought of the photo of Cherry all hugged up with Charles Holmes. Olivia had said Cherry hung out with Charlie—like an old married couple . . . people who had a connection. Holy shit.

"How did Charlie figure out you were his sister?" Finley asked, sidestepping to put herself in front of Cecelia. "Had you figured it out, or did he?"

Cherry blinked. Frozen in place, her arms dangling at her sides, mouth slightly open. "What're you talking about?"

"He found you. You're his family." Finley studied the curve of her cheek. Her nose. And then she knew. "You went to see him every month in prison . . . until just recently."

Cherry was shaking her head. "I don't know what you're talking about." She took another step backward.

"Lance wouldn't let you go." Finley saw the whole picture now. "You fought. No one was supposed to be home, except Cecelia had gotten ill and was holed up in her room. She heard the shouting and came to see what was going on. By then the argument had escalated, and you had grabbed a weapon."

Another step backward. "You're as crazy as she is. We should call the police. You're scaring me."

"No," Finley said, certainty rooting deep inside her. "I'm wrong. You brought the weapon with you, didn't you? Did Charlie give it to you to protect yourself? You don't really seem the type to carry a switchblade."

No one moved. They all stared at each other as if they'd reached some sort of impasse. Finley's last words seemed to ring on and on in the thick air. Anger and frustration, triumph and determination—it all burst inside her. The answer had been right in front of them all along.

"It was her," Cecelia repeated softly. "I know it was her."

Cherry remained frozen . . . seemingly unable to speak or to run.

"I'll bet Charlie will confirm it for us," Finley said. "He's not happy with you right now, is he, Cherry? That's what all this is about, isn't it? You stopped visiting him, and he decided to show you just what he could do from that prison cell." Finley's anger turned to outrage. "He even gave you a scapegoat—Cecelia. All you had to do was fall back in line."

Another beat of tense silence.

"He just wanted me to be happy." Cherry looked around as if hoping to find some miracle that would rescue her. She shrugged. "He said I was his sister and he wanted to take care of me. He killed our father for me. The bastard intended to kill me and Charlie after he killed our mother, but Charlie stopped him."

The image of a little boy picking up a shotgun and shooting his father to save his baby sister seared through Finley's mind. Horror quaked through her.

"How did he find you?" Finley asked, her voice hollow. She would bet money Penelope Keaton hadn't told him where his sister was.

Cherry leaned one shoulder against the wall as if the weight of her story were too heavy to continue carrying without support. "He found out a long time ago. He said he tracked down the cop who investigated his parents' case and got the truth out of him. He had been watching me since." She touched the shape on her cheek. The one Finley had noticed the last time they'd talked. "He said my mother had this same birthmark."

Finley wanted to hate Cherry for what she had done to the Legard family. But she was a victim the same as the twins. The outrage whooshed out of Finley and left her feeling empty and exhausted. "When did the two of you meet?"

"Five years ago. He saw me at the Paradise." Cherry hugged herself again. "We became very close. It was surreal. Like an angel God had sent to save me from my mistake. I told him about Lance, and he told me I should protect myself." She shook her head. "But I never expected to . . . I was just so angry. I'd only meant to scare Lance off, but things got out of control."

"You called your brother, and he came to your rescue," Finley guessed.

"He came over and cleaned up everything. He told me not to worry, that he would take care of it. He knew how." She exhaled a big breath, traced a crack in the wall with her forefinger. "I thought when he went to prison it would be over, but it had just begun. He wouldn't go away. He sent his followers to check up on me, and when I stopped visiting and decided to go on with my life, he started this new nightmare. He wanted me to see there was no escape. I knew he could change his story at any moment, but I was willing to take the risk. To call his bluff." She stared directly at Finley then. "I had to. It was the only way to protect my son. No one could know what really happened."

Except everyone had to know the truth. This was the moment in a case when Finley usually felt jubilant, satisfied that she had accomplished her goal. Those feelings were oddly missing in this instance.

"Come on, Cherry," Finley said as she extended her hand toward the other woman. "Let's go. Your son will wonder where you are."

Cherry pushed away from the wall and walked toward Finley. Next to her, Cecelia stiffened. Finley slid an arm around her and whispered, "It's okay now."

Finley wasn't sure she would ever fully understand how she managed to usher the two women out of there without one attacking the other, but somehow she did. When they reached the outside, the sounds of sirens filled the air, and lights flashed from the tops of police cruisers and at least one ambulance.

Finley couldn't recall when she'd been so glad to see the cops.

Matt came rushing toward them. Jack was right behind him.

Finley blinked back the moisture collecting in her eyes. Not tears. Just something in her eyes.

The case hadn't ended the way she had expected, but that was life. You rarely got to choose the ending.

33

Saturday, July 16

9:30 a.m.

The Murder House
Shelby Avenue
Nashville

Finley sat in the rickety glider on her porch. It, too, had come with the house. The yellow paint was flaking and there was some rust, but she didn't care. She was content just sitting there with the biggest mug she owned filled with freshly brewed coffee.

Been a hell of a week.

An understatement for sure. A big one. Cecelia Legard was being evaluated at Vanderbilt Psychiatric Hospital. She had been the one to thrust the knife into her mother's chest. The effort was to somehow tie her death to their father's, since she believed Olivia had killed them both. Cecelia had been treated for borderline personality disorder since she was twelve. After murdering her twin sister, she appeared to have developed dissociative identity disorder.

The truth was, no one could actually say if it was Olivia who was dead or Cecelia. None of the medical records mentioned identifying marks or characteristics of either twin. The truth had died with Sophia.

The remains of the murdered twin were being excavated from the Legard backyard.

Charles Holmes would get a new trial, but it wouldn't be the one he wanted. He had murdered Officer Keaton—he'd admitted the crime to his sister. His sister, Cherry Prescott Inglewood, was only too happy to use that information to lighten her own sentence. She was taking a plea deal for the murder of Lance Legard. Charles refused to give a statement for or against her. Funny thing was, if he hadn't been trying to wield control over his sister after she stopped visiting him, none of this would have happened. He'd done exactly what he'd hated his father for doing—trying to control the people he cared about.

A truly sick, sadistic man.

Cherry had admitted to taking Alisha Arrington's driver's license. They'd been in the same deli, and Cherry was desperate to figure out a way to go see Charles, thus keeping him happy without officially being tied to him.

District Attorney Briggs hadn't said a word to Finley, but he had congratulated Jack for saving the taxpayers the cost of a new trial in the Legard case and for helping to see that justice was done.

The case was closed. Finley had rescheduled her trip to the lake house with her dad. She needed some time away, and her dad deserved some of her attention.

All work and no play have never led to happiness.

Derrick had reminded her all the time that she worked too hard, but he'd never complained. Never tried to change her.

Why did you lie to me, Derrick?

Like the identity of the surviving twin, the answer was one she might never find. Could she live with that?

Maybe. She thought of her dad and Jack and the firm. Matt too. She could probably live without the answer. There were people who needed her. People who loved her.

But she wasn't giving up on proving who killed her husband. The bastard who'd taken him would not get away with what he'd done. The two remaining minions who had carried out his order wouldn't either. No one could blame her for wanting justice. She wasn't planning anything, but if the opportunity arose . . .

Finley sipped her coffee.

It was an oddly cool morning for mid-July. Her favorite weather guy had promised that would change by noon and the temps would hit near triple digits. It was going to be a long, hot summer.

Jack's Land Rover rolled to a stop in front of her house. She sat up straighter. She hadn't expected to see him this morning. He was supposed to be spending the weekend relaxing.

"Morning," he called as he climbed out and walked to the back of his vehicle. He wore paint-stained jeans and a tee.

"Morning." She stood, sipped her coffee again before putting it aside. "What're you doing here?"

Not that she wasn't happy to see him. He pulled two cans of paint from the Rover and headed up her walk.

"I came to paint," he announced. He plopped the cans on the porch and strode back to his vehicle.

She walked over, stared down at the cans, read the label. *Serene Blue.*

"Blue?" She didn't have a problem with blue, but did she want to be surrounded by it?

"It's calming," he announced as he returned to the porch with an armload of painting tools. Pan, brush, roller, and cover.

"You think I need calming?"

He glanced at her, gave a wink. "Don't we all?"

He was right, she supposed. "So you're not feeling the need for a drink?" Playing the part of fixer-upper seemed to be his primary coping mechanism when the urge grew too strong.

"Nope. Just tired of looking at this dump."

Good point. "You want coffee?"

"Absolutely."

"I'll make a fresh pot."

While Jack hauled in drop cloths and more paint, she set another pot to brew. She wandered to the porch behind him and out to the sidewalk. He grabbed two more cans of paint and headed back in.

She should change and give him a hand. The physical activity would be good. She'd already decided to start running again. When she turned back to the house, the door of her mailbox snagged her attention.

A couple of envelope corners jutted out of the partially open door. Jesus, she couldn't remember the last time she'd checked her mail. She opened the door, and mail tumbled out. Not in a while, obviously.

She gathered the pile and went back into the house. "Give me a minute, and I'll change so I can help."

"It would definitely go faster that way." He was already draping drop cloths around the living room.

She couldn't say she would miss the grayish-white, stained walls. She and Derrick had talked about using earth tone natural colors. But blue worked.

In the kitchen she opened the trash can and started tossing junk mail. She set the utility bills aside. The hand-addressed letter stuck between two mail-order catalogs seemed out of place. She pulled it free of the junk mail, threw out the rest, and wandered back to the living room.

No name of the sender or return address on front or back. She ripped the envelope open and found a single folded page. Handwritten. She glanced down the page at the signature.

Martin Wellman.

Her gaze shot back to the top of the page. The letter was dated Wednesday, July 6. The day he died.

Her heart thumped harder as she read the words.

> Finley,
> I'm sorry I couldn't find any answers for you. I hope you will move on with your life. What you believe happened is way off the mark. I have every reason to believe this awful thing had nothing to do with you and everything to do with Derrick's past. You can't change what happened, and maybe a better detective can find the truth you need.
> Goodbye,
> Martin Wellman

Finley stared at the letter, at the words. She and Wellman weren't exactly friends. Why would he feel compelled to write her a letter before eating a bullet?

Anger and frustration tore at her. She was not wrong about who'd killed Derrick.

"Knock, knock."

Finley looked up to find Matt standing in the open doorway, a large box from the local doughnut shop in hand.

"Jack said I should bring doughnuts."

She tossed the letter onto the coffee table. Couldn't think about that right now. "I see how it is. You two have been plotting against me."

Matt grinned. "Just against your house."

Jack grabbed the box from Matt. "I hope you got chocolate covered."

"Course I did. Would I let you down?"

He wouldn't. This was one answer Finley knew without a doubt. Matt would never let her or Jack or anyone else he cared about down. He wouldn't lie either.

"I'll take one." She reached for the box next.

"I guess this is where we're starting," Matt said as he poured himself a cup of coffee.

Jack swallowed a chunk of doughnut. "I hope you're as good with a paintbrush as you are at smooth talking reporters."

Matt laughed. "That sounds exactly like a challenge, my man." He reached for a brush. "I guarantee I can hang with you."

Finley laughed. "I'll change and grab a roller."

The banter between two of her favorite guys followed her to the bedroom. She pulled off her tee and paused. This was the first time she'd felt like laughing in this house since that night.

In the other room Matt laughed at something Jack said.

He's in love with you. You know that, right?

Don't be silly, Derrick. We're just good friends. Best friends.

Finley shook off the memory and grabbed one of her rattiest tees. She finger combed her hair and reached for a hair tie. She checked her reflection and headed back to join the others. She paused at the window. Frowned. Helen Roberts stood in the middle of her yard, her dog under one arm, the water hose in her other hand. She stared at Finley's house.

Maybe she was lost in thought and wasn't even aware she was staring.

Strange woman.

"We can have pizza delivered for lunch," Finley offered, returning to the living room.

Matt stopped pouring paint into a smaller plastic bucket. He smiled. "Sounds good to me."

Jack was across the room on his cell.

"The Judge," Matt said as he reached for the paint pan next, "mentioned the firm in a conversation with the trinity yesterday."

"Really?" Finley could imagine any remark she made was a less-than-complimentary one.

Matt nodded, passed her the pan filled with paint. "She said Metro and the city owe the firm a debt of gratitude."

Finley almost dropped the pan. "You're lying." Which was ridiculous because Matt never lied.

Matt grinned. "Those were her words. I heard them myself."

"Oh. My. God." Finley laughed. "The world is ending."

"Hope not," Jack announced, joining the conversation. "We just landed the biggest client in Music City, and he's in one hell of a fix."

There will always be another case, Fin. And you will always win. Because you're the best.

Derrick was right about that first part anyway. There would always be another case. She wouldn't have time to be looking back.

Only forward . . . at least for a while.

ACKNOWLEDGMENTS

I've taken the liberty of giving some of the characters, particularly attorneys, in this series a few shady traits. Made them a little self-serving and sometimes a lot uncaring. These characters are wholly fictional and not based on anyone I know. One of my dearest friends is an attorney, and I adore her completely. She is a wise and strong woman I would trust with my life. Another of my favorite legal eagles is a guy who represents the epitome of a brilliant attorney with a heart that makes him a simply awesome human. You know who you are.

The relationship between Finley and her mother (a.k.a. the Judge) is tough, but sometimes mothers and daughters go through difficult times. It's how you fare in those times and the end result that matters. Life is not perfect, and sometimes we hurt the people we love most. I look forward to this journey with Finley and the Judge.

Nashville is one of my favorite cities. A perfect blend of old and new, amazing and daunting. A place filled with inspiration. I love exploring the settings for my stories, and I most often take the inspiration found and create something fictional with only the slightest basis in fact. It's important to me that my characters live in real neighborhoods, so I search the perfect places to suit each one. Anyone who knows me will tell you one of my favorite hobbies is exploring houses.

My thanks to Nashville Metro Police Department, the Davidson County District Attorney's Office, and the Davidson County Mayor's Office. You have my utmost respect.

Last but never, ever least, I am always blown away by how my amazing editors, Megha Parekh and Charlotte Herscher, are able to help me reach deeper and stretch further, ultimately taking my stories to the next level. Thank you for all your hard work!

ABOUT THE AUTHOR

Photo © 2019 Jenni M Photography LLC

Debra Webb is the *USA Today* bestselling author of more than 150 novels. She is the recipient of the prestigious Romantic Times Career Achievement Award for Romantic Suspense as well as numerous Reviewers' Choice Awards. In 2012 Webb was honored as the first recipient of the esteemed L. A. Banks Warrior Woman Award for courage, strength, and grace in the face of adversity. Webb was also awarded the distinguished Centennial Award for having published her hundredth novel. She has more than four million books in print in many languages and countries.

Webb's love of storytelling goes back to her childhood, when her mother bought her an old typewriter at a tag sale. Born in Alabama, Webb grew up on a farm. She spent every available hour exploring the world around her and creating her stories. Visit her at www.debrawebb.com.